HER COUNTRY GENTLEMAN

HER COUNTRY GENTLEMAN

Sian Ann Bessey

Sarah M. Eden

Rebecca Connolly

Mirror Press

Copyright © 2022 Mirror Press
Paperback edition
All rights reserved

No part of this book may be reproduced in any form whatsoever without prior written permission of the publisher, except in the case of brief passages embodied in critical reviews and articles. These novels are works of fiction. The characters, names, incidents, places, and dialog are products of the authors' imaginations and are not to be construed as real.

Interior Design by Cora Johnson
Edited by Meghan Hoesch, Lisa Shepherd, Joanne Lui, and Lorie Humpherys
Cover design by Rachael Anderson
Cover Photo Credit: Lee Avison / Arcangel

Published by Mirror Press, LLC

Her Country Gentleman is part of the Timeless Romance Anthology® brand which is a registered trademark of Mirror Press, LLC

ISBN: 978-1-952611-21-6

HER COUNTRY GENTLEMAN

Spring at Tribbley Hall
by Sian Ann Bessey _____ 1

Love of My Heart
by Sarah M. Eden _____ 99

Miss Smith Goes to Wiltshire
by Rebecca Connolly _____ 203

TIMELESS REGENCY COLLECTIONS

AUTUMN MASQUERADE
A MIDWINTER BALL
SPRING IN HYDE PARK
SUMMER HOUSE PARTY
A COUNTRY CHRISTMAS
A SEASON IN LONDON
FALLING FOR A DUKE
A NIGHT IN GROSVENOR SQUARE
ROAD TO GRETNA GREEN
WEDDING WAGERS
AN EVENING AT ALMACK'S
A WEEK IN BRIGHTON
TO LOVE A GOVERNESS
WIDOWS OF SOMERSET
A CHRISTMAS PROMISE
A SEASIDE SUMMER
THE INNS OF DEVONSHIRE
TO KISS A WALLFLOWER

TIMELESS VICTORIAN COLLECTIONS

SUMMER HOLIDAY
A GRAND TOUR
THE ORIENT EXPRESS
THE QUEEN'S BALL
A NOTE OF CHANGE
A GENTLEWOMAN SCHOLAR

TIMELESS GEORGIAN COLLECTIONS

HER COUNTRY GENTLEMAN

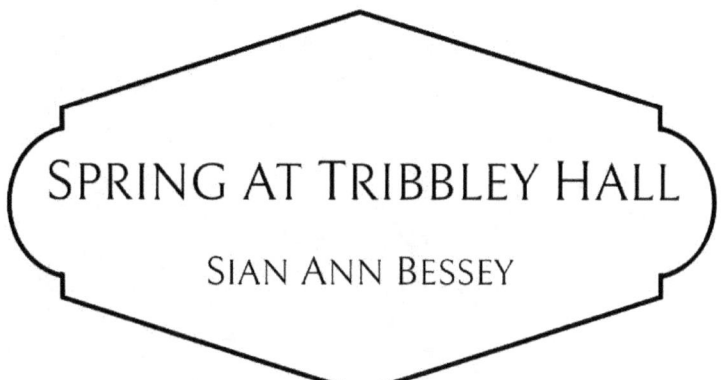

Spring at Tribbley Hall

Sian Ann Bessey

CHAPTER 1

London, 1784

GRANDMAMA MADE HER STUNNING announcement at the breakfast table. Charlotte's father had just finished the last sausage on his plate. Across from him, her mother and sister, Margery, were reviewing their long list of appointments for the day. Charlotte was nibbling on her toast, hoping she might have enough time before she finished it to conjure up a worthy excuse to stay at home rather than join them in yet another shopping expedition for Margery's trousseau.

"I am going to the country," Grandmama said. "Norfolk, to be precise. If you would be so good as to make a carriage available, Edward, I should like to leave tomorrow."

The elderly lady would not have garnered a more stunned reaction had she told her family that she was visiting the moon.

Charlotte's mother was the first to recover.

"To Norfolk?" She set her teacup in its saucer, the slight rattle of the china a fitting reflection of her obvious shock. "Tomorrow?"

"That's right. And if she is willing, I should very much like Charlotte to accompany me."

Charlotte's heart leapt. Had she heard correctly? Not only had Grandmama formulated her own plan of escape from the prenuptial madness that currently surrounded them, she had engineered one for Charlotte also.

Her mother's expression moved from stunned to aghast. "But we have Margery's wedding in a month."

"I am aware," Grandmama said dryly.

Charlotte bit her lip to hide her smile. The entire house had been turned on its end in preparation for Margery's upcoming marriage to Viscount Rothsey. Indeed, for the last few weeks, breakfast had been the solitary hour of calm before the whirlwind of daily premarital activities resumed.

"My good friend, Lady Cheston, has written to invite me to visit. Her home is located not more than five minutes from the coast. Given all the chimney smoke hanging over London these past few weeks, I believe the sea air will do me good."

"I have no doubt you are right, Mother." Charlotte's father had taken one look at his wife's face and had obviously determined that he had best enter the fray. "But there *is* the matter of Margery's wedding."

Grandmama released a frustrated breath. "I have no intention of missing my own granddaughter's wedding, but I hardly think my presence is needed here before then. Nor Charlotte's either, come to that. Constance already has things well in hand, and I would hazard a guess that Margery will fare perfectly well without her old grandmother's and younger sister's advice. Is that not so, Margery?"

Margery blinked, clearly unprepared for the question. She turned to Charlotte.

"Would you like to go, Lottie?"

Charlotte hesitated. She loved her sister, but an

opportunity to be by the sea did not present itself often. Their family's small country manor was in landlocked Leicestershire, and unlike most of their friends and acquaintances who divided their time evenly between the country and the city, her family rarely spent time away from London. Her father's business demanded that he be in Town more often than not, and since her mother preferred the hustle and bustle of London over the slower pace of village life, she opted to stay with him.

"If Grandmama is sure that we will be back to see you marry your viscount, and you feel that you can manage without me until then," she said, "I believe I would."

Grandmama's gratified smile was instant, and Margery gave her an understanding nod.

"I daresay choosing linens is not a terribly exciting endeavor when one will never see them again no matter which are chosen."

Charlotte laughed. "You forget, Margery. I intend to visit you in your new home often, and I shall pay particular attention to the towels you have out."

"As will everyone else," their mother warned. "Such things say a great deal about the mistress of a house."

"I believe that with your expert guidance, I shall not go awry, Mother," Margery said.

"Well, be that as it may," their mother said with a sniff, "Charlotte would learn a great deal by coming with us. It will surely not be long before she is choosing her own linens."

Charlotte was all too aware of their mother's desire to marry her two daughters off in quick succession, but as she had sighed with relief when every eligible gentleman who had come to call on her this Season left the house, she sincerely hoped that matrimony was not in her immediate future.

She met Margery's eyes and saw humor shining there.

"When that day comes, I shall happily assist Charlotte," Margery said. "I think she should be allowed to go with Grandmama."

"But to leave tomorrow? How ever will you be ready in so short a time?"

"I received Daphne's invitation only this morning," Grandmama said. "She is anxious that we be there in time for a dinner party she has planned on Saturday, and as it will take us two full days to reach Tribbley Hall by carriage, we have little choice but to leave tomorrow."

"Tribbley Hall," Charlotte said. "Is that the name of Lady Cheston's residence?"

"It is. And it is quite lovely."

"You've been there before, then?"

"I have. Many years ago," Grandmama said. "Daphne and I have been friends since childhood. When she married, she moved to Norfolk, and since I was in Leicestershire, we rarely saw each other. She had five daughters—all of them now married and living elsewhere—and then twelve years after her youngest daughter was born, she gave birth to a son. Her husband died three years ago, and her son became Lord Cheston. From what Daphne tells me, he is taking his responsibilities quite seriously and is already making better use of the estate's many acres."

"What is he doing exactly?" Charlotte asked, intrigued.

"I cannot tell you," her grandmother said. "But I daresay Lord Cheston will be happy to enlighten us both."

The thought of being forced to listen to a middle-aged man extol the virtues of his wheat and barley fields was almost enough to dissuade Charlotte from making the trip. But not quite. Tribbley Hall was near the sea. She had seen the ocean only twice—both times from a carriage on a short excursion to Brighton—and she longed to actually walk the beach and perhaps even dip her fingers into the water.

"May I go, Mother?"

Her mother sighed. "Very well, as long as your grandmother ensures that you both return in plenty of time for the wedding."

"Wild horses could not keep us away," Grandmama said.

"Do they have wild horses in Norfolk?" Charlotte asked, rather hoping that they did.

"Not to my knowledge." Her grandmother smiled. "But they certainly have sheep. Lots and lots of sheep."

William Falkner, Lord Cheston, looked up from the report on his desk, a frown marring his forehead.

"What the blazes is happening, Thomas? Five sheep a fortnight ago. Another four this week. Sheep don't simply disappear. Either the tally is wrong or we are being robbed."

His steward shifted uncomfortably. "I would suggest that it's the latter, my lord. Ralph maintained his own count while we were moving the flock from the lower pasture to the upper one. His numbers were the same as mine."

"Blast it all." William rose to his feet and ran his fingers through his dark hair. "This has to stop. We can't afford to lose any more. Especially now, with lambing season upon us."

"I agree, my lord."

"Then what are we going to do about it?"

"With the flock grazing so far from the house, it's quite possible that the sheep are being taken during daylight hours, but it may take setting watchmen around the clock to deter the thief. We can separate the ewes who are about to give birth and put them in the barn. If we lose them, we lose the mother and the lambs."

William nodded. He'd sunk a great deal of money into increasing Tribbley Hall's flock, counting on recouping his costs and making a substantial profit when shearing time came around. His desk contained hard-fought contracts with wool merchants in Antwerp and Genoa. He'd promised those gentlemen a certain quantity of Norfolk wool, and every sheep that went missing put his ability to deliver at greater risk.

"I could make some inquiries in the village," Thomas continued. "There may be laborers looking for work who'd be willing to stand guard in the fields."

"If we could guarantee that we weren't bringing on the very man who is stealing the sheep in the first place, I'd agree," William said.

Thomas inclined his head. "We'd be foolish not to consider that possibility."

"We would, indeed. And until we've uncovered the identity of the thief, no one outside this room is above suspicion. Not even our own workers."

"May I suggest that we include Ralph in our circle, my lord."

It was a fair request. The old shepherd had been at Tribbley Hall since William was a boy and was as protective of his flock as most people were of their own children.

"I believe that goes without saying," William said.

The sheep headcount had started dropping by one or two a week as long ago as November, but in the last month, they'd seen losses closer to four or five a week. Either the thief was getting greedy or he was becoming overconfident.

William paced the study, mentally reviewing the short list of employees he'd taken on since November. Other than a scullery maid, there was one young lad who'd started training as a groom, and two men who'd helped with the shearing in July and had asked to stay on as shepherds under Ralph.

"Harry and Simon are the only others who have reason to be out in the fields," Thomas said, following William's train of thought without prompting.

"Have either of them given you or Ralph any cause for complaint?" William asked.

"No, my lord. They do their work without being supervised and have learned to signal the dogs well enough to get by."

The dogs. William paused his pacing. Why had the sheepdogs not barked a warning about intruders in the fields? Dex was Ralph's shadow. If Ralph was in the fields, his faithful dog was too. But what of Patch?

"Do Harry and Simon take Patch with them when they're in the fields?"

"They have in the past, my lord. Seeing as she just delivered her litter, we're down to only Dex at the moment."

Of course. He was not thinking clearly. He'd stopped by to see the puppies in the barn only yesterday.

"Tell Ralph to have Dex patrolling the fields on a regular basis. I want at least one man in the pastures around the clock until we've caught the perpetrator of this crime."

"We are trusting Harry and Simon with this assignment, then?"

William set his jaw. "We have to. It's too big a job for three men to do alone."

"Three men?" Thomas looked at him questioningly.

"I wish to be put in the rotation," William said. "Write up a schedule and inform the others. It is to be effective immediately."

His manager bowed his head. "Right away, my lord."

A knock sounded on the door, and both men turned to see William's mother walk in. Her white hair was coiffured to perfection, and her lilac gown billowed out around her. In one hand, she held the ivory handle of a walking cane; in the other hand, she held a letter.

"Good day, Lady Cheston." Thomas bowed lower.

William's mother breezed into the room without bothering to ask if she were interrupting. "Good day to you, Thomas," she said. "I assume you are well."

"Yes, my lady."

"Good." She turned her attention to William. "A word, if you please, William."

William attempted to curb his irritation at her peremptory approach, but Thomas evidently recognized the dismissal.

"If you will excuse me, my lord, my lady," he said. "I have much to do."

"Yes, of course," his mother said.

William nodded his appreciation. "I shall expect the schedule by day's end, Thomas."

"Yes, my lord." He slipped out of the room, and William's mother lifted the letter in her hand.

"Speaking of schedules, William, I hope you have remembered the dinner party I have arranged for this Saturday."

Lud. His brain must have developed a leak. First Patch's puppies and now the dinner party his mother had been talking of for the last fortnight. He would have to tell Thomas that he was unavailable to be in the fields on Saturday evening.

"How could I forget?" he said, hoping his mother's enthusiasm for the event would blind her to the fact that it had obviously slipped his mind. He spent a moment dredging his failing memory. "Mr. and Mrs. Fitzroy, their daughter, and Mr. Ryland. Is that correct?"

His mother pursed her lips. "It is. But as I told you only yesterday, I have also invited Mr. Wellington."

William pinned a smile to his face. He wasn't sure who was the greater bore: Mr. Ryland, who spoke incessantly about the flora and fauna indigenous to the Norfolk Broads, or Mr. Wellington, who took his position as magistrate so seriously that he felt obliged to share every detail of his responsibilities each time they met.

"Forgive me. So you did."

"Yes, well, I shall now need to also reach out to Mr. Beeker. It is late notice, I realize, but it really would be preferable to have an even number of gentlemen and ladies, and I daresay the minister would be happy to receive an invitation to dine out."

It appeared that not only was his memory failing him, his ability to count was also in question.

"I would have thought that adding Mr. Beeker to your guest list would skew the numbers in favor of the gentlemen," he said.

"Not at all." With a pleased look, his mother waved the letter in her hand. "I have just heard from my friend, Mrs. Marion Densley. She is coming to visit, and she is bringing her granddaughter with her."

Thankfully, William's numerical reckoning skills returned when he needed them most. He silently—and without error—counted to six before trusting his voice.

"Mother, you are aware that lambing season has begun, and therefore it is the worst possible time to entertain guests at Tribbley Hall, correct?"

His mother bristled. "No matter what the sheep are doing, we need to eat, William. Inviting a few people over for dinner will have no bearing on what is happening in the fields."

"A single dinner party is one thing," he said. "House guests is quite another. No matter what else you have planned,

I will not be available, and neither will I allow a child to run freely on the property when every servant's attention is so wholly consumed elsewhere." He refrained from mentioning that he also wished to protect the child from encountering those who thought nothing of stealing sheep.

"Charlotte Densley will hardly be running freely," his mother said.

"No matter how well behaved the girl may be, if you would be so good as to write to suggest that your friend and her granddaughter delay their visit by a fortnight, I believe they would have a far more enjoyable time."

"I cannot do that," his mother said. "Marion and I have decided to embark upon a project that necessitates her being here."

William eyed his mother warily. Her past "projects" ranged from donating food baskets to the poor to purchasing a pony for his eight-year-old nephew without first consulting the boy's parents. The former was perfectly acceptable; the latter was not.

"A project," he said.

"Yes." She flicked her hand as if to dismiss the subject. "Think nothing of it. You have other concerns that are far more pressing. Besides, it is too late. They are already on their way."

Counting was of little value at this point. "I shall attend your dinner on Saturday, Mother, but as my presence will likely be required in the fields and the barn for the next few weeks, you will have to make my excuses to your guests for the remainder of their stay."

"If it comes to that, I shall," his mother said, but she did not look the least put out. Indeed, if anything, she appeared rather pleased.

The first hint of unease wiggled its way past his irritation.

What was she not telling him? "I am quite serious about this, Mother."

"Yes, I can see that, but I believe Marion's visit will turn out very well regardless." She started back across the room, her cane clicking against the polished wood floor. When she reached the door, she turned. "I am off to have Mrs. Underhill make ready the yellow and green guest chambers. Good luck with your lambs."

William watched her disappear into the passageway before dropping into his chair with a groan. Surely something would go right before this day was over.

Chapter 2

"Over there, Charlotte." Grandmama pointed out the carriage window. "Do you see it?"

Charlotte leaned closer. Gently undulating fields dotted with white sheep stretched out like a deep green blanket marked with hedgerow seams. Small groves of trees and an occasional cottage interrupted the rolling pastures, and in the distance, where the sky met the land, a narrow strip of blue sparkled in the sunlight. Her breath caught. They had reached the sea.

"Do you think we would hear the waves if we were to lower the windows?" she asked.

Her grandmother laughed. "Not yet, perhaps, but it is quite possible that you may be able to hear them from Tribbley Hall."

"Really? Are we getting close?"

Grandmama nodded. "Very close. I believe the house will come into view around the next bend."

Charlotte waited impatiently as the carriage slowed to take the turn in the road. They rolled past a handful of large sycamore trees, and then the vista opened up. Not more than half a mile away, a gray slate roof topped with a dozen or more chimneys showed above a tall hedgerow.

"There it is," Grandmama said, sounding uncommonly pleased. "Tribbley Hall."

Charlotte supposed that she could have made a polite comment about the height or number of chimneys, but instead, she waited, watching quietly as the carriage rumbled closer. They turned another slight bend, this time passing between two stone pillars that marked an opening in the hedge. The drive curved slightly to the right and, all at once, they were pulling up before a magnificent red-stone house.

"Oh my." The words left Charlotte's lips in a whisper.

Her grandmother looked pleased. "I am glad to see that it is just as I remembered."

"I've rarely seen such a beautiful house," Charlotte said.

A white portico hung over half a dozen stone steps leading to an imposing set of double doors. On either side of the doors, rose bushes—which would undoubtedly be a mass of color later in the year—filled narrow flower beds. Beneath the gabled roof, three stories of white-framed windows lined the front of the home.

As they watched, the doors opened, and two footmen came out to meet the carriage. Behind them, a lady with white hair, an exceptionally fine floral gown, and a walking cane appeared in the doorway.

"Is that Lady Cheston?" Charlotte asked.

"It is, indeed," her grandmother said.

The woman's bearing spoke of high breeding, but her somewhat severe expression softened into a welcoming smile when one of the footmen opened the carriage door and helped Grandmama out.

"Marion, you are come at last." With the aid of her cane,

Lady Cheston descended the stairs and moved to greet her old friend with a kiss on each cheek. "It has been far too long."

"It certainly has," Grandmama said.

"And this must be your granddaughter." Lady Cheston's attention shifted as Charlotte stepped out of the carriage.

"Yes." Grandmama waited for Charlotte to join them. "Charlotte, this is my dear friend, Lady Cheston. Daphne, this is Miss Charlotte Densley."

Charlotte curtseyed. "It is a pleasure to meet you, Lady Cheston."

"The pleasure is mine, Miss Densley," Lady Cheston said. "I have heard a great deal about you from your grandmother." She studied Charlotte carefully. "And I must say, you are just as lovely as she claimed."

Perhaps Lady Cheston's eyesight was not what it had once been. Charlotte's yellow silk gown was covered in wrinkles. After having slept with her head resting against the carriage seat for well over an hour, she was quite sure that her blonde hair was falling from its pins beneath her bonnet. And although others had commented on the unusually blue color of her eyes, she knew full well that her nose sported far too many freckles to be considered attractive.

"You are very kind, my lady," she said.

Lady Cheston smiled and slid her free hand through Grandmama's arm. "Come. After such a long journey, you both must be travel-weary. Let us go inside."

An hour later, Charlotte had marveled at the splendid great hall with its swooping banister rail, marble tile floors, and enormous oil paintings in gilded frames. She'd admired the tastefully decorated drawing room and neighboring, more personal, parlor. And she'd fallen in love with her assigned bedchamber. When her grandmother had declared her need for some quiet time, Charlotte had tried—and failed—to take a nap on the comfortable, four-poster bed covered in a pale green and white striped bedspread. She had then stood at the window admiring the view for at least ten minutes before finally succumbing to her excitement and opting to take her exploration outside.

Tying the ribbons beneath her bonnet, she nodded her thanks to the butler who opened the front doors for her. She stepped outside, and closing her eyes beneath the portico, she took a deep breath. The air was fresh and carried the song of birds and the bleating of sheep. Opening her eyes again, she took in her surroundings. The drive curved around the front of the house, looping back to join the main thoroughfare on the left and branching off to go around the back of the house on the right. Curious as to what lay behind the stately home, Charlotte chose to go right.

The gravel drive cut through manicured lawns. Flower beds with the last of the season's daffodils and tulips were a splash of color against all the greenery. If the grass's verdant color and the small puddles spotting the drive were any indication, Tribbley Hall had received significant rain this spring.

Up ahead, the drive ended in a small courtyard surrounded by three buildings. Based on their size, Charlotte assumed one was the stables and one was a carriage house. The function of the third escaped her. A small copse of trees and shrubs stood nearby, the undergrowth more tangled and wild than the flower beds she'd recently passed. She moved closer. And then she heard a cry. Or at least, she thought she did. Veering left, she approached the shrubs cautiously, pausing to look through the foliage. The cry came again. This time it was louder and more urgent.

Charlotte pushed back the branches of an alder and stepped into the small wilderness area. The barbs of a blackthorn bush snagged her gown. She frowned and tugged the fabric. It was a mistake. A two-inch-long tear appeared just below her knee. She groaned, stepping free of the wicked thorns only to have her shoe sink in a patch of mud.

"Botheration!" she muttered.

A yelp sounded at her left and something shifted beneath a wide fern. She froze. It had to be an animal. Fully prepared to leave the creature to its own business, she took a step back and stumbled over a root. Moments later she was on the ground, surrounded by a cloud of yellow silk and petticoats.

"Blast it all!"

Her mother would be horrified at her vocabulary, but landing in a mud puddle within two hours of arriving at Tribbley Hall was worthy of far more than a mild "botheration." How on earth was she to regain her bedchamber without half the household catching sight of her in this state?

The fern shifted again, and a little black puppy stumbled out from the undergrowth, falling headlong into Charlotte's skirts.

"Oh!" she gasped as the small dog floundered in the billowing fabric. The pup yelped again, and she reached out, lifting it off the ground. It whimpered and Charlotte drew it closer.

"How ever did you come to be in these bushes?" she asked.

The puppy's response was a lick on Charlotte's chin.

"Not good enough, little fellow," she said with a laugh. "You need a better reason than that."

Tucking him tightly in the crook of one arm, she scrambled to her feet. After making a futile attempt at brushing off some of the dirt clinging to her gown with her free hand, she pushed past the blackthorn bush to return to the drive. No sooner had she set foot on the gravel, however, than a low menacing growl brought her up short. A full-grown sheepdog stood not more than ten yards from her, its shoulders low, advancing on Charlotte as though she were its quarry.

William was closing the pen gate on the laboring ewe in the barn when he heard Patch's warning growl. He swiveled, his eyes immediately drawn to the pile of blankets in the far corner, where Patch and her litter of puppies had been living for the last three weeks. Patch was gone. William made for the open door. There were not many things that would take his sheepdog from her puppies, but an intruder intent on stealing sheep might be one of them.

He reached the courtyard in time to see Patch's ears pull back. She growled again. William's gaze flew to the object of his dog's ire, and he came to an abrupt stop. A young woman was standing near the alder tree. She wore a yellow gown smattered with mud, and her full attention was on the dog before her.

"Go away, dog!"

She retreated a step and something in her arms whimpered. Patch barked and the young woman started. The brim of her bonnet hid her face from him, but William recognized the fear in her voice and the puppy in her arms. He put his fingers to his mouth and blew a piercing whistle. Patch froze, and William stepped out of the shadow of the barn. The young woman gasped and stumbled, her gown catching on the nearby blackthorn's barbs.

"Patch is a well-trained dog," he said, "but maternal instinct is strong. You'd best put that puppy down if you wish to leave here unscathed."

She turned toward him and fixed him with a pair of the bluest eyes he'd ever seen. "Is . . . is this her puppy?"

"It is." He folded his arms, his elbows pressing against the thinning threads of his old work jacket. "And I should like to know how you came to be holding it."

The young woman set the puppy on the ground and straightened. "I rescued it."

"You rescued it?" He did nothing to hide his skepticism.

"Yes. I heard him yelping in the bushes and I went in to get him."

If the young woman's current state of dress were any indication, she had also dropped to her hands and knees in the bushes. He relaxed fractionally.

"That will do, Patch," he said.

The puppy was already loping across the gravel toward its mother, and at being freed from his whistled command to stand back, Patch rushed to pick up her offspring in teeth that had gone from menacing to protective in a moment. Lifting her puppy off the ground, Patch trotted toward the barn without a backward look.

The young woman tugged at her skirts. The blackthorn's barbs released them with the distinctive sound of tearing fabric. She muttered something under her breath before facing him again. A hint of pink colored her cheeks.

"I thank you for your assistance with the dog," she said, holding her head high. "I shall leave you to continue with your work now."

She was dismissing him? He stared at her. Who was this woman, and what was she doing on his property?

"May I be so bold as to ask what prompted you to visit the Tribbley Hall stables unaccompanied by a member of the household?"

If anything, the color in her cheeks deepened. "As a newly arrived guest of Lady Cheston, I was unaware that an escort was required to walk the grounds."

A newly arrived guest. William's mind raced. His mother had told him that she was expecting her friend, Mrs. Densley, and the lady's granddaughter. Had his assumption that the granddaughter would be as young as his sisters' children been a mistake? The alarming realization that his oldest niece would soon be celebrating her fifteenth birthday hit him like a bludgeon. If Mrs. Densley started her family a few years before his mother had done, there was every likelihood that the young lady before him was, in actuality, her granddaughter.

"No escort is required. Except perhaps to enter the barn," he said.

Her eyebrows rose. "Because your master keeps a vicious dog within?"

His master? Was it possible that she did not know to whom she was speaking? A vision of how he must appear flashed across his mind: dark hair falling loose from the strip of leather he'd used to tie it back, a jacket so worn at the elbows as to show the white of his shirt beneath, and breeches and boots as old as they were muddy. It was no wonder. He did not resemble a baron in the least.

"You are mistaken, Miss . . ."

"Densley," she said. "And I hardly think so. If you had not appeared when you did, that dog would have attacked me."

He shook his head. "Patch is a trained sheepdog, not a hunting dog. She was simply protecting her puppies. In her eyes, you were the predator."

She blinked. "But I was only trying to help."

"She did not know that." He paused. Perhaps a second introduction to Patch would be worthwhile. "Would you care to see what she is protecting so fiercely?"

Her eyes darted to the barn, and a flicker of fear crossed her face. "How many dogs are inside?"

"Five," he said. "Patch and her four puppies."

"There are four puppies?" Her eyes widened and he chuckled.

"Unless Soot has wandered off again. He has a tendency to do that, but he usually finds himself in the sheep pens."

"His name is Soot?"

"Yes. He's the only one that is all black."

Her smile was unexpected. "It's a perfect name for him." She glanced at the barn again, indecision written on her face. "Will Patch growl if I go in?"

"Not if you are with me."

She gave a brief nod. "Then I should very much like to see her other puppies."

CHAPTER 3

CHARLOTTE WAS UNCONVINCED THAT the presence of the handsome farmhand with the amber eyes would be enough to placate a wary sheepdog. But the opportunity of seeing Soot with his siblings was too big a draw to ignore. As a child, she had longed for a pet of her own, had even gone as far as to sneak scraps from the kitchen in their London townhouse to put outside for the alley cats. She'd come to recognize the regulars—the limping tabby and the skittish white one—but had never been quite brave enough to allow them indoors. Her mother would have confined her to her room for weeks for breaking their house rules so flagrantly, and that would have meant the cats would have gone without food.

She stood at the barn doorway, waiting for her eyes to adjust to the dimmer light. From inside, the rustle of movement in the straw and the bleat of a sheep echoed in the cavernous building.

"You said there are sheep in here," she said. "Why are they not out in the fields with the others?"

The man walked in ahead of her. "These are the mothers

with new lambs and the ones that will deliver their young very soon."

"Oh."

He spoke as if such things were everyday occurrences. Charlotte had never been closer to a sheep than looking at them over a hedge through a carriage window.

"Would you care to see some lambs while you are here?"

She was fairly sure that viewing newborn lambs and laboring ewes was not on her mother's list of approved activities for young ladies. Then again, neither was foraging through underbrush to rescue puppies or leaving out food for stray cats.

"Are they close by?"

She saw his teeth glint in the semidarkness and was fairly sure he was smiling. "Look to your left."

Charlotte turned. A lantern burned low atop the corner post of a nearby wooden pen. As she moved toward it, a plaintive bleating was echoed by another. Setting her gloved hands on the top of the gate, she peered into the small enclosure. A sheep was lying in the straw, and curled up beside her were two tiny white creatures with long, spindly legs and black noses. One of the lambs nudged the other and snuggled in closer.

"How old are they?" She did not try to hide the thrill in her voice.

"Two days," he said. "We'll keep them inside until they're a little steadier on their feet, then they'll go out to the pasture."

"And Patch will watch out for them."

He chuckled. "Well, she has her own little ones to care for at the moment, but we have another dog called Dex who is equally vigilant."

"He's in the fields now," she guessed.

"That's right." He moved past the doorway to the corner of the barn. Without being prompted, she followed.

"It looks like Soot found his rightful place once more," he said, standing aside so she could see.

A blanket lay piled on the floor. Burrowed within its folds was the large sheepdog she'd encountered outside, with four wriggling puppies climbing all over her. One of the puppies tumbled into the straw. Offering the humans no attention whatsoever, Patch nosed the little one back onto its feet, and the puppy immediately wiggled its way into the shifting pile of black and white furry bodies. It was, quite possibly, the most heartwarming sight Charlotte had ever seen, and for a few moments all she could do was watch, mesmerized by the miracle of it all.

"Patch has done remarkably well with them," the man said, finally breaking the silence. "I'm surprised Soot made it out of the barn without her noticing."

"She has her hands full," Charlotte said. "What are the names of the others?"

"The one with the white nose is Lady," he said. "She's the only female in the litter. The other two are Wyatt and Tinker."

She nodded, not wishing to look away. "It was good of you to show them to me."

"It seemed only fitting that you see the wanderer back where he belonged. And should you walk this way again and come across another escapee, you now know where to return it."

"Yes." She glanced down, suddenly remembering her state of dress. "Although for the sake of my gowns, I should probably refrain from entering the wilderness area again."

The benefit of being in the company of an unknown farmhand whilst covered in mud was that she need not fear that word of her misadventure with the puppy would ever reach her mother—or anyone else in London, for that matter.

It was likely that Grandmama was still resting in her

bedchamber, and even if she were to learn of Charlotte's unorthodox activities this afternoon, Charlotte felt sure she was safe. Years ago, Grandmama had caught her wrapping a piece of the fish on her dinner plate in her serviette. By unspoken agreement, she'd accompanied Charlotte to feed the alley cats that night and had kept her secret ever since. No matter her grandmother's response to today's adventure, however, she would rather not meet Lady Cheston, or, even worse, Lord Cheston, in her present condition.

As though he'd read her mind, the farmhand pointed to the manor just visible through the barn doors. "Do you see the door beside the large water barrel?"

"Yes."

"That's the servant's entrance. If your preference is to access your rooms privately, you can enter the house there and reach the upper floors via the back staircase."

Charlotte accepted the information gratefully.

"You have my thanks," she said. "And now I really should go."

He inclined his head. "Good day, Miss Densley."

She offered him a small smile, and lifting her muddied hem a fraction of an inch, she hurried out of the barn.

Chapter 4

William stood still, his chin raised while his valet, Geoffrey, straightened his cravat. He was an idiot. That was all there was to it. Not only had he neglected to properly introduce himself to Miss Densley outside the barn, thereby perpetuating her mistaken belief that he was a servant, he was also going to have to make a grand entrance in front of all his mother's guests because he was late. Not fashionably so. Embarrassingly so.

"That will do, Geoffrey." The piece of silk may not be placed quite as perfectly as his valet would like, but he had no more time for fussing. "My shoes, if you please."

Geoffrey reached for William's shoes, and William attempted to reset his thoughts. He could not go downstairs consumed by the mental image of the two lambs that had just made their appearance in the barn. They would surely have died had Ralph not arrived from the fields in time. It had taken both men working side by side with the exhausted ewe to deliver them safely. The creatures' first shaky steps had been a moment to celebrate, and William would have preferred to stay in the barn to watch them further, but according to the schedule Thomas had drawn up, it was Ralph's rotation in the barn. And William was needed elsewhere.

"Will there be anything else, my lord?" Geoffrey asked.

"No. Thank you, Geoffrey. That will be all."

"Very good, my lord."

His valet moved away to gather up William's soiled work clothes, and William's thoughts flew back to Miss Densley. Had she reached the guestrooms in her tattered and dirty gown without being seen? He smothered a smile. It had been refreshing to be with a young lady who was more interested in newborn lambs and puppies than in the state of her gown. Is that what it was like for his servants when they associated with young ladies who'd been raised in the country? His smile fell. Those few moments of unaffected conversation in the barn were doubtless all he would be allowed. Once Miss Densley realized who he was, he would be fortunate if she deigned speak to him again.

Straightening his shoulders, he opened the door to his bedchamber and started down the passageway. Under normal circumstances, he would be bracing for his mother's censure at his overdue appearance. This evening, however, he found himself far more worried about Miss Densley's reaction.

The rumble of male voices interspersed by light female laughter reached him as he approached the drawing room. The door was open, and William took a moment to scan the room before entering. Mr. and Mrs. Fitzroy were talking to his mother and the local minister, Mr. Beeker. All four were white-wigged, but whereas the gentlemen wore jackets and breeches of conservative brown and blue respectively, the women were resplendent. Mrs. Fitzroy wore pale pink with layers of lace. His mother's turquoise silk gown shimmered in the light coming from a nearby silver candelabra, her skirts even wider than Mrs. Fitzroy's.

Not far away, Mr. Ryland was in deep conversation with Miss Fitzroy. The botany enthusiast was appropriately dressed in green, and his untamed hair resembled a dandelion gone to seed. He must have been talking to Miss Fitzroy about one of his latest projects on the Broads for some time because the poor young woman wore a slightly glazed expression. Beside the fireplace, Mrs. Marion Densley stood beside Mr. Wellington and Miss Densley. It had been many years since William had seen the older lady. She'd aged but appeared to be in good health.

Sparing the rather pompous and self-assured magistrate, Mr. Wellington, little more than a passing glance, William turned his attention to Miss Densley. Like Miss Fitzroy, Miss Densley had opted to forgo a wig in favor of a light dusting of hair powder. He had caught only a glimpse of her golden hair beneath her bonnet, but now it lay piled upon her head in a mass of ringlets. She had replaced her muddy yellow gown with a pale blue one that accentuated her tiny waist and matched her eyes. As he watched, she raised a hand to emphasize something she was saying, and Mr. Wellington—who had yet to take his eyes off her—laughed.

William looked away. It was time. With a quick tug at the ends of his navy and gold striped waistcoat, he entered the room.

His mother saw him immediately. "Ah, William!" Her voice was welcoming even as she met his eyes with a steely look. "Here you are at last."

William inclined his head. "Forgive me for keeping you waiting, Mother. There was an emergency."

"With the sheep, no doubt," Mr. Fitzroy said.

William ignored the hint of mockery in his tone. "Indeed."

"A critical time of year for sheep farmers," Mr. Ryland

said. "Although, I will say that when it comes to giving birth, the ewes raised in the wild on the Norfolk Broads are far stronger than those living in farm pastures."

"So I imagine." His mother's swift response barely masked Mrs. Fitzroy's gasp, and if the deepening color in Miss Fitzroy's cheeks were any indication, she was as discomforted by Mr. Ryland's inappropriate remark as was her mother. Unfortunately, it seemed that the gentleman was blissfully unaware of the ladies' discomposure.

"I would recommend that everyone devote extensive time to studying the local wildlife," Mr. Ryland continued. "Only then can one truly understand that humans are nothing more than interlopers on the Broads."

"Yes, well, now that Lord Cheston has joined us, I believe it is time to eat," his mother said in a valiant effort to redirect the conversation. "Let us all relocate to the dining room."

A general murmur of approval was quickly followed by movement. William's mother crossed the short distance between them.

"I certainly hope your emergency warranted being over half an hour late to your own dinner party, William." There was no mistaking her softly spoken reproof.

"It did." He refrained from reminding her that this was *her* dinner party, not his.

"Hm." Appearing unconvinced, she took his arm and turned him toward the fireplace. "Come. I wish you to meet your dinner partner."

Meet his dinner partner? Since Mrs. Densley was the guest of honor this evening, William had assumed that he would be escorting her to dinner. But as a longtime friend of his mother's, she needed no introduction. Indeed, there was only one person in this room whom he had yet to meet. As far as his mother was concerned, at least.

The walking cane his mother carried did nothing to diminish her regal gait as she guided William across the room toward their visitors. William kept his eyes on Mrs. Densley, who offered him a warm smile.

"Marion," his mother said, "you remember my son, William."

"Of course." The older lady curtsied. "It is a pleasure to see you again, Lord Cheston."

"Likewise, Mrs. Densley. I hope your journey from London went well."

"Very well, my lord. And already, I am enjoying the invigorating sea air in this beautiful part of the country."

He smiled. "I am glad to hear it."

Mrs. Densley gestured to the young lady at her side. "May I have the pleasure of presenting my granddaughter to you, Lord Cheston."

"Of course." William braced himself. He had yet to meet the young lady's eyes.

Mrs. Densley smiled. "Charlotte, I should like you to meet our host, Lord Cheston. My lord, this is my granddaughter, Miss Charlotte Densley."

William inclined his head as Miss Densley dropped into a curtsey.

"Welcome to Tribbley Hall, Miss Densley," he said.

"Thank you, my lord." She straightened, and he found himself looking into a pair of blue eyes flashing with barely repressed anger. "We are only recently arrived, and yet my short time here has already proven to be most diverting."

William had expected embarrassment and awkwardness. Indeed, he'd been fully prepared to offer the mortified young lady an apology for keeping his identity from her. But it appeared that Miss Densley was no shrinking violet, and upon meeting her eyes, the words of regret died on his tongue.

"I am happy to hear that Tribbley Hall can offer diversion to someone who is used to experiencing the many amusements of London."

"Yes," she said. "It really is quite remarkable. Although the city often boasts things that are not what they seem, I had not thought to find the same in the country."

"Forgive me for being blunt, Miss Densley," William's mother said, "but it would seem to me that deceit of any kind should be avoided no matter where it is found."

Miss Densley offered her a small smile. "I completely agree, my lady."

Swift and sure, William's feelings of remorse returned. Clearing his throat, he offered Miss Densley his arm. "May I escort you to dinner, Miss Densley?"

She hesitated, and for one awful moment, he thought she might refuse. A fraction longer, and her civility rose to the fore.

"I would be honored, my lord," she said, and turning her face away from him, she set her hand upon his elbow.

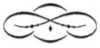

Charlotte kept her eyes to the front as she walked with Lord Cheston to the dining room, indignation vying with embarrassment. Had he been secretly laughing at her during their interaction at the barn? She'd been foolish to assume that Lord Cheston was closer to her father's age than her own. Her grandmother had made mention of the fact that the baron was significantly younger than his sisters. Why, oh why, had she not taken the time to think through the numbers?

Her astonishment when Lady Cheston greeted the handsome, young gentleman at the drawing room door as her son had been nothing to her shock when she'd realized that he and the farmhand were one in the same. True, the baron had never offered her his name, but surely good breeding should have impelled him to identify himself. Especially after requiring her to disclose her name.

She released a frustrated sigh, and she felt Lord Cheston glance at her.

"I believe I owe you an apology, Miss Densley." His voice was low, cautious. "Although it was never my intent to deceive you at the barn, I allowed you to leave unaware of my identity. That was remiss of me."

"If you had forgotten to tell me Soot's name, it would have been remiss, my lord. To not share that you were the master of the house rather than a simple laborer was both ungentlemanly and unkind."

His arm tensed beneath her fingers. "Although it may be hard for you to believe, I think this may be the first time I have ever been accused of those things."

She hazarded a glance at his face and was taken aback by the chagrin she saw reflected there.

"Perhaps I was too—" she began.

He shook his head slightly. "No, Miss Densley. You are correct. Now that I have had the chance to view the situation from your perspective, I can see that my actions were indeed ungentlemanly and unkind. I appreciate your willingness to be honest with me. Too often, people tell me only what they wish me to hear, and that offers me little opportunity for improvement." His frown was fleeting. "I shall endeavor to make today the first and last time I am accused of such undesirable traits."

They were approaching the dining room doors, and their opportunity for private conversation was coming to an end.

"In that case," Charlotte said, offering Lord Cheston a tentative smile, "perhaps we should begin again, as though we truly had never met."

He recognized the olive branch for what it was. "I should like that very much."

Her smile widened. "Would you tell me more about Tribbley Hall and this area of Norfolk?"

"Of course." He guided her to her chair. "What would you like to know?"

"Well," she said, "I have always been rather fond of animals. My grandmother gave me to understand that you have increased the number of sheep at Tribbley Hall, and it made me wonder if perhaps you have any trained sheepdogs." She looked at him, wide-eyed. "Or maybe even some puppies that you plan to train in the future."

Lord Cheston chuckled softly. "Why, yes, as a matter of fact, we have a new litter of puppies born only three weeks ago." He raised an eyebrow. "Would you be interested in seeing them?"

His question was an echo of the one he'd asked when she'd been standing in the small yard covered in mud, but this time she was not the only one to hear him.

"I say, Cheston, did you say that you have puppies?" Mr. Wellington had sat down next to Charlotte, her grandmother at his other side. "They wouldn't belong to that rather marvelous border collie you own, would they?"

"Yes, as a matter of fact, Patch is the mother."

"Well, now." Mr. Wellington leaned a little closer. "I don't suppose you're interested in selling any of them, are you?"

"Not at present," Lord Cheston said. "They're too young to leave their mother."

Mr. Wellington did nothing to hide his disappointment. "Keep me in mind when the time comes, would you? I could use a sheepdog like yours."

"Do you keep sheep, Mr. Wellington?" Grandmama asked.

"I do, although not nearly so many as Lord Cheston."

"Every single sheep is important, Mr. Wellington." Mr. Beeker joined the conversation, his tone reminiscent of a Sunday sermon. "The Bible tells us that repeatedly."

"A lovely reminder, Mr. Beeker." Mrs. Fitzroy smiled sweetly at the minister who acknowledged her compliment with a nod.

"Thank you, Mrs. Fitzroy. I have found that there are a great many ways to relate the teachings of the Bible to Norfolk's sheep."

"It's a shame that they are such malodorous creatures," Miss Fitzroy said. "Have you ever had occasion to be in the presence of a wet sheep, Miss Densley?" She wrinkled up her pert little nose as though she could smell one in the dining room.

Charlotte lifted her serviette to her mouth in an effort to hide the giggle that was threatening to emerge.

"I . . . I cannot say that I have," she managed.

Lady Cheston's initial look of displeasure at the dinner conversation's subject matter was rapidly becoming a glare, but Charlotte had rarely been so entertained. Did all dinner gatherings in the country include such diverting characters and open dialogue?

"Well, then, I will warn you to not get too close," Miss Fitzroy said, blithely unaware of Lady Cheston's mounting irritation. "For not only do sheep smell terrible, they also bite."

"If they were allowed to roam freely on the Broads, sheep would live quite happily, and you would find no reason to be offended, Miss Fitzroy," Mr. Ryland said passionately. "It is unfortunate that people take offense so readily. Indeed, the vast majority of us could learn a great deal by becoming more like a sheep or an owl or a beetle."

Lord Cheston's cough sounded suspiciously like a

smothered laugh. It did not help Charlotte's efforts to maintain a placid expression.

"No matter where the sheep live, I appreciate the warning regarding their tendency to bite, Miss Fitzroy," she said. "Although I'm not sure that I shall ever be that close to them."

"I would not be so sure, Miss Densley," Mr. Fitzroy said. "You cannot go ten yards in this part of Norfolk without encountering the blasted creatures."

Charlotte did not know why the gentleman seemed to hold all sheep in contempt, but thought it best not to ask. Perhaps, for Lady Cheston's sake, a change of subject was due.

"I shall be on my guard for them, sir, but in truth, one of the things I am most looking forward to is visiting the sea."

"It is something you must do," Lady Cheston said with understandable enthusiasm for the new topic. "This part of the coastline is truly magnificent."

"It is, indeed," Mr. Beeker said. "And when the fishermen are out on the water, it reminds me greatly of the stories Jesus told at the Sea of Galilee."

This time, when Lord Cheston coughed, Charlotte dared a glance at him. Mirth danced in his amber eyes, and an unexpected warmth filled her. She was not quite sure what to make of this baron who dressed as a farm laborer and found humor in the world around him, but there was a part of her—an alarmingly significant part—that rather hoped she would have the opportunity to come to know him better.

CHAPTER 5

If William had not been obliged to listen to every word, he wouldn't have believed it possible. But the clock on the mantle did not lie. The gentlemen had joined the ladies in the drawing room over twenty minutes ago, and Mr. Ryland had been talking about the great crested newt the entire time.

"And that is the tragedy of the situation, you see, my lord," Mr. Ryland said.

"Quite," William said. It was a safe response when one was still unsure as to which of the supposed calamities occurring in the Norfolk Broads the gentleman had determined was greatest.

"People are unaware that the natural order of things must not be undone. Every frog, toad, and newt is vital to the balance of the marshland."

"I could not agree more, Mr. Ryland," Mr. Beeker said.

William smothered a sigh of relief as the minister joined them. If there was one gentleman in the room who may be able to outtalk Mr. Ryland, it was Mr. Beeker.

"Good of you to say so, sir." Mr. Ryland turned his

attention to his new audience, and William allowed his gaze to traverse the room. His mother, Mrs. Densley, and the senior Fitzroys were seated, chatting near the fireplace, while on the other side of the room, Mr. Wellington appeared to be entertaining Miss Densley and Miss Fitzroy with a dramatic story that had the ladies alternately gasping, then smiling.

William watched Miss Densley's expressive face light up at something the magistrate said. All evening, the lady had exhibited remarkable poise. No one would ever guess that she had been forced to go in to dinner with someone who had treated her in an ungentlemanly and unkind manner. He winced. Her accusation had hit its mark. His negligence in sharing his name and position with her had been beneath him. And, although they had spoken pleasantly at dinner, he had an uncommonly strong desire to prove that he could do better.

"Excuse me, gentlemen," he said, stepping away as Mr. Beeker and Mr. Ryland launched into a discussion about the difference between the doves of the Bible and the turtledoves of the Norfolk Broads.

He crossed the room. Mr. Wellington had his back to William, but Miss Densley saw him coming. She smiled, and his responding smile was instant. She dipped her head, turning her attention back to Mr. Wellington.

Beside her, Miss Fitzroy spotted his approach for the first time. "Lord Cheston," she said, bobbing a curtsy.

Mr. Wellington swung around. "Ah, Cheston. There you are." His jovial tone sounded forced.

"Mr. Wellington has just been telling us about the smuggling that occurs along this portion of the coast," Miss Densley said.

"Such terrible goings on, my lord." Miss Fitzroy's face was pale. "I had no idea that being a magistrate was so dangerous. Mr. Wellington does us all a great service by being willing to tackle such lawlessness."

"And he does it essentially single-handed," Miss Densley added.

If William had not spent over an hour watching the young lady flawlessly navigate the conversation at the table, he might have been fooled by her serious expression. As it was, he caught the merriment in her eyes. He was impressed. Miss Densley had known Mr. Wellington for only a few hours, but it appeared that she had already taken the man's measure.

"Mr. Wellington is an extremely brave gentleman," he said.

"Yes, well . . ." Mr. Wellington blustered. "I would not go so far as all that."

"Oh, but you are, sir," Miss Fitzroy gushed. "The few encounters with evildoers that you've shared this evening would be far too perilous for a lesser man."

Miss Densley coughed, but the muffled sound behind her gloved hand could not fool someone so used to strangling a laugh by the same method.

"Tell me, Wellington," William said. "How recently have smugglers been spotted off our shores?"

"Not more than a week ago, my lord. It was Mr. Fitzroy who notified me when he saw lights above Brindle Bay."

All trace of humor left William. Tribbley Hall land ran directly into Brindle Bay, and as far as he was aware, it would be almost impossible to see lights flickering on that remote beach from any other location.

"How was Mr. Fitzroy able to see lights in Brindle Bay?" he asked.

"He was out fishing," Mr. Wellington said.

"At night?"

"Yes, my lord," Miss Fitzroy said. "My father has been

suffering from terrible sleeplessness. He finds it more restful to be out on a boat than pacing his bedchamber."

It was a plausible, albeit highly unusual, excuse, but it also placed Mr. Fitzroy near Tribbley Hall land at the time that sheep had been mysteriously disappearing. Could the gentleman who had never had anything good to say about the animals be behind the thefts?

"Are you quite well, Lord Cheston?"

Miss Densley's question brought William back to his situation with a start. The young lady was too perceptive by half.

"Yes, thank you," he said. "I was merely wondering if Mr. Fitzroy has discovered whether or not the fish bite better at night."

"I should say so." Miss Fitzroy grimaced. "It seems to me that we eat fish for dinner almost every day."

"Then I shall have to speak to him about it," William said. *Along with a few other things*, he added to himself.

Charlotte peered out of the carriage window, her excitement mounting. They were close; she could feel it.

"The driver will take us to the end of the road," Grandmama said. "From there, we should have only a short walk to the beach."

Upon learning of Charlotte's desire to visit the seashore, Lady Cheston had insisted upon organizing the outing right away. The fact that they had awoken to clear skies and mild temperatures had solidified the plan. Lady Cheston had ordered the carriage be brought around immediately after breakfast, and although she'd declined to join them because of her difficulty in walking across the sand, she had sent Charlotte and her grandmother on their way with two chairs, a table, a small picnic basket, and an enthusiastic wave.

Charlotte could admit to a little disappointment that Lady Cheston had been the only one to see them off. She'd seen nothing of Lord Cheston since the other guests left Tribbley Hall last night. She had not spoken to him since he'd crossed the drawing room to join Mr. Wellington, Miss Fitzroy, and her. And even that had been a brief interaction. He had moved on, soon afterward, to speak with Mr. Fitzroy. She supposed it was expected that a host float between the small clusters of guests gathered in his drawing room, but she had hoped he would stay a little longer. After her indignation over his earlier behavior had faded, she had enjoyed her interaction with the baron far more than she would have anticipated. But even though she'd felt his eyes upon her more than once after dinner, he had scarcely spoken to her again.

"There! Look!"

At Grandmama's exclamation, Charlotte ceased her woolgathering to focus on the sight before them.

The dirt road ended at a narrow strip of grass. Beyond that, the grass gradually gave way to a sandy path, which rose over a gentle incline before disappearing between craggy rocks.

For the first time since they'd embarked on this outing, Charlotte's enthusiasm gave way to unease. "Can you manage it, Grandmama?"

"I am determined to manage it," she said. "After all, the footman will assist me, if necessary."

Charlotte should have known better than to ask. Her grandmother rarely allowed obstacles—physical or otherwise—to get in her way. The fact that they were both here a mere four weeks before Margery's wedding was proof enough of that.

The carriage rolled to a stop, and moments later the footman appeared. Charlotte waited only until he had opened the door before climbing out. She stood on a patch of sand and watched a seagull soar overhead. Its piercing cry was echoed by another bird, and then in the silence that followed, she heard the sea. Like the earth's heartbeat, the rhythmic ebb and flow of waves filled her ears. She reached for Grandmama's arm.

"May I be the one who assists you?" she asked. "I'd very much like to have us reach the water together."

Grandmama smiled. "As would I." She turned to the footman. "Would you be so good as to follow us to the beach with the furniture and the picnic basket?"

"Yes, ma'am."

She patted Charlotte's hand. "Very well. I believe we're ready."

The grassy tussocks made the terrain uneven, and the sand shifted beneath their feet, but Charlotte guided her grandmother slowly up the path to the rocky ridge. And suddenly, the vista opened up before them. Cliffs, standing like a protective wall around the semicircular sandy bay, and beyond that, water as far as the eyes could see.

"There," Grandmama said, coming to a stop beside a large boulder. "What do you think of that?"

Charlotte gazed at the sight in wonder. "It is magnificent."

They stood together, silently watching the whitecapped waves roll in for a few moments longer, and then Grandmama gave Charlotte's arm a squeeze. "Shall we go closer?"

She nodded, and together they descended the rocky slope until they reached the hard, wet sand. They walked to the water's edge. Grandmama stood a few feet from the lacy foam, but Charlotte lifted her skirts and dared move a little closer. The water rushed in, touching the tips of her boots. With a squeal, she stumbled back a few steps. The wave receded, and she moved forward again, waiting. This time, as the water approached, she bent over just enough to run her fingers across its surface. It was ice-cold and smelled of salt and seaweed.

"Be careful, Charlotte," her grandmother called.

She did not heed the warning quickly enough. A larger wave rolled in, instantly wetting the lower three inches of her gown.

"Oh no!"

Backing up farther, Charlotte took hold of the layers of fabric and shook them. Tiny grains of sand rained down. She studied her gown helplessly. Mud one day, seawater and sand the next. She had most definitely not packed enough clothing for a stay at Tribbley Hall.

Turning, she started up the sand toward her grandmother, who was now safely ensconced in one of the two chairs Lady Cheston's footman had set down in the shade of the cliffs.

"Are you terribly wet?" Grandmama asked as she drew near.

"No." Charlotte gave her a chagrined smile. "It seems that this young lady from the city has much to learn about the fickle nature of ocean waves."

Her grandmother chuckled. "Sit with me for a while. If you allow your skirts to dry a little, they will be less likely to attract the sand."

Charlotte accepted her grandmother's advice and claimed the chair beside her. She sat, watching the sunlight dance upon the water.

"Thank you for bringing me here, Grandmama."

"You deserve it, my dear."

She turned to face her grandmother. "I'm not sure that I have done anything worthy of this outing."

"Does patiently enduring endless hours of discussion, decisions, and shopping for a wedding that is not your own count for nothing?"

Charlotte wrinkled her nose at the memories. "I was not always very patient."

"You were a saint," Grandmama said. "And your increased desire to be excused from it over recent weeks was simply your intelligence shining through."

Charlotte laughed. "I shall cling to those words when Mother chastises me for not offering an opinion on the color of Margery's wedding flowers."

Grandmama muttered something under her breath. "I am only willing to put up with inconsequential matters being made important if truly vital issues are given equal treatment. When those things are ignored, it is time to step in and do something about it."

Charlotte searched her memory for something in her grandmother's life that may have been inadvertently overlooked. She could think of nothing.

"I am terribly sorry, Grandmama. I am sure that if you were to make Father aware of whatever has been neglected, he would see to it."

She leaned over and patted Charlotte's hand. "I think not, my dear. But do not fret. Lady Cheston and I have embarked upon a scheme, and we are both quite hopeful regarding its outcome."

When Charlotte considered how determined Lady Cheston might be if she set her mind to a project, her concerns lessened.

"I am glad." She looked at her grandmother curiously. "Is that why you chose to come here? To gain Lady Cheston's assistance?"

"Yes. And to give you an opportunity to meet people

beyond the pathetic circle of would-be-suitors whom you have been entertaining while your mother is consumed with Margery's wedding."

Charlotte stared at her. She had been flattered by the number of gentlemen callers she had received over the last few weeks.

"Lord Haversham is an earl."

"He is a sap."

"What of Mr. Ledbetter? No one could accuse him of being a sap."

"Of course not, because he is too cocky by half."

"And Mr. Wilmore?"

"Have a care, Charlotte. He is three times your age. With his money, he should have no difficulty finding a kindly widow to keep him company in his dotage."

Charlotte was beginning to see where this conversation was leading. She brushed sand off her gown with feigned nonchalance.

"Why did you not tell me that Lord Cheston is significantly younger than Father?"

"It did not seem important."

"Grandmama," Charlotte's exasperation was obvious. "You have just told me that Mr. Wilmore's age is of the utmost importance. You cannot now tell me that Lord Cheston's is not."

"Would you have agreed to come if I had told you that a handsome and eligible baron lived in the house?" her grandmother challenged.

Would she? Charlotte attempted to set aside her indignation long enough to analyze the question. Truth be told, she'd been secretly glad that she'd felt nothing more than flattery for the attention offered her by the aforementioned gentlemen in London. After having been involved in the rigmarole surrounding Margery's wedding preparations, she had little desire to enter that state herself.

"It would have depended upon whether or not you had told me that I could spend a full day at the sea," she said.

Her grandmother chuckled. "You are a delight, Charlotte."

Charlotte shook her head. Somehow it felt wrong to accuse her grandmother of being sneaky, wily, or meddling, even though she was all of those things.

"Just remember, I am at Tribbley Hall as your companion and to visit the seaside. Lord Cheston can have no interest in someone so wholly removed from his world, and I refuse to be one of those silly young ladies tripping over themselves to get in his way." She looked at Grandmama sternly. "And I also refuse to be further manipulated by my scheming grandmother."

"Very well," Grandmama said.

"Very well?" It was not the response Charlotte had anticipated, and her grandmother appeared far too smug for someone whose underlying motives had just been exposed.

"Absolutely," Grandmama said. "Daphne and I have done what we set out to do."

Heaven help her. Lady Cheston was in on the scheme too. "And what exactly was that?"

"Simply to have you and Lord Cheston meet each other."

It was true; they had accomplished that much. Charlotte looked away and brushed another clump of sand from her skirts. This was probably not the time to tell Grandmama that at their first meeting, Lord Cheston had been dressed as a farmhand and she'd been covered in mud.

CHAPTER 6

THOMAS REINED HIS HORSE to a halt in front of William. "That's the last of them, my lord. We've not found a hole in any of the property's hedges or walls that's large enough for a sheep to use as a means of escape."

William nodded. He'd guessed as much. Ensuring that the sheep were safely enclosed was a priority, and he'd never known his steward to let something so important slide. But it had been essential that he make one last check.

"I believe we can rule out wandering off as the reason for our loss of sheep," he said.

"Yes, my lord." Thomas's expression was grim. "Which leaves us with thievery."

"Indeed." William sat in his saddle and surveyed the rolling pastures. "But we are no closer to discovering who to hold accountable."

With a grunt of frustration, he swung his horse around. Thomas followed his lead, riding beside him as they started back toward the barn.

"If there's any good news to be had in all of this," Thomas

said, "it is that Harry and Simon don't seem to be involved. Sometime in the last eighteen hours, we lost two more sheep. During that time, both men were either with me or with Ralph."

Thomas was right. Knowing that he could trust his new hires was a huge boon. "Inform them of what we are up against," he said. "The more men we have watching for signs of mischief, the better our chances of catching the perpetrator."

"Simon handles a horse well, my lord. If you're agreeable, I'll have him ride the perimeter of the estate tonight while Harry and I watch the fields closer to the house."

"Very well," William said. "And I shall take a shift in the barn so that Ralph can get a few hours' sleep before he relieves you in the fields."

Thomas nodded, but his attention was on the road. "A rider, my lord. And he looks to be heading this way."

William spotted him immediately. The lone man wearing a dark jacket and breeches turned his brown stallion onto the Tribbley Hall drive. By the time the rider had reached the first bend, he'd recognized him. Mr. Wellington. What business did the local magistrate have at Tribbley Hall? Touching his heels to his mount's sides, William urged the horse into a canter. Thomas kept pace until, with a clatter of hooves, they entered the small courtyard near the barn. Mr. Wellington was waiting for them.

"Well met, my lord," Mr. Wellington said, inclining his head.

"Wellington." William returned the gesture. "What brings you to Tribbley Hall again so soon?"

"I am come to ask about the puppies you mentioned last evening."

William frowned. "I thought I made it quite clear that they are not of an age to leave their mother."

"Indeed, you did." The gentleman was looking distinctly uncomfortable. "And although I have no desire to be an irritant, I find myself in a rather difficult situation. I wondered if I might secure a guarantee that you will sell me one of them at the earliest possible date."

"May I be so bold as to ask what is so urgent?"

Mr. Wellington looked as though his cravat might be strangling him. "Sheep stealers, my lord."

"I beg your pardon?"

The magistrate swallowed. "A few of my sheep have gone missing. Not many, mind you, but sufficient to cause concern. I understand that it does not bode well for the community if the magistrate himself cannot maintain the law on his own property." He withdrew a handkerchief and mopped his brow. "I thought that perhaps if I were to acquire a dog that could be both a sheepdog and watchdog, I might have success in apprehending the criminal."

"A young puppy is hardly a trained sheepdog, Mr. Wellington." It was an obvious observation, but William used it to buy himself time to absorb this stunning new development.

"I realize that, my lord, but border collies are born for this work. It will not take one long to learn to do the job."

"They are fast learners, I grant you. But surely not so fast as all that." He kept his eyes on Mr. Wellington's face. "Are you aware of any others who have lost sheep?"

"Mr. Crawley down Biddington way wrote to say that he had lost half a dozen ewes over the last three weeks."

The Crawleys' land was about ten miles south of Tribbley Hall.

"Any others?"

"Only the four of my own, my lord."

That was ten. And there may be those who, like him, had

not reported their losses. By the last count, William was missing over two dozen head. The criminal had already amassed a decent flock.

"Five weeks from now, you may have first pick of the litter," William said. "But until that time, you had best exert your efforts to apprehending the thief yourself." He paused. Should he mention his own losses? He had only just drawn Harry and Simon into his circle of trusted men. Unfortunately, no matter his elevated position in the community, Mr. Wellington had yet to pass muster.

"May I ask that you inform me of any further developments in your efforts to catch the thief?"

"Of course, my lord." Now that he had taken one small step toward solving his problem, Mr. Wellington's self-assurance was reemerging. "I shall not allow such criminal behavior to go unchecked. Have no fear. I will get to the bottom of this."

"I certainly hope so, Wellington. The more people affected by this thievery, the harder it will be to hide."

Mr. Wellington blanched. "How right you are, my lord. I believe I shall make a visit to Mr. Crawley straight away."

Charlotte had walked farther than she'd intended. She'd followed the curve of the bay, collecting seashells and marveling at the beauty of the rugged coastline along the way. To her right, the tide was steadily advancing up the beach. To her left, the cliff face, which had been little more than a few feet high where the carriage was parked, now towered above her head like a castle wall.

A shadow flickered across the sand ahead of her. She stopped, looking up in time to see a man's head and shoulders disappear beyond the upper rim of the cliffs. Who could it have been? She turned. Grandmama was still sitting in the shade on the other side of the bay, the footman who'd assisted them visible a few yards away. It was unlikely that their carriage driver would roam so far from the vehicle since they'd given him no indication of how long they intended to stay.

Charlotte gave the spot where the figure had disappeared one last look. She was fairly certain that the land butting up against the bay belonged to Lord Cheston. Could it have been him? Her heart tripped. What had Grandmama been thinking to orchestrate an introduction for Charlotte with the gentleman? A baron who was so devoted to his land that he worked in the barn delivering lambs could have no interest whatsoever in a young woman raised in the city who'd never even owned a pet rabbit. And she could have no interest in him. The logic was sound. Unfortunately, at that precise moment, she wasn't feeling especially logical.

Pushing away the memory of Lord Cheston's humor-filled amber eyes, she turned and started back toward her grandmother. A sheep bleated, a solitary, mournful cry. It sounded remarkably close. She paused once more to scour the cliff. Perhaps the man she'd seen had been a shepherd in search of a missing sheep. If so, he appeared to have moved on, for there was no sign of him on the ridge.

By the time she reached the waiting chairs, her shoes and hem were caked with sand, and she was panting slightly.

"Forgive me, Grandmama. I should not have left you alone for so long."

"Nonsense," Grandmama said. "We have both filled our time with the very things we came for—fresh sea air for me and walking the beach for you. Besides, I was not alone. Frederick was nearby the whole time."

"Thank you, Frederick," Charlotte said, glad to know the footman's name.

"My pleasure, miss." He moved a little closer. "Will you and Mrs. Densley be returning to the carriage now?"

Grandmama was already coming to her feet.

"I believe so," Charlotte said.

"Very good, miss."

He waited until Grandmama had tucked her arm through Charlotte's and they had started back up the rocky slope before gathering up the chairs and the empty picnic basket.

"I must say," Grandmama said. "I'm beginning to think there really might be something to the claim that sea air improves one's appetite. I have rarely looked forward to a meal as much as I am anticipating dinner this evening."

Charlotte smiled. She, too, was looking forward to dinner at Tribbley Hall. But whether it was for the food or the company, she could not tell.

Ralph ran a callused hand over the sheep's abdomen. "Not much longer, m'lord. I reckon the little one'll be 'ere within the hour."

"I certainly hope so," William said. "She's been through enough already."

"Aye, she's had a rough go of it, this one," Ralph said, sitting back on his heels as the ewe panted through her discomfort.

"I'm only sorry that you did not get the rest you were due after spending all day in the fields."

Ralph shrugged and gave him a craggy smile that showed his missing teeth. "That's 'ow these things go, I reckon. You'll 'ave all these mothers waitin' and waitin' fer their time t'come, and then all of a sudden they're all goin' through it at once. Somethin' to do with the moon, is what I'm thinkin'."

"You might be right," William said. "These lambs seem to prefer to arrive in the dead of night."

Ralph chuckled. "I reckon they don' know what's day and what's night, m'lord. They're jus' ready to stretch them long legs of theirs."

There was no denying that. Watching a newborn lamb come to its feet within minutes of its birth was something he would never take for granted. It was a miracle every single time.

He pulled his watch from his pocket and glanced at it. The dinner hour was long gone. Most of the household would be abed already. Disappointment that he'd missed seeing Miss Densley lingered, surprising him in its intensity. He had not planned on dining with his mother's guests beyond the dinner party last night, but thoughts of Miss Densley had remained with him throughout the day, and he had caught himself watching for her whenever he was near the house.

That the young lady was attractive went without saying; her golden hair and blue eyes were stunning. But what set her apart from other young ladies of his acquaintance was her willingness to openly share her emotions. There was no hiding behind fans for Miss Densley. He had yet to see her feign indifference or enthusiasm. Her fear of Patch had been real, as had her thrill at seeing the lambs and puppies. She had not covered her embarrassment over their first meeting, but neither had she withheld her forgiveness. To see the humor shining in her eyes over the ridiculous dinner conversation had been as heartwarming as it was unusual.

He shook his head as though it would somehow rid him of all perplexing thoughts of the lady. He had no time for such unsettling contemplation now. The sheep and their lambs needed his attention.

Chapter 7

Charlotte could not sleep, and she had no good reason for it. Dinner had been divine. The roast duck could not have been more tender, the treacle tart more sweet. Lady Cheston and Grandmama had done an admirable job maintaining a lively conversation, but it had lacked the entertainment of the evening before, and Charlotte had found herself missing Lord Cheston's presence rather too much for comfort.

She released a frustrated breath and rolled onto her back. Moonlight was peeking through the curtains, illuminating the finely furnished room. The bed was soft, the blankets warm. She was perfectly comfortable, and yet sleep remained elusive. If she had been at home, she would have slipped downstairs to the kitchen and heated up some milk. Cook swore by that simple remedy for insomnia, and Charlotte had relied upon it often enough that Cook had taught her how to rekindle the banked fire just enough to warm the milk in a pan.

She paused her train of thought. Could she heat up some milk in the Tribbley Hall kitchen? The household staff would be asleep by now, and she had no desire to disturb them.

Surely a jug of milk and a small pan would be easy enough for her to find. Sitting up in bed, she reached for the flint on the bedside table and lit the candle beside it. Its light augmented the moonlight well enough for her to locate her slippers and dressing gown. After putting them on, she raised the candle aloft, opened the door to her chamber, and tiptoed into the passageway.

The house was silent except for the creak of the stairs as she made her way to the kitchen. The faint smell of roast duck lingered in the large room, but the table was clear. Shelves hung on the far wall, covered with piles of dishes, bowls, and jugs. Some of the dishes were covered. Setting her candle on the table, Charlotte moved closer and reached for a large bowl covered in a cloth. She lowered it and raised the cloth, wrinkling her nose at the pungent smell that assailed her. Yeast. Tomorrow must be bread-making day at Tribbley Hall.

Replacing the bowl on the shelf, she took down an earthenware pitcher covered with a small plate. She lifted the plate, peered inside, and smiled. Milk. Carrying it to the table, she set it down beside the candle and walked across the room to the fire. A few of the coals still glowed. She knelt down and blew softly. The corner of one of the coals turned bright orange, and a wisp of smoke drifted upward. Taking the tongs from the nearby coal scuttle, Charlotte placed two pieces of coal atop the glowing piece and blew again. The fresh coal shifted. She blew one more time. A little more smoke appeared and then a crack sounded. Sparks flew, and one of the new coals began to burn.

Satisfied that the fire was strengthening, Charlotte eyed the row of pans hanging from one of the large beams running across the ceiling. Taking the small one on the end, she poured a little of the milk into the bottom before taking the milk jug back to the shelf and claiming a cup. Setting the pan over the tiny flames, she pulled a wooden chair closer and sat down to watch. Experience had taught her that the milk went from tepid to boiling over in an instant.

The first tiny bubbles were just beginning to form in the milk around the edges of the pan when the door to the kitchen burst open. Charlotte leapt from the chair, her heart hammering.

"L-Lord Cheston!"

The gentleman staggered to a halt. He was wearing his working clothes again, and in his arms, he carried a bundle of sacks.

"Miss Densley," he said. "Whatever are you doing here?"

Warmth flooded Charlotte's face. She had considered meeting the baron while covered in mud to be humiliating. It was nothing compared to this mortification. How did one gracefully make excuses for helping oneself to things in her host's kitchen in the middle of the night, let alone doing so while wearing nightclothes? She was quite sure it could not be done.

She cinched the cord around her dressing gown tighter. "Forgive me, my lord, I—"

He did not allow her to finish. "What do you have in the pan?"

"Milk."

"Thank the heavens."

He hurried across the room and dropped to his knees in front of the fire. One corner of the sack fell back, exposing the face of a tiny lamb. Charlotte gasped, but he ignored her. Taking a piece of the sack in each hand, he began to furiously rub the lamb's limp body.

"What are you doing?" Charlotte asked.

"Trying to save his life," he said through gritted teeth.

Charlotte did not ask anything more. Reaching for the

tongs, she tossed four more pieces of coal onto the fire before picking up the poker and coaxing the fire to spread.

"The milk," Lord Cheston said. "How hot is it?"

She checked the pan. Wisps of steam were beginning to rise. She dipped her finger into the milk. "Warm, but not hot," she said.

He nodded, continuing to rub. "Would you take it off the heat?"

She did as he asked.

"Somewhere on the shelves, you'll see a pewter bubby pot," he said. "I need you to pour the milk into it."

Charlotte had no idea what a bubby pot was, but she ran to the shelf, searching for anything made of pewter.

"How big is it?" she asked.

"Small. It looks like a miniature teapot."

"This?" she asked, holding up a metal cup with a spout connected to its base.

"Yes."

She hurried back, and setting the bubby pot on the floor beside Lord Cheston, she poured the steaming milk into it.

"Now what?" she asked.

"A scrap of fabric to cover the spout." His attention shifted momentarily from the lamb on his knee to his clothing. "If you can find a knife, we can cut a piece off my shirt sleeve."

Within seconds, Charlotte had a knife in hand. "There's a pile of clean rags in a basket in the corner," she said.

"Can you cut a piece off one of them? A few inches will suffice."

Charlotte pierced the rag with the tip of her knife and sawed off an inch-long strip. "Will this do?" she asked, holding it up so he could see.

"Perfectly," he said.

She hurried back to him and picked up the bubby pot, noticing for the first time that the spout was enclosed except for three small holes. "Where do I attach the fabric?"

"It needs to be tied to the spout in such a way that when we tip the pot, the milk will soak the fabric and the lamb can suck on it."

Charlotte hesitated. "Have you done it before?"

"Yes."

"Let me take the lamb," she said. "I don't want its life taken because of my incompetence. You ready the bubby pot, and I shall endeavor to keep the lamb warm."

Lord Cheston raised his eyebrows. "You are sure?"

"Yes." Setting the pot and fabric down, she knelt beside him and extended her arms. Carefully, he transferred the lamb from his knee to hers. Charlotte wrapped the sack around the small creature and pulled it closer. It made no movement. "Hurry, my lord."

Lord Cheston was already cinching the fabric around the spout. He lifted the pot, tipping it slightly. Seconds later a drip of milk fell from the small piece of fabric hanging from the spout. He leaned closer, pried open the lamb's mouth, and allowed the milk to dribble in.

"Come along, little fellow."

Charlotte rubbed the lamb's back as she'd seen Lord Cheston do. "Please, little one. Just try it."

Lord Cheston pressed the fabric to its mouth.

"There! Did you see?" Charlotte cried. "His nose twitched."

"He very likely smells the milk. Now, if we can just get him to start sucking."

Dipping his finger into the milk, he transferred it into the lamb's mouth. The lamb's head shifted, and its jaw started to move.

"He's doing it," she whispered.

Lord Cheston nodded, slowly easing the bubby pot's spout into the place his finger had occupied in the lamb's mouth. The lamb kept sucking. Charlotte barely breathed for fear that any movement she made might interrupt the miracle at work. Minutes passed, and the only sounds breaking the silence were the lamb's sucking and the crackle of the fire. Finally, the lamb's legs jerked, and his head rose from Charlotte's knee.

"Look at him." Charlotte could not hide the tears in her eyes. "He's trying to sit up."

William smiled. He was not sure what touched him most: the lamb's valiant fight for life or Miss Densley's part in it. He watched as she untangled the lamb's legs from the sack. Although her dressing gown covered her body completely, it was impossible not to notice her feminine form. Her golden hair fell in a mass of unruly curls halfway down her back, and as she guided the lamb upright, a gentle smile tugged at her lips. He tore his eyes from the scene to set the bubby pot down.

"It was fortunate that you already had the milk warming," he said. "This little fellow's mother rejected him. Lambs do not survive much more than an hour without the warmth and nutrients of their mother's milk. Cows' milk is not quite the same, but it was the best we could do, and it seems to have done the trick."

Concern filled Miss Densley's eyes. "But what will happen to him now?"

"We'll try him with another ewe. If she won't take him, we'll keep feeding him with the bubby pot."

"Oh, the poor dear!" She ran her hand across the lamb's back. It lowered its head again and nestled into Miss Densley's knee. She smiled, and William tried not to stare. How many young ladies of his acquaintance would willingly sit on a kitchen floor and embrace the opportunity to have a newborn lamb on their lap?

He cleared his throat. "I thank you for all your assistance, Miss Densley. I would have been hard-pressed to save him alone."

"I am glad I was here." Her cheeks colored as awareness of their somewhat unseemly situation returned. "I . . . I could not sleep. And I thought perhaps some warm milk might help."

"Then we should heat up some more for you," he said, coming to his feet.

"Oh no, please do not trouble yourself, my lord." The color in her cheeks deepened, and she attempted to rise.

"Wait. Allow me to relieve you of your squirming bundle." William reached for the lamb.

She relinquished it with a small laugh. "It's marvelous to see him moving so much."

"It is."

He tucked the lamb under one arm and extended his free hand to her. She took it. Awareness of her touch hummed through him. Her small hand fit perfectly within his larger one, her soft skin so unlike his own. He helped her to her feet.

"Thank you, my lord," she said, but he did not immediately release her hand.

"William," he said. "After all we have shared this evening, I believe we have moved beyond being general acquaintances."

"Thank you, William," she repeated, her smile causing his pulse to quicken. "My name is Charlotte."

The lamb squirmed, attempting to wriggle free of his arm. Reluctantly, William released Charlotte's hand to calm the creature.

"I'd best return him to the barn," he said. "My head shepherd, Ralph, will know what to do with him."

Charlotte tipped her head to one side, studying him curiously. "If we are to be friends, may I ask why you are working in the barn this late at night? You have already admitted to having at least one shepherd who is surely trained for such work."

William considered his response. It would be very easy to offer a vague answer about lambing season being a time that required extra hands, or that he preferred to be intimately involved in the workings of his farm. But for some reason, he felt that he owed Charlotte a more honest reply. Besides, if there was anyone whom he could fully absolve of involvement in the recent rash of sheep stealing, it was the lady before him.

"I am always more heavily involved in the farm during lambing season," he said, "but this year, my presence in the fields and barn is all the more important. Over the last few months, someone has been stealing sheep from Tribbley Hall. My men are spread thin trying to monitor the flock and the new births, so I take my turn with both."

Her eyes widened. "How many sheep have you lost?"

"Over two dozen."

She gasped. "That number must be a severe blow."

"It is, indeed, and I cannot afford to lose another." He set his jaw. "Unfortunately, it would seem that the felon does not consider the fact that the crime is punishable by death to be deterrent enough."

"Do you have any idea how he is managing it?"

"No." William released a frustrated sigh. "It could be that he is taking the sheep from the estate at night. Alternatively, he could be luring the sheep from the fields by day and hiding them somewhere on the property until he returns at night to remove them."

"Do you have men watching the fields at night?"

"Every one of them except Ralph, who is needed with the laboring ewes," he said.

She wrinkled her brow, as though deep in thought. "What kind of place would a thief use if he wished to hide the sheep until he could return?"

William shrugged. "An abandoned hut or walled enclosure, a cave, or a ravine. I have ridden the length and breadth of my land searching for just those things, but to no avail. Other than the woodland to the north of the upper pasture, my land is predominantly open fields."

If anything, her blue eyes were even wider now.

"What if he took the sheep and hid them just beyond your fields. Close enough that he could remove them quickly, but far enough that you would not see or hear the animals before he returned for them?"

"If such a place existed, I have no doubt a thief would take advantage of it," he said.

"I believe it does, my lord." She took a small step closer to him, her expression eager. "My grandmother and I spent a good portion of the day at the beach. Whilst she rested in the shade, I walked almost the entire length of the bay. Just before I turned around to return to Grandmama, I saw a man disappear over the ridge above the cliffs. And then I heard bleating. I could not tell exactly where the sound came from, but it seemed closer than the pasture above."

William stared at her. His father had planted hedges along the tops of the cliffs to prevent the sheep from falling. He and Thomas had checked the hedge's integrity only two days ago. But there was a gate on the far corner of the upper pasture that connected to a public footpath. It would allow a man easy access to the cliffs. Was it possible that the upper cliffs boasted caves large enough to hide a sheep or two?

"When daylight comes, would you be willing to show me exactly where you heard the bleating?" he asked.

She shook her head. "We cannot wait until then. Do you not see? If the man I saw was your thief, then the sheep I heard had already been taken from the flock. He will undoubtedly move them from the cliffs before morning."

She was right, deuce take it. But he could not ask her to go out in the dark, dressed in a nightgown.

"As soon as I return the lamb to the barn, I will locate my steward, Thomas. He's currently watching the lower pasture, but I will take him with me to the bay."

Again, she shook her head, but this time she also seized his hand. "Let me go with you. In the time it will take you to return the lamb to the barn and locate Thomas, I can be dressed. If we ride out to the bay now, I can show you exactly where to look."

Her suggestion was ludicrous. It was one thing for him and Thomas to be riding the beach at night, searching for missing sheep and a criminal. It was quite another for a young lady to do the same—particularly one who was here as his mother's guest. And yet, with her hand on his, he was finding it exceptionally difficult to refuse.

"Do not hesitate, William," she urged. "Every minute we waste may cost you another member of your flock."

He could not deny the truth of her words. "Very well," he said. "I will send a stable boy to the lower pasture for Thomas and will have a horse saddled for you. We will meet you outside the barn in twenty minutes, but if you choose not to come, I shall know that you allowed common sense to prevail."

Her eyes sparkled. "I rarely allow common sense to prevail, my lord. Particularly when it comes to stray cats, puppies, lambs, or righting a wrong."

And then, before he could so much as formulate a response, she had taken the candle on the table and exited the kitchen on running, slippered feet.

Chapter 8

Protecting the flickering flame of her candle with one hand, Charlotte hurried up the stairs and along the passageway to her bedchamber. When saving William's flock had become a priority, she did not know. But somehow, it had. She'd enjoyed the baron's presence enough last night to miss it today, but that early connection had become something much stronger as they'd battled together to revive the lamb. She'd felt it when he took her hand, had seen the flicker of awareness in his eyes. And when he'd asked her to call him by his given name, she'd known he'd recognized it too.

She reached her room and stepped inside, the magnitude of what she had agreed to do hitting her for the first time. Pushing aside her misgivings, she crossed to the wardrobe. Her first challenge would be dressing in a timely fashion. She did not know where Lady Cheston's ladies' maids slept, and she had no time to find out.

Opening the door, she rifled through the clothing hanging there until she found her riding habit. She took off her dressing gown, and eyeing her stays with trepidation, she loosened the ties just enough to slip it over her head, fumbling to tighten the laces. It was impossible to keep the two sides even. With a frustrated tug, she cinched the back as tight as she could and tied the laces in a haphazard knot.

Sparing herself the additional encumbrance of a hooped petticoat over her shift, she put on her habit, tugged on her riding boots, and tied back her hair with a piece of loose ribbon. Guessing that the beach would be more exposed to the sea breeze than was the house, she tossed her cloak across her shoulders. Picking up her candle once more, she left her room as quickly as she'd entered it.

At the top of the stairs, she hesitated. Under normal circumstances, she would leave the house by the front door. This did not constitute normal circumstances however, and she would prefer to avoid alerting anyone in the household to her departure. Realizing that William had likely left the servants' door unlocked, she retraced her steps to the kitchen. Already, the fire had dimmed. The empty pan and bubby pot sat on the table. Charlotte placed her candle beside them and blew it out. By the faint glow of the coals, she crossed to the door and pulled it open.

Moonlight shone down on the drive, outlining trees and bushes near the house. Dark oblong shapes in the distance marked the position of the barn and stables, and over the rustle of leaves in the breeze, she heard the distinctive sound of a latch lifting, followed by the clatter of hooves against the gravel. William was bringing out their horses. Closing the door behind her, Charlotte picked up her skirts and ran.

William rode between Thomas and Charlotte, his thoughts swirling. If, as Charlotte suspected, someone was hiding his sheep in a cave and removing them under cover of darkness, where were they taken next? It seemed to him that there were only three possibilities. One was to take them back across the pasture or down the public footpath, but Tribbley Hall lands were extensive, and it would take considerable time to cross it from the cliffs—especially in the dark. Another possibility was to remove the animals by sea. It would not be difficult to steer a small craft into the bay, load up a sheep or two, and take off again, only to dock elsewhere. Regardless of his obvious disdain for the creatures, Mr. Fitzroy had already admitted to being out in a boat by night.

If the tide were out, the easiest exit strategy for someone droving sheep would be to take them across the sand. Around the headland to the north, the Tribbley estate gave way to Mr. Wellington's land. Beyond his, was Mr. Fitzroy's. To the south, Mr. Ryland's estate butted against William's and was bordered on the other side by the wetlands surrounding the Broads. Mr. Crawley, the gentleman who had reported missing sheep to the magistrate, owned the property beyond the waterways. It was notable that each of those individuals had acreage that terminated at the sea.

He glanced at the sky, grateful for the bright moon. He and Thomas knew the road well enough to ride it in the dark, but the pale light would undoubtedly make it easier for Charlotte to find her way back to the spot where she'd heard bleating earlier today. As desperate as he was to reach his sheep before they disappeared, the thought that the three of them might appear on the beach at the same time as the thief had not escaped him. He and Thomas had taken the time to arm themselves with the emergency pistols he kept locked in the stables, but Charlotte—the most vulnerable of them all—was defenseless.

Mindful of how well sound traveled at night, William kept his voice low. "Would you ride on the other side of Miss Densley, Thomas?"

Without a moment's hesitation, his steward slowed his horse and waited for them to continue ahead of him before crossing the road to move up alongside the lady.

"Do you anticipate trouble, my lord?" Charlotte asked softly.

"If you are right about what is happening at the cliffs, I pray we will arrive before the villain. In that case, all will be well."

"What if I am correct, but he is there ahead of us?"

"If there is any hint of a confrontation, I would ask that you return to the house immediately. Thomas will accompany you."

"I think not."

He swiveled to look at her in the dark. "I beg your pardon?"

"Forgive me," she said. "I did not mean to be discourteous. It's simply that if we happen upon the villain, you and Thomas must face him together."

"I would not have you return to the house alone."

"Then we are at an impasse, my lord."

William's frustration vied with his admiration. "There was no sign of your common sense when you returned to your chamber, then."

"Not so much as a smidgen," she said. "But I shall attempt to locate it as quickly as possible."

If he had not been so concerned for her, he would have chuckled. As it was, he redoubled his silent prayers that they would reach the cliffs without encountering anyone.

"The entrance to the bay is up ahead, my lord," Thomas said.

"I see it," William replied. The gravel ended at a dark swathe of sand and scrub. "Be aware that once we cross the remaining rocks, we will be clearly visible to anyone on the beach."

"Let us hope any other visitors to the bay are similarly blessed," Thomas muttered.

The clatter of hooves against the rocky entrance seemed especially loud. When they reached the sand, Charlotte pointed to the left. They started that way without speaking, hugging the cliffs so that they might take advantage of the protection afforded by the rock wall. The waves rushed in and out, rattling the pebbles as they rolled over them. The breeze strengthened, and up ahead, the chalk and sandstone of the rising cliffs reflected the moonlight.

Charlotte led them a considerable distance, and at just about the time he considered questioning if she would have walked so far, she stopped.

"We are close," she whispered. "I remember standing near that outcropping and realizing it was long past time to return to Grandmama."

"Did you go any farther?" William asked.

"No."

He nodded and studied the cliff face above them. Were there any caves hidden in the pale-colored rock?

"My lord." Thomas's voice could barely be heard over the waves. "Look. A few feet below the tree."

A lone tree stood at the edge of the cliff, and as William searched the rock surface beneath its crooked trunk, he spotted a dark figure moving along the cliff face.

"There must be a path," he said. "He's moving too quickly to be looking for footholds."

"A sheep would not need anything very wide," Thomas said. "But did he access it from the beach or from above?"

William's heart pounded. Finally, they had the thief in their sights, and it appeared that he was going after the sheep. If he brought the animals down, they would have him. If he took them up to the ridge, they would have no chance of catching him from here.

"We must find a way up," he said, already scouring the base of the cliffs for anything that resembled a trail. "He must be heading for a cave."

"He's gone." At Charlotte's startled whisper, William's head jerked back up.

"Where?"

"About halfway down, my lord," Thomas said. "I reckon there must be a cave there, or a crevasse large enough to contain a few sheep."

"Do you see a boat out at sea?" he asked.

"It's hard to tell with how dark it is out there," Thomas said.

"I don't think there is one," Charlotte said. "Listen to the waves. There's no slap of water against a hull and no creak of ropes or oars."

She was right. It had been too long since he'd taken the time to simply listen to what the sea could tell him.

"It seems like this blighter's going to make his getaway on foot," Thomas said.

"I agree," William said. "But will he go up or down, Thomas? What do you think?"

Thomas slid out of his saddle, his feet landing soundlessly on the sand. "What I think is, we shouldn't take a chance that he'll walk into our waiting arms. We need to get closer before he reappears."

"Wait." Charlotte's low voice rang with urgency. "I think I see his horse."

"Where?" William asked.

"A few yards ahead. It must have turned its head just right. I saw its eyes in the moonlight."

Thomas walked forward a few steps, and out of the darkness, a horse snorted nervously.

"She's right, my lord. Looks to be a black stallion."

"A mount that blends well in the darkness," Williams muttered. "I should have expected nothing less."

"It would seem that your thief can access the cave from the top and the bottom," Charlotte said. "Earlier today, I saw him on the ridge, and yet it appears that he started from the beach this evening."

"And he will be returning this way to reclaim his mount," William said. "I am grateful to you, Charlotte. Your observational skills are second to none."

"Then may I make one more, my lord." The moon caught a portion of her upturned face. She was studying the cliff face again. "I believe there are two sheep traversing the same path the man was on moments ago."

Charlotte had barely finished speaking when a rattle of small rocks rained down the cliff face. Moments later, a sheep bleated.

"I see our man," William whispered. "He's following after the sheep."

Thomas appeared beside them, leading a large stallion. "I have his mount," he said quietly. "I'll tie him to mine." His teeth flashed in the moonlight. "No sense in leaving his ride available to him, is there?"

"As soon as you've done that, escort Miss Densley back to the house," William said.

"No, William." As much as Charlotte did not wish to make that journey alone in the darkness, it was nothing when compared to how much she did not wish William to confront a criminal by himself. She swung her horse around so it was facing the way they had come. "Thomas must stay with you. I can make my own way."

"Charlotte, please."

"He is coming, my lord." Thomas's insistent whisper cut off any reply she may have made.

Another shower of rocks bounced off the cliff, and seconds later, two white smudges materialized on the sand. Charlotte heard a muffled curse, followed by a male voice.

"Jasper. Where the devil are you?"

The stallion attached to Thomas's mount nickered.

"Your horse is quite safe," William said, his voice steely. "I certainly hope the same can be said for my sheep."

"Lord Cheston!"

"It appears you have an advantage over me, sir. Your name, if you please."

The dark shadow up against the white cliffs stepped forward. "We need no introduction, my lord."

William inclined his head. "So it would seem. I had not expected to see you here, Mr. Ryland."

"Nor I, you, my lord," Mr. Ryland said.

Charlotte bit back her gasp at his calm response. Mr. Ryland had dined at the baron's house not more than two days before. The gentleman was William's neighbor and friend.

"You have just come from my land and are stealing my property, sir." William's posture was ramrod straight, his tone glacial. "My presence should not be terribly surprising."

"What I am about is hardly stealing, my lord."

"Then how exactly would you define the taking of my sheep under the cover of darkness?"

Mr. Ryland's shoulders straightened. "I am merely setting them free."

Charlotte stared at the gentleman. His eyes shone unnaturally bright in the moonlight. There was something about him that put her on edge. She shifted in her saddle and his gaze darted to her.

"Miss Densley," he said, bowing his head. "This is an unexpected pleasure."

"I would not go so far as to say that, sir."

"Come now." His smile sent a trickle of unease down her spine. "We spoke together quite pleasantly at Tribbley Hall. Indeed, I told you that very evening of my mission to have the marshlands around the Broads be a place of refuge for all of England's marvelous flora and fauna. The opportunity to grow and roam in their natural environment belongs to all creatures." He raised his chin, turning back to face William. "Norfolk's sheep do not belong penned in by walls and hedges. They deserve to be as unrestricted as the county's native deer and rabbits."

"If you wish to populate the Broads with sheep, Ryland, you may do so," William said. "But they will be animals purchased with your own purse, not mine."

"A baron, such as yourself, has such deep coffers, you have no need of sheep," Mr. Ryland scoffed.

"The depth of my family's coffers has no bearing whatsoever on the fact that I have given my word to several noteworthy merchants that Tribbley Hall will provide them with a large quantity of high-quality wool—a promise that will be almost impossible to keep since you have stolen over twenty-five of my sheep."

William's vehement rebuke had its effect. Mr. Ryland took a step back, appearing suddenly less sure.

"It was for the sake of the sheep, my lord, I was simply—"

William did not allow him to finish. "In case you have forgotten, Mr. Ryland, sheep stealing is a crime punishable by death. You may offer your excuses to the magistrate, but as he has also fallen victim to your nefarious activities, I would advise you to choose your words wisely. Indeed, as Thomas and I intend to escort you to Mr. Wellington's residence right away, you may take the entire journey to consider your speech because, quite frankly, I do not wish to hear anything more."

Thomas stepped toward Mr. Ryland. The gentleman saw him coming and bolted, startling the meandering sheep. With a fearful bleat, they ran directly into Thomas's path. The steward stumbled backward. William turned his horse to cut off the sheep, and Mr. Ryland leaped onto a boulder beside Charlotte's mount. The horse skittered sideways, but before Charlotte could settle him, Mr. Ryland tore the reins from her fingers and swung himself up behind her.

In one swift movement, he wrapped his free arm around her in such a way that her arms were pinned at her sides, and then he dug his heels into the horse's sides. The horse shot forward, and Charlotte was thrown back against Mr. Ryland. He grunted but did not let go of her.

"William!" Charlotte cried, but already, her horse was galloping down the beach.

CHAPTER 9

A SHEEP WAS IMMEDIATELY in front of his horse's hooves. William pulled on the reins and his mare swerved to the right, barely missing the second sheep. Out of the corner of his eye, he saw Thomas run for his horse, but his steward would be of little help in pursuing Ryland with the man's stallion tied to his mount. Thomas would have to untie Ryland's horse if he were to take up the chase.

"Gather the sheep," William shouted, and then he took off after Charlotte.

Ryland was pushing the horse hard. Already, William had to strain to see the vague shadow of the mare and its riders, but the steady cadence of galloping hooves against the wet sand echoed the pounding of his racing heart. There was no accounting for what a man so delusional would do to someone he kidnapped. He took a ragged breath. If something were to happen to Charlotte, her grandmother and his mother would never forgive him. More to the point, he would never forgive himself.

Lowering himself in the saddle, William gave his horse

its head. "Come on, Bella," he muttered. "We have to catch them before he reaches the promontory."

Ryland's advantage was that he'd obviously ridden this stretch of beach several times in the last few weeks; William's advantage was that he was riding solo. Bella's hooves thundered around the bay, sending sand flying in their wake, and gradually, the distance between the horses began to narrow.

William raised his head slightly. He could make out Ryland's form, but it was impossible to see Charlotte. He'd heard nothing from her since she'd called his name. Was her silence of her own doing, or was the fiend threatening her in some way? His stomach twisted. She was the most fearless young lady he'd ever met. And the only one whose smile and blue eyes could distract him so completely from his work. He pushed aside the vision of her holding the lamb in the kitchen and focused on the horse ahead. No matter Ryland's end goal, William would reach Charlotte first.

Charlotte attempted to quash her rising panic. If Mr. Ryland's ragged breathing and ever-tightening grip on her arms were any indication, the gentleman was close to the breaking point. And with the rocky promontory drawing closer, that did not bode well for either of them. A fall from a horse traveling at this speed could be deadly; landing on the rocks made it almost certain. She tensed her right leg around the pommel of the sidesaddle in a desperate attempt to retain her seat on the galloping horse.

"Do you aim to kill us both, sir?"

The wind caught her words and flung them away, but Mr. Ryland was close enough to hear.

"You have nothing to fear, Miss Densley." He leaned

closer, his mouth at her ear. "Once we are out of this bay, we are free."

Charlotte strained against his arm. She wanted no part of Mr. Ryland's warped sense of freedom. All she wanted at this moment was to be with William. A sob caught in her throat as awareness of her growing feelings for the baron overtook her. The unexpected revelation was quickly followed by a surge of determination. She would escape—no matter how impossible it seemed. She and William had witnessed one miracle already this evening. Surely another was possible.

They were reaching the tip of the bay. Straining to see the terrain in the darkness, Mr. Ryland slowed the horse to a trot. At their right, the land jutted into the sea in a steep, rocky promontory, which appeared as a jagged black shadow against the night sky. On their left, the sea was an enormous pool of ink. And behind them, above the sound of the wind and the waves, Charlotte heard the thunder of hooves. Her heart lifted a fraction. It had to be William. And, unless the sea breeze was distorting the sound, he was close.

Mr. Ryland must have come to the same conclusion. He touched his heels to the horse's side, urging it into the water.

"He shall not catch us, Miss Densley." He spoke with brash assurance. "The tide is coming in too quickly for Lord Cheston to navigate the remaining distance on horseback."

Charlotte said nothing. If Mr. Ryland wished to believe that all would be well for him once he was beyond the bay, he could do so. It would have no bearing on her. One way or another, she would be gone before then.

The horse forged on, the water now up to its forelegs. Water was seeping into Charlotte's boots, and she could feel the weight of her skirts increasing as they became wetter. It was an unpleasant state, but if she were forced to choose, she would rather drop into the water than onto the rocks. There was no way of knowing when her opportunity would come, but she must be ready to seize it when it did.

Using the horse's unsteady gait to hide her movement, Charlotte slowly eased her right leg up and over the pommel, gradually shifting until it was free of the horn. A wave hit the horse's chest, splashing seawater at both riders. Mr. Ryland cursed, wiping his forehead on his shoulder. Unable to remove the drips from her face, Charlotte used the distraction to slide her left foot out of the slipper stirrup. Both legs now hung free. She twisted her hips slightly to the left until the only thing keeping her in the saddle was Mr. Ryland's crushing arm-hold.

Another wave rolled in, wetting Charlotte's riding habit above her knees and causing the horse to misstep. Behind her, she heard echoing splashes. William's horse had entered the water.

"Come on!" Mr. Ryland tugged on the reins.

With a snort, the horse shook its head, and suddenly the black silhouette of a huge rock appeared in the water before them. The rush of water filled the air.

"Watch out!" she cried.

Mr. Ryland reacted instinctively. Releasing his hold on Charlotte, he grabbed the reins in both hands just as an enormous wave rounded the headland and barreled down upon them. The horse's legs buckled. It staggered sideways, struggling to stay upright. Clinging to the reins, Mr. Ryland cursed again, and Charlotte let herself fall.

As she slid out of the saddle, her feet hit the water, her skirts expanding around her as she sank. The sudden cold stole her breath, and for one awful moment, she was not sure that she could take another. She opened her mouth, but instead of air, she gasped seawater. Coughing, she floundered, trying to find her footing. Her knee hit a rock. Pain radiated upward from the injury. The water was up to her chin. She took two more unsteady steps away from the horse before her leg gave way and she dropped below the water's surface.

William tightened his hold on the reins as another wave crashed into Bella. As far as he could tell, they were only a few yards from the promontory's tip. At this point, the battling currents on either side of the rock formation caused the waves to hit with greater fury. Ryland was a lunatic to attempt passing it on horseback with the tide coming in so rapidly. If the man had been riding alone, William would have let him test fate without doing the same himself. It would have been a long, hard ride, but crossing to the other side of the headland by road and meeting the fiend on the other side would have been far safer. As it was, William was not willing to lose sight of the horse carrying Charlotte.

Ryland was almost around the tip now. Only a moment ago, William had heard loud splashes. He'd hoped the stronger waves would slow the horse enough for him to close the distance between them further, but the man was pressing on relentlessly. The gentleman's white cravat stood out above his dark jacket. Charlotte's navy riding habit was almost invisible, but her blonde hair . . . William strained to see through the darkness, a pit widening in his stomach as he searched in vain. There was no one on the horse but Ryland.

Another wave caught him off guard. Bella sidestepped. William loosened the reins, allowing Bella to steady herself as he scoured the water around him. Charlotte had been on the horse when Ryland had entered the sea. He was sure of it. Just as he was equally sure that she was not in the saddle now.

"Charlotte!" he shouted.

The sea breeze snatched his voice. Another wave came in. Bella moved closer to the promontory.

"Steady girl!" The last thing William needed right now was an injured horse. He guided her back out into the water. "Charlotte!" he yelled again.

Something slapped against his foot. He looked down. Fabric. He reached for it, pulling the sopping mass out of the water. His heart pounded as he held it up. It was a cloak. Charlotte's cloak. Swallowing the bile in his throat, he scoured the water around him.

"Charlotte!"

A splash up ahead had him urging Bella forward.

"Here!" Her voice was weak, but he heard it. He swung to his right. Another wave rolled by, and he saw her face seconds before it disappeared beneath the surface.

Keeping the reins firmly in one hand, William leaped out of his saddle. He landed on his feet, the water reaching his chest. Wading forward, he raked the water in ever-increasing circles until he felt her arm. Grasping it, he pulled her up. She emerged, spluttering and flailing her limbs. Releasing his hold on Bella's reins, he pulled her against his chest.

"Calm yourself," he said. "I have you."

"I . . . I . . . c-cannot . . . s-swim." A racking cough overtook her, and she clung to him so tightly he thought he might lose his own ability to breathe.

"But I can," he said. "And if you will trust me, I will get you to safety." He pried her fingers from around his neck and swept her into his arms. "Come. Before the next wave hits."

"B-but, M-Mr. R-Ryland. Y-you m-must go a-after him."

William waded over to his horse and caught Bella's floating leather straps in between his fingers. "You are infinitely more important than Mr. Ryland."

Her wide eyes met his, but then she tensed and was seized with another bout of coughing. Tightening his arms around her, he started back for the beach.

The water had dropped to his thighs by the time her hacking calmed, and with no water to offer buoyancy to her clothing, the weight of her sodden riding habit pulled at his shoulders. He dragged his feet through the last remaining inches of seawater, grateful when Thomas materialized out of the darkness and took Bella's reins from him.

"I have the sheep secured, my lord," he said. "What more can I do?"

"Lend me your jacket," he said. "Mine is too wet to be of any use, but we must get Miss Densley out of these sodden clothes and into something warmer."

Charlotte gasped, squirming to be free of his arms. "N-no, W-William."

"Hold still or I shall drop you," he said, clasping her more tightly. "This is not an issue of modesty or propriety, Charlotte; this is a matter of life and death. If you were to attempt riding home in these wet clothes, you would perish from cold before we reach Tribbley Hall."

"W-will you at l-least t-turn away?"

"Thomas and I will both turn away. If you need assistance, however, you have only to ask." He paused. "Are you ready to try your feet?"

"Y . . . yes."

Slowly, he set her down. She was trembling with cold. He waited, not moving his arms away until he knew she was steady. "Very well. Thomas will hold his jacket out for you and we will both face the other way."

He took a few steps and stood beside Thomas with his back to her. He waited. He heard the slap of wet fabric, followed by a rip. And then Charlotte's voice.

"I-I c-cannot, William. M-my fingers w-will not . . ." Her voice broke.

"I'm turning around, Charlotte." He pivoted. Her teeth

were chattering so violently, he could hear them. He eyed the dark swathes of fabric clinging to her legs. "How do I undo these ridiculous outer garments?"

"T-the s-skirt is t-tied. Th-there's a knot."

"Show me."

Her trembling hand reached for his and she placed it on her hip. "Th-there."

He felt the ribbons. They were wet and tied tightly. "Thomas," he said. "Do you have a knife on you?"

"Yes, my lord."

"Hold it out to me, if you please."

Moments later, a short blade glinted in the moonlight at the end of Thomas's extended arm. William reached for it, pulled the ribbons free of the skirt, and sliced through them. He tugged at the heavy fabric and it shifted. Charlotte took ahold of it and pulled. It slid to the sand in a wet heap, leaving her standing in her shift.

William took a breath. "Now the jacket."

"B-buttons in f-front," she said.

He circled her. She lifted her trembling chin slightly and met his eyes. Even in the pale moonlight, he recognized the trust shining there.

"As soon as it's off, you shall have Thomas's," he said softly. "It will be warm and large enough to cover you well."

She gave a small nod, and before he could second-guess himself, he reached for the button below her neck. His fingers fumbled and brushed against her skin. It was soft and smooth, but icy-cold. Grateful for the poignant reminder of her critical condition, he hurriedly undid each of the remaining buttons and peeled the sleeves off her shaking arms. When Charlotte's jacket landed on the ground atop her skirt, he reached for Thomas's coat.

He threaded her pale arms into the sleeves and buttoned

up the jacket. It hung from her slender shoulders like a shapeless sack, but William had rarely been so thankful for an article of clothing.

He cleared his throat. "Thank you, Thomas." he said. "Would you hold Bella while I set Miss Densley in the saddle?"

"Yes, my lord."

His steward drew William's horse closer and stood at her head, holding the straps.

"Come," William said to Charlotte. "We must get you home."

He placed his hands on her waist. A gust of wind blew off the sea and she shivered. William lifted her onto his mare and climbed up behind her.

"I'll take care of the lady's outerwear and the sheep, my lord," Thomas said, handing William the reins. "You get Miss Densley home."

"You have my thanks, Thomas," William said, already wheeling Bella around.

Charlotte coughed and pressed her cheek against his damp jacket. He threaded his arm around her, drawing her close as Bella broke into a canter.

"Th-thank you f-for s-saving me, W-William," she said.

This was not the time to tell her that if he did not have her in front of a fire very soon, her battle to regain full health would be in serious jeopardy.

"You must do everything my housekeeper, Mrs. Underhill, tells you, so that you regain your strength quickly," he said.

He felt her nod. "I w-will. I-I must. I have a l-lamb to f-feed."

His heart ached at her simple declaration, and he pressed his lips to the top of her head. "Indeed, you do."

Chapter 10

Slowly, Charlotte became aware of women's voices talking nearby.

"She's been sleepin' soundly this whole time, ma'am."

"So she's had nothing to eat or drink?" Grandmama sounded worried.

"No, ma'am."

"Run down to the kitchen and fetch a tea tray, would you, Sally? She cannot continue much longer without nourishment."

"Yes, ma'am. Right away."

A door closed, and Charlotte forced her eyelids open. Sunlight, bright and warm, filled the room. She blinked, struggling to get her bearings. She was in her guest bedchamber at Tribbley Hall, lying beneath a mountain of blankets. And she was no longer shivering.

Memory of her condition when William handed her off to Mrs. Underhill came flooding back, bringing with it a rush of warmth to her cheeks.

"Grandmama?" Her voice was croaky.

"Charlotte! You're awake at last." Her grandmother took the chair beside the bed and reached for her hand. "How are you feeling?"

"Thirsty," she said.

Grandmama nodded. "I've just sent Sally for some tea. It will be here shortly."

"What time is it?"

"Quarter past four."

Charlotte stared at her. "In the afternoon?"

"Yes, child. You've been asleep for almost fifteen hours." Anxiety filled her eyes. "We've all been worried sick about you. Mrs. Underhill and Sally have watched over you from the moment Lord Cheston walked into the house with you in his arms. Lady Cheston has stopped by every hour since she arose. And Lord Cheston has almost worn a hole in the carpet in the passageway from all the pacing he's been doing outside your room." She squeezed her hand. "Honestly, Charlotte, whatever possessed you to do something so rash?"

"We needed to save the sheep before they were stolen, and . . ." She paused as her grandmother's words sank in. "Did you say that Lord Cheston has been pacing?"

Grandmama chuckled softly. "Like a man possessed."

If it were possible, the warmth in Charlotte's cheeks intensified.

"Why? He has so many important things to see to." Not least of those was the capture of Mr. Ryland.

"I get the impression that you rank rather highly on his list of important things."

"Is he outside the door now?"

"No. I believe the magistrate arrived at the house about half an hour ago, and he was called downstairs to speak with him," Grandmama said.

Had the magistrate brought news about Mr. Ryland?

Charlotte pulled back the covers. "I must get dressed."

"Absolutely not!" Her grandmother was horrified. "After what you've endured, you will not leave this room until I am fully satisfied that you are completely well."

"I am completely well." Charlotte tugged one of the blankets so that it fell across her leg. Until she'd moved it, she had forgotten about her encounter with a rock when she dropped into the sea. The large purple welt on her knee was commensurate with the throbbing pain she was experiencing, and if Grandmama were to spot it, she would not be allowed out of the room for a week.

"When Sally brings the tea tray, you shall sit up in bed and partake of some refreshment," her grandmother said. "Afterward, if you feel up to it, you may attempt a turn around the room. For now, that is as far as you will go." Her grandmother waggled her forefinger at her. "And you know full well that it is a great deal more than your mother would allow."

Just because Grandmama was right did not make it any easier to bear. With a sigh, Charlotte pulled the pillows up against the headboard and repositioned herself so that she might lean against them. She had no doubt that her grandmother would watch her like a hawk when she circled the room. Somehow, she was going to have to hide her bruise and her limp simultaneously.

"I cannot imagine where he might be, my lord," the magistrate said. "Immediately after your steward arrived to tell me what had occurred at the beach, I rode to Ryland's house to detain him. There was no sign of the gentleman. According to his butler, he had arrived home an hour or so before and had awoken his valet, ordering him to pack trunks for an extended time away. He changed into dry clothing, left the house, and has not been seen since. His trunks are sitting in the hall still."

William paced the length of his study. He'd sent Thomas to the magistrate's house in the early hours of the morning. Since he'd heard nothing from Mr. Wellington in the intervening hours, he'd assumed that the magistrate had apprehended Ryland long ago. Learning that the gentleman was yet at large did not sit well.

"Where have you searched?"

"I left a man watching Ryland's house. He's to get word to me the moment Ryland reappears. I have spent the day visiting each of his neighbors, from Mr. Crawley in the south to Mr. Fitzroy in the north." Mr. Wellington scowled. "There's been no sign of him anywhere."

Running his fingers through his hair, William did another circuit of the room. Where would the man go? Surely he would not order his trunks to be packed only to leave without them. Unless he was using them as a ruse. William paused his pacing. Was Ryland that devious?

"Have you checked his stable and carriage house?"

"Yes, my lord. His conveyances are all accounted for. He exchanged your horse for one of his own. I believe your steward has returned the one Ryland left at the beach and has reclaimed your mount already."

So Ryland was on horseback. That opened up his destination to an almost impossible number of possibilities.

"Did you ask Ryland's butler if he knew where the man might have gone?"

"I did. He said that his master rarely journeyed anywhere beyond the Broads."

William swung around. "That's it!"

Mr. Wellington gave him a puzzled look. "I beg your pardon, my lord?"

"That is where Ryland has gone." When Mr. Wellington showed no sign of grasping his meaning, William continued. "The man is fixated with the Broads. If he were to contemplate leaving the area, he would undoubtedly visit his favorite spots one last time."

Mr. Wellington's expression cleared. "By Jove, I daresay you're right. It would be just like Ryland to stay in the marshland longer than he'd intended."

"Indeed," William said.

"A thorough search will require additional men," Mr. Wellington said.

"I suggest you begin in the areas closest to Ryland's land," William said. "Since he's been driving sheep along the beach, I will search the marshland that borders the sea."

Mr. Wellington did nothing to hide his relief. "I am most grateful for your assistance, my lord."

"I want the man apprehended, Wellington." He opened the bottom drawer of his desk and withdrew a pistol. "And we've wasted enough time already."

A light knock sounded at the door, and Sally walked in carrying a tray.

She bobbed a curtsy before approaching. "Mrs. Densley thought you might like some tea, miss."

Charlotte smiled. "Thank you, Sally."

"Of course, miss." She set the tray on Charlotte's knee. "An' if you don' mind me sayin' so, it's right good to see you lookin' more like yerself."

"Thank you, Sally. And I believe I have you to thank for taking care of me when I arrived here, wet and bedraggled."

"Mrs. Underhill is the one t' thank, miss. She knew just what t' do."

"I shall be sure to express my appreciation to her too."

Sally offered her a shy smile and bobbed another curtsy. "Will there be anything else, miss?"

"No. Actually, yes." Charlotte avoided looking at her grandmother. "Do you happen to know if Mr. Wellington is still meeting with Lord Cheston?"

"No, miss. The magistrate left about twenty minutes ago."

"I . . . I see." Charlotte swallowed her disappointment. William was no longer occupied with the gentleman, yet he had not returned. "Thank you, Sally."

The maid turned to go and another knock sounded. Charlotte's hope rose again, but when Sally opened the door, it was Lady Cheston who entered.

"Well, this is a sight for sore eyes," she said. "I am most grateful to see you sitting up in bed, Miss Densley."

"Thank you, Lady Cheston. I am very sorry for all the trouble I have caused."

"Nonsense, my dear. The only person in this house who has been trouble over the last twenty-four hours has been my son. I can assure you that I will be speaking to him regarding what he put you through."

Charlotte shook her head. "There is no need, my lady. I am the one responsible for placing myself in danger. In actuality, Lord Cheston saved my life."

She raised one eyebrow. "Is that truly how you see it?"

"Yes, my lady. He deserves nothing but heartfelt thanks."

The older lady exchanged a meaningful glance with Grandmama. "Well, then, perhaps there is hope for him yet."

William turned his horse toward the distant grove of trees. The vast expanse of marshland to his right left few places for a man or horse to remain hidden. If Ryland was there, he was lying amidst the reeds. There would be no finding him unless one literally stumbled upon him. The trees, however, provided plenty of cover and ample wildlife for the nature enthusiast.

He urged his horse forward. The sun was setting, and it would soon be too dark to search without lanterns. If he found no sign of Ryland in the trees, he would return to the house with the hope that Mr. Wellington or one of his men had discovered their quarry.

As he approached the nearest oak tree, a loud rustle of leaves preceded a flutter of wings. Suddenly, a flock of coots took to the sky. William watched them go.

"Did we startle them, or was it someone else, Bella?" he muttered.

Slowing his approach, he entered the trees. The sound of water increased, and through the branches, he glimpsed the slow-moving river on the other side of the copse. He spotted a flash of white. Withdrawing his pistol, William reined his horse to a stop and slid from the saddle. Using the trees as cover, he inched forward until he had a clear view of the riverbank.

A horse stood grazing on the grass, his leather straps trailing the ground. A few yards away, Ryland was pulling a sheep from a boggy patch by its front legs. The gentleman was knee-deep in dirty water, and the sheep was more brown than white. The animal gave a frightened bleat, and the sound was echoed by two more sheep standing at William's left. He glanced at the animals; their ears bore the distinctive clipped mark of the Tribbley Hall flock.

Gritting his teeth, he stepped out from the protection of the trees. "The magistrate wishes to speak with you, Ryland."

With a start, the man swung around, dropping the flailing sheep to the firmer ground. He scrambled out of the reeds, his eyes darting toward his horse. "I have no time to see him today," he said.

William took another step toward him. "Then you must make some."

Ryland bolted for his horse, and William raised his pistol. He was not sure that Ryland cared much for his own life, but he most certainly cared about the marshland.

"If you force me to shoot, there is no telling how the sound—or, worse, a misdirected bullet—might affect the wildlife," William warned.

Ryland froze, one hand on the reins and the other on the pommel. He took a juddering breath and dropped his head.

"It was for the sake of the animals," he said. "That is why I took them. Sheep used to roam free on the Broads. They belong here."

"You may explain that to the authorities," William said. "You are a gentleman of means. When you have replaced all the sheep you have stolen around the district, perhaps they will listen to you."

"My intentions were good."

"Your intentions came at the expense of law and order and endangered Miss Densley's life," William said.

Ryland's shoulders slumped, and like a light extinguished, the fight left him. "I should not have taken her mount."

"There is a great deal that you should not have done, Ryland," William said. "But this is neither the time, nor the place, to discuss it." Keeping his gun trained on Ryland, William seized the reins from the man's hand. "I will lead your mount behind my own," he said. "You, on the other hand, will walk." He pointed back the way he had come. "That way. And be quick about it. Neither of us wishes to have this journey take all night."

Chapter 11

William crossed the short distance to the barn with purposeful strides. The dew on the grass glistened in the early morning sunlight. It would not be more than an hour before the sun rose high enough to warm the day. By then, he hoped Charlotte would have awoken and he could finally visit her.

The positive reports he'd received from Mrs. Underhill and his mother when he'd arrived home late last night were everything he'd prayed for, and they had helped allay his overarching concern for the young lady. And yet, he wished to see the color in her cheeks with his own eyes, hear that she was well from her own lips. In truth, he simply wished to be with her.

Despite the early hour, the barn door was open. It did not surprise him. Ralph was undoubtedly checking on the new lambs before starting his work in the fields. William stepped inside. The familiar rustle of animals in their stalls was punctuated by a single bleat and the low rumble of Ralph's voice.

"That's it, miss. Keep it nice 'n' steady, jus' like that."

"Ralph?" William scanned the open space, searching for the shepherd in the dim light. Movement in the stall to his left caught his eye, and Ralph's head appeared above the upper slats.

"'Mornin', m'lord."

"Good morning. How are the lambs today?"

"Gettin' along nicely. The only one I've bin worryin' about is the little fella who got rejected, but 'e's taken a likin' to Miss Densley, and she's managed t' persuade 'im t' take the bubby pot right well."

William stared at him. "When did Miss Densley feed him?"

"Well, she's doin' it now, m'lord."

William was at the shepherd's side immediately. Ralph stepped aside to allow him a clear view inside the stall. Charlotte, dressed in a pale green floral gown, was sitting on a small stool in the corner. A brown wool blanket lay across her knee, and sitting on it was the lamb they'd rescued. In her hand, she held the bubby pot. The spout was pressed to the lamb's mouth, and the little creature was avidly guzzling the milk dripping from the scrap of fabric on the spout's end.

He stepped into the stall, his gaze shifting from the lamb to Charlotte. Her blue eyes met his and she smiled. His heartbeat quickened. Lud, she was beautiful.

"Whatever are you doing here?" he asked.

The lamb flinched.

"Feeding Snow," she whispered. "Shhh. He's almost finished."

William stood, silently watching as the lamb finished the last of the milk.

Charlotte set the bubby pot down. "He took it all, Ralph," she said.

The shepherd gave her an almost-toothless smile. "That's

grand, miss." He reached for the squirming lamb. "I'll put 'im back with the others, then."

She relinquished the animal and blanket, rose to her feet, and brushed a few pieces of straw off her gown.

With a slight nod directed at William, Ralph carried the lamb out of the stall and headed toward the back of the barn. Charlotte watched him go and then slowly turned to face William. The air stilled between them.

"You named the lamb Snow," William said. Given that all intelligent thought had unaccountably fled his mind, it was the best he could manage.

"Yes." She shrugged slightly. "It seemed fitting since the puppy that started my adventures at Tribbley Hall is called Soot."

"I'm afraid young Soot has a great deal to answer for."

The smile he had expected did not come. Instead, she lowered her head.

"I believe I do too," she said. "Because of me, you were unable to capture Mr. Ryland, and you lost a valuable horse. Forgive me. I owe you my life but have repaid you very poorly."

He closed the distance between them, placed his finger beneath her chin, and gently raised it until she was looking directly into his eyes.

"Charlotte, you have nothing to apologize for. It was your quick thinking and observational skills that spared the sheep Ryland took yesterday. Not only that, you helped save Snow." A hint of a smile touched her lips at his use of the name she'd given the lamb. Encouraged, he continued. "Were it not for you, we would still be searching for an unknown thief. As it is, Mr. Wellington is currently escorting Mr. Ryland to Norwich to face charges of sheep stealing, and Thomas has reclaimed my horse from his stable."

Her eyes widened. "Truly?"

"Truly." He smiled. "Mr. Wellington came to the house yesterday to ask if I would assist in locating Mr. Ryland. I had hoped to speak with you after you awoke last afternoon, but by the time I returned, it was too late."

"I... I watched for you, hoping that you would come."

Was it his imagination or was there more color in Charlotte's face now than there had been moments ago? He slid his fingers from her chin to softly brush her cheek. She held perfectly still.

"Then it is I who should apologize."

She shook her head. "I guessed that you were about some important business."

"Only the capture of Mr. Ryland would have kept me away." He touched a curl, tucking it gently behind her ear. "Tell me," he said softly. "How is it that you have been at Tribbley Hall for only a few days, and already I cannot imagine my life without you in it?"

"I . . . I do not know," she said. "But I have been wondering the same of you."

He slipped an arm around her and drew her closer. She came willingly, fitting into his arms as though she'd always been meant to be there. She raised her face, the look in her eyes telling him all he needed to know. One heartbeat passed, and then he lowered his head to claim her lips with his.

The heady scent of roses mingled with straw filled his senses, and from somewhere far away, a sheep *baa*ed.

"Charlotte?" he murmured, as awareness of his surroundings slowly returned.

"Yes?" Her voice was little more than a whisper.

"When lambing season is over, would you allow me to call upon you in London?"

Her lips curved upward, and he barely resisted the temptation to kiss her again.

"I should like that very much," she said.

"May I come every day?"

She laughed softly. "As much as I would love to see you in London every day, you would miss your work at Tribbley Hall too much to be gone for long."

Marveling that she could know him so well, he shifted his head so he could see her more clearly. "Then I think I may need to persuade my mother and your grandmother to act as chaperones so that you may visit me here."

Her beautiful eyes sparkled. "I do not think they will need much persuading. I have a feeling they have been working to that end all along."

A memory surfaced of his mother standing in his study telling him of Mrs. Densley's and her granddaughter's pending arrival, and of a project she and her friend were undertaking.

He chuckled. "I believe you may be right. I shall have to thank them."

Outside the barn, a rooster crowed. Charlotte gasped. "What time is it?"

William was not about to release her to withdraw his pocket watch. "I imagine it is close to nine o'clock."

She pulled away. "I must go before Grandmama arises and discovers that I escaped my room without permission."

"Ah, I wondered how you came to be here so early."

"If I am caught, I daresay she will place me in solitary confinement for the remainder of my stay."

"She cannot do that. Snow would not survive."

Charlotte looked aghast. "Do you really think so?"

"No," he admitted. "Ralph would take care of him. But I'm not so sure that *I* would survive."

A smile lit her face. "Then perhaps we should return to the house together and tell my grandmother that her host's very life depends upon me being free to visit the barn at any time."

William pressed a kiss to her forehead before offering her his arm. "That, my dear Charlotte, is the best suggestion I've heard in a very long time."

Sian Ann Bessey was born in Cambridge, England, but grew up on the island of Anglesey off the coast of North Wales. She left her homeland to attend Brigham Young University in Utah, where she earned a bachelor's degree in communications with a minor in English.

She began her writing career as a student, publishing several magazine articles while still in college. Since then she has published historical romance and romantic suspense novels, along with a variety of children's books. She is a *USA Today* best selling author, a Foreword Reviews Book of the Year finalist, and a Whitney Award finalist.

Although Sian doesn't have the opportunity to speak Welsh very often anymore, she can still wrap her tongue around, "Llanfairpwllgwyngyllgogerychwyrndrobwllllantysiliogogogoch." She loves to travel and experience other cultures, but when she's home, her favorite activities are spending time with her family, cooking, and reading.

You can visit Sian on the web at www.sianannbessey.com

LOVE OF MY HEART

SARAH M. EDEN

Chapter 1

London, 1790

CORDELIA WAKEFIELD KNEW NO home other than London. She'd lived in the bustling metropolis for the entirety of her twenty years and could not imagine passing so much as a single day as a resident of any other part of the world.

In London, one had that world at one's fingertips. Drapers, milliners, dressmakers, and booksellers of the highest stamp could be found in England's foremost city. The very best of food and company, the perfect balance of imposing architecture and glorious green spaces filled it to bursting. She was not so naive as to think her beloved home city was devoid of suffering and struggle, or that the experiences of all who called it home were as pleasant as her own.

But with all its flaws, she loved it.

Her younger sister was equally enamored. In fact, on a late-March morning, the two young ladies were spending time as they often did, making a slow circuit of the gated green near their home. The day was a bit blustery, as was often the case in Town, yet they could not have been happier with their location and the diversions it offered. The very earliest bulb flowers were emerging from their winter slumber. Soon, London itself would awaken as well, with the return of those who divided their time between their country estates and their Town residences. Cordelia felt heartily sorry for them. One ought to never be required to quit such a glorious city.

"Do you suppose Mother and Father will allow me to finally have my Season this year?" Cordelia asked.

"I do hope so. I'll not ever have mine if they don't allow you yours."

Cordelia shook her head at Seraphina's teasing declaration. Her sister did, in fact, wish to join Society herself in the next year or two, but she was too good a sister and too good a person to not wish Cordelia happy.

They passed Mrs. Seaver—a widow of advancing years who lived nearby—and her companion on the path that circled the green. Both ladies offered greetings, which the sisters returned in kind. This was an established routine between them. Cordelia loved the familiarity and calm of her life in London. She knew the people, and they knew her. The only thing marring her adoration of Town was her longing to truly become part of Society.

She would so enjoy attending dinner parties and balls, having full access to musicales and the theatre. She would, of course, still make ample time for painting, her true passion. Watercolors were deemed entirely acceptable for young ladies. Though Cordelia did enjoy the challenge of that particular medium, she was more enamored of oils, a less characteristic choice for a woman.

"Do you suppose Father and Mother have not allowed you your Season because they feel you ought to be older?"

Seraphina asked once they'd fully passed Mrs. Seaver and Miss Greene.

"Perhaps. Though, I hope not. Most young ladies making their first foray into Society have done so by my age. I'll be ancient in comparison if made to wait too many more years. I nearly am already."

"And that would mean *I* would, of necessity, be required to wait just as long." Seraphina's sigh was heavy with frustration. "I would very much like to dance the allemande with someone other than Monsieur Benoit."

Their aging dancing tutor had provided them a more than adequate education in the various dances one was expected to execute, but he smelled very strongly of cloves mingled with a putrid sort of tobacco and powdered his hair so heavily and inexpertly that a cloud of wafting white followed him everywhere he went. They did not dislike the Frenchman, but he was sometimes a bit uncomfortable to spend time with. Surely, there were gentlemen at the balls they'd heard so much about who did not leave residue everywhere they went.

"Perhaps Father and Mother have denied you your Season because of the expense," Seraphina said.

There had been some tightening of the family purse strings the last couple of years, but nothing terribly severe.

"Perhaps they fear I will spend all of my time amongst Society haranguing anyone and everyone on the topic of painting," Cordelia suggested with a teasing smile.

"Which means they will *never* permit me a Season, as I am even more likely to make a nuisance of myself, though on the subject of music."

They made light of the situation as they continued their leisurely walk. Cordelia hadn't the first idea why her parents had thus far denied her the entrée into Society she'd been expecting. She knew better than to ask. Her parents did not discuss difficult things with their children. Neither Cordelia nor Seraphina were certain their parents discussed difficult things even with each other.

And thus, the sisters spent a great deal of time speculating and guessing and uncertain about the whys governing their present or the whats to come in their future.

"Miss Wakefield!" The sound of her name spoken in urgent tones stopped Cordelia on the spot.

One of the chambermaids was only just catching up with them. She did not appear to have come in search of Cordelia for a calm or insignificant reason.

"Has something happened, Nora?"

She nodded and motioned back in the direction of their house. "Your mother's insisting you return directly, miss."

"Only Cordelia?" Seraphina asked.

Nora shook her head. "The both of you."

Cordelia exchanged a glance with her sister. Mother didn't often call them back to the house, and she very seldom showed significant emotion in front of the servants. Whatever had led to this departure from decorum, it must have been urgent.

An immediate return home was unavoidable.

The scene she found upon entering the sitting room was nothing short of chaotic. Servants rushed about, simultaneously offering Mother restorative teas and attempting to stay entirely out of her way. Cordelia's parents did not allow their tempers to flare in front of the staff. The servants' avoidance of Mother likely resulted more from confusion than fear.

"Why in heaven's name were you gone so long?" Mother pressed her handkerchief, clutched tightly in her hand, to her embroidered stomacher.

"We were away no longer than usual," Cordelia said.

"I am quite certain you were absent much longer. I have been in great distress waiting for you both."

Seraphina looked every bit as confused as Cordelia felt. "We returned the moment we were sent for."

"You should not have left to begin with." Mother had never before objected to their daily exercise.

Cordelia crossed to her. "What has distressed you so entirely?"

Mother did not dismiss the staff nor request her daughters accompany her to a more private corner of the house. She declared, with passion and volume, neither of which she usually employed, "Your father is requiring that we retrench."

Retrench? Cordelia had seen no indications that the family coffers were in danger of emptying. They'd certainly not been drastically economizing.

"What are we meant to quit in the name of retrenchment?" she asked. How she hoped it was not her painting supplies or Seraphina's music instructions.

It was not her mother who answered, however. Father's voice quite unexpectedly filled the room from the doorway. "London," he said. "We are to quit London."

Chapter 2

Teviotbrae, Scotland

Sebastian Coburn had been born on the same estate where he now lived. One might think he'd not gone anywhere or seen anything other than this corner of Scotland. But one would be mistaken.

He had spent much of his life traveling Britain and even attending Eton as a boy. His father had died when he was very young. Upon the untimely death of his mother nearly four years ago, he had returned to Teviot Castle, where his grandfather lived. As the principal landowner in the area, his grandfather was styled Angus Coburn, Laird of Teviotbrae. Sebastian, himself, would acquire the same dignity upon his grandfather's passing.

For now, he was known simply as "Sebastian of the Home Farm." All the local people, of course, knew his connection to the laird. But Grandfather had decided that Sebastian needed to show the people living in the vicinity that he would both be a good steward of the land and a valuable addition to the area.

And thus, Sebastian had been assigned to work the home farm on the Teviot Castle estate, living in the humble home there, tilling the fields, repairing the buildings, depending upon the income generated from his efforts to sustain himself, rather than calling upon the income he received from his late father's accounts or living on the land nearby that he had inherited upon his father's death.

In making the Teviot Castle home farm his home and his occupation, he had gained an ever-increasing love for the land and for the people. He further found himself increasingly humbled to know that the well-being of the area would one day depend so much on the decisions he made. But he didn't know if he was making any difference to anyone.

"I think your mind is off in the clouds again, Sebastian," young Connall McCrory said, rightly acknowledging that Sebastian was distracted. "Best snatch up your thoughts and bring 'em back to earth."

"While I do that," Sebastian tossed back, "why don't you snatch up those nails we pounded straight so we can finish this up before the storm brewing breaks."

Sebastian didn't sound as Scottish as the others who lived here did. He'd been away too long, educated in England and raised by an English mother. He'd picked up a bit of it during his four years as Sebastian of the Home Farm, but knew he'd likely always sound a bit out of place. The people of Teviotbrae had accepted him anyway, a bit of mercy for which he was deeply grateful.

"Do you suppose the foxes'll manage to get into the hen house after this?" Connall was quite careful with the nails as he brought them over to where he and Sebastian had been working. The bits of metal came dear; they didn't dare risk losing one.

"I wish I could say they won't," Sebastian said. "But they manage to outsmart us more often than I'd care for."

"Are you saying we're nae so clever as foxes?"

"This is the third time we've rebuilt the hen house, thinking we'd managed to thwart them," Sebastian said. "Draw your own conclusions, lad."

They began hammering the last boards of the newly reinforced wall in place. Connall often worked with Sebastian on the Teviot Castle home farm. It was too much work for one man alone. It was very nearly too much for him and his fourteen-year-old farmhand. Still, they managed it.

"M'sister's found herself a new position," Connall said.

"Has she?"

"Aye." Connall held out another nail for him. "She's to be an upstairs maid."

An upstairs maid? Only the castle employed enough servants for the maids to be so specifically employed. "Whereabouts is she working? Has she had to leave Teviotbrae entirely?"

"Nae." Connall shook his head. "Though she does have to live at Burnwick House, in the servants' quarters."

Burnwick House was empty. Had been for a year now. "It's been let, has it?"

"Aye. And a full staff brought on."

A full staff meant the house had been taken by someone of means, likely a family. "Odd that the laird didn't tell me of these new arrivals."

"The laird does nae usually whisper his thoughts in the ears of the home farmer." Connall tossed him a knowing look. All the area knew Sebastian's identity, and all the area knew the laird required that home farmer be the entirety of his identity for now.

"What do you know of the people who'll be calling Burnwick House home?" Sebastian asked.

"From what the whispers say, it's a Mr. and Mrs.

Wakefield. We believe they've children, though how many or how old, no one seems able to say. And they're coming directly from London."

London was a fair bit away from Teviotbrae, and in more than merely miles. The wealthy of the capital city had decided ideas about what gave a place and people value. And none of those things could be found here: deep coffers, bustling streets, endless strings of frivolous Society activities. Sebastian had known a bit of that world during the one Season he'd spent there.

He had not enjoyed Town overly much. But Town, it seemed, was coming to him whether he wished for it or not.

Chapter 3

"You told me nobility could be found in this area of Scotland," Mother said, in that same tight tone of voice she had employed nearly constantly since their departure from London.

"I did not," Father said, wearing the look of annoyance *he* had been employing for just as long. "I very clearly said the area had a laird."

"How is that meant to impress me?" Mother demanded. "There are squires throughout England. A Scottish laird is hardly different."

"You seem to forget the squires in various corners of England do have some influence. They are generally members of Society. And in this small and secluded area of Scotland, the local laird holds a great deal of significance."

"Small, secluded area." Mother shook her head, even as the description fell from her lips in tones of sorrow. "I understand needing to tighten our purse strings, but did we truly have to relocate so far from everything?"

"The house's remote location is the reason we can afford

the rent." Father spoke through tightened teeth. "Everything available that was closer to London proved beyond our means."

"The girls now have no Society, no prospects. And who am I meant to invite over for tea? The local milkmaids?"

Cordelia didn't like to think that her mother was truly pompous, but there were moments, like this one, when she couldn't entirely deny that Mother was a bit haughty. She also knew that Mother was lonely and grieving.

Upheaval brought out the worst in some people. She hoped as their time here stretched on, Mother's grief would lessen, and her kindness would reemerge, though Cordelia harbored a great many doubts that Mother would ever forgive Father. Cordelia herself was struggling to do that. She did not know how he had managed to spend all their money, nor did she know for how long this difficulty had been looming on the horizon without him giving them so much as a whisper of it. Had they known the family funds were more meager than they'd once been, everyone could have done some additional economizing, which might have prevented this relocation.

"The laird is meant to call today," Father said. "From him, we can learn what, in terms of society, we can expect in Teviotbrae."

"I think you know perfectly well what we can expect. Nothing." Mother crossed to the window, a look of absolute suffering on her face.

Cordelia alternated between frustration with her parents and pity for them. Neither was enduring the situation with any degree of decorum. She suspected Mother felt betrayed more than angry, and Father felt more embarrassed than indignant. Whatever their actual emotions, they were making their daughters miserable. Cordelia and Seraphina sat a bit apart from them, both bent over their needlework and, at least on Cordelia's part, pretending not to hear all that was spoken around them.

The disagreement between Mother and Father might've continued and grown more pointed, but in that very moment, their newly installed butler, a local man by the name of McCrory, announced to the room, "Angus Coburn, Laird of Teviotbrae."

Cordelia and Seraphina rose to greet the highest-ranking person in this "small and secluded area of Scotland." The man was likely in his sixties. His ice-blue eyes took in the room and its occupants in one quick sweep. His bow was everything that was proper and dignified.

"How pleased we are to have you call," Father said. "I have only just been telling my wife how very much she will enjoy coming to know you."

Father made quick work of the introductions around the room. The laird declared himself pleased to meet them all. He did not speak with so obvious a tone of Scotland as the staff Father had hired since their arrival, but there was more than a hint of it there. Cordelia would wager the man had been educated either in England or by English tutors. But he had clearly lived a large portion of his life here. A place where one passed so much time could not help but leave a mark on a person.

Everyone was soon situated comfortably in the drawing room. Tea was called for. Mother was more calm and at ease in the role of hostess than she had been since their arrival in Teviotbrae.

"Other than yourself, laird," Mother said, "I fear we have not made the acquaintance of any of our neighbors."

"Other than myself, you haven't any. Of course, there are a few merchants in the local village, and families surrounding it who have children who work at the castle or, now, here in your home. And there are plenty of families employed in working the land."

"There is none but yourself with claim to the gentry or Society?" Father asked.

"None in Teviotbrae," the laird answered. "But Teviot Castle has quite a reputation for being welcoming and comfortable for visitors. I have been known to host quite a few from that sphere. And we've a few fine families in neighboring areas."

"I do hope many will come to visit," Mother said. "And I do hope that when they do, you will let us know, so that we may call on them as well as ask them to do so here at Burnwick House."

"Of course," the laird said.

"In the meantime," Mother said, "a few things in the house need addressing."

"That is true," Father said. "Updated furnishings and wallcoverings and such."

"And I should very much like to see the grounds beautified," Mother said.

"The family that lived here before you was, I fear, neglectful of the grounds." The laird shook his head in slow disapproval. "I suspected you would find a great deal in need of attention. I have taken the liberty of asking Sebastian of the Home Farm to come have a look and offer his recommendations."

Father appeared to ruffle up a little at that. "We are not looking to install a home farm. A kitchen garden, of course. But we wished most of the grounds to be ornamental."

The laird, thankfully, didn't look offended by Father's near rejection of his generous offer. "I assure you, Sebastian is well-versed in both. He can help you determine whether you need a single groundskeeper or an entire team of gardeners."

Regardless of what they were in need of, Cordelia knew they would not be hiring an entire team of anything. She and Seraphina were not merely sharing a lady's maid—they were sharing *Mother's* lady's maid, sometimes waiting hours in the morning for her to be available to help them dress. The two sisters were far from helpless, but current fashions made dressing oneself nearly impossible. If Father could not afford to give such minimal consideration to his daughters, he certainly could not afford an enormous expenditure on the grounds.

"And as you are in search of updated furnishings," the laird continued, "I suggest a trip to Edinburgh. It is, of course, not so fashionable as London, but you'll find a great many things that will more than meet your expectations. In fact, I would find a journey there to be quite to my liking."

"We would very much like to join you on such a journey." Father's chest swelled and his expression turned smug. Though their neighbor was only moments earlier dismissed as a mere country squire, Father was finding his approval and compliments quite to his liking.

Mother looked excited at the prospect of the journey to a larger city. "Oh, I am in need of new silk to hang in a few of the rooms. Can such be obtained in Edinburgh?"

The laird nodded. "Of course."

By sheer force of will, Cordelia kept her thoughts to herself. They had quit her beloved London, left behind all her friends, every familiar street, every hope for the future. They'd come to this place where they knew no one and could, for all intents and purposes, go nowhere, and all on account of having insufficient funds to continue in Town. And yet, how eagerly her parents were anticipating spending money updating furnishings and wall hangings and other things that, though perhaps a bit faded with time, were perfectly usable in their current condition. It was all too frustrating.

In as sweet and unassuming a voice as she could summon, Cordelia asked if she and Seraphina might be excused. Her parents were too distracted by the prospect of Edinburgh and their pleasure at the laird's attention to care very much about what their daughters did. They were dismissed with hardly a glance and quitted the drawing room without even a moment's hesitation.

Stepping out of the house onto the large expanse of lawn to the east of their new home, Cordelia took a lungful of cool and refreshing air. She let her gaze linger on the view afforded her from this spot. She loved London and always would. But the wild beauty of this place had proven a balm. Seeing it in this moment, when she was deeply frustrated, worked better than any medicine. No matter her sorrow and grief, no matter her parents' thoughtlessness, this view would help her endure the years to come.

Seraphina, never as content as Cordelia was to spend hours on end gazing at a lovely prospect, was quick to make a suggestion. "Shall we take up a game of battledore and shuttlecock? All we need can be found in the small outbuilding just there." She motioned to it.

"You know I haven't the grace or agility for such things as you do," Cordelia reminded her.

"It is only meant to be fun. We need not be the world's foremost experts. Besides, I could see quite clearly how frustrated you were with Mother and Father. Hitting the shuttlecock as hard as you possibly can over and over again will, I do not doubt, prove the perfect means of relieving your mind of that frustration."

Even if the theory proved unfounded, it would, at the very least, provide a much-needed distraction.

The needed equipment was soon found, and the game undertaken.

They were both quite out of practice. The first few attempts resulted in no more than two or three times batting the shuttlecock between them before the ball with its crown of feathers fell to the ground. But they soon found their stride. Seraphina managed to look quite graceful, even when lunging in desperation after Cordelia's poorly aimed return hit. Cordelia, more often than not, tripped over her own feet and only just managed to keep herself from falling entirely.

Had they been in company, or on any of the greens in London where they might have been seen, she would have been horrified. But in this quiet corner of the world, with only her beloved sister privy to her graceless attempts, she found she could laugh. And Seraphina, likely reassured by her sister, found humor in the undertaking as well.

They soon managed a very successful back and forth, having hit the shuttlecock between them more than a dozen times. Seraphina batted it over Cordelia's head. Determined not to be the reason this volley ended, Cordelia ran backward, swinging her racket behind her head, ready to lob the shuttlecock back. But before she could begin the forward swing once more, it stopped, making the most horrific cracking sound.

It was not the sound of the racquet itself breaking on something. She very much feared the racquet had, instead, broken something else.

Seraphina's gasp was her first warning that what she had hit with such tremendous force was something she ought not have. The muffled moan of a deep voice was her second clue.

She spun about. A man stood directly behind her, his hand clutched to his nose, clad in the clothes of a farmer, wavy black hair spilling in riotous abundance. And to her horror, blood seeped from between his fingers. Had she broken his nose?

Cordelia pulled from her sleeve the handkerchief she always kept there, trying desperately to offer it to him, all the while too embarrassed to speak a word. He didn't accept it. Whether he was objecting to her handkerchief on account of not wanting to ruin it or because he was angry at her, she couldn't say.

Seraphina was there in the next instant, offering an unending stream of apologies and expressions of concern for his well-being. As luck would have it, their groomsman passed by in the very next moment

She waved him over. "This man has suffered an accident." She was too embarrassed to describe it further.

"That there's Sebastian of the Home Farm," the groomsman said. "Looks to me like he's broken his nose."

It was precisely what Cordelia feared.

Sebastian was muttering, though Cordelia hadn't the first idea what he was saying. Though she couldn't see his nose or mouth, she could see his eyes. The look he gave her bordered on a glare.

Flustered and humiliated and overwhelmed with all that had happened in the last two weeks, she felt immediately on the verge of crying. Having embarrassed herself enough in front of this stranger, she wrapped her dignity around her and did her best to maintain her calm.

"Will you accompany him to the kitchen?" she asked the groomsman. "And see to it that he is given a poultice for his nose?"

The groomsman agreed. Sebastian of the Home Farm dipped the tiniest of head-only bows, muttering something that sounded suspiciously like "the woman's a menace."

She was too flustered to even take offense at the comment.

Seraphina, however, seemed anything but flustered. "I suspect he is very handsome when he's not bleeding."

"Handsome or not, he's now convinced I'm an utter menace. This was not the sort of first impression I'd hoped to make in this area."

"Let us hope, for your sake, that home farmers are not terrible gossips."

But if there was one thing Cordelia felt certain about in matters pertaining to small, isolated villages, it was that nothing traveled through them faster than a diverting tale.

Chapter 4

"Merciful heavens!" Mrs. Calhoun, the newly installed housekeeper at Burnwick House, declared as Sebastian stepped into the kitchen. "What's happened?"

Sebastian would have answered, but he was currently quite occupied with attempting to hold back the blood pouring from his nose. Though he'd had only the briefest interaction with the woman who'd hit him, he had no difficulty identifying her: She was a daughter of the house, a lady of Society.

He'd not always been well received by the London set. This was, however, the first time a fine lady had physically assaulted him.

Ewan, who'd been tasked by the Misses Wakefield to see Sebastian deposited in the kitchen, took up the tale. "Miss Wakefield and Miss Seraphina were undertaking the game of battledore and shuttlecock on the lawn. Somehow or another—I didn't see the thing actually happen—one of them mistook Sebastian's face for the shuttlecock and batted it heartily."

It was a humorous version of what had actually happened, but not terribly far off the mark.

Cook arrived on the scene in the very next instant, with a fresh dishcloth in hand. She handed it to Sebastian. "Hold your nose tightly. See if you cannae stop the bleeding. Do you suspect it's broken?"

Sebastian shrugged, pressing the cloth against nose. His voice emerged oddly pitched and toned, as was always the case when a person's nose was closed off. "I've been prone to nosebleeds since I was a lad. Doesn't take much for this to happen."

Still, it hurt like the dickens. Whichever of the two sisters had been the racket-wielding assassin had done a fine job of laying him low.

Connall's sister Glenna, a chambermaid at Burnwick house, wandered into the kitchen as well, and Mrs. Calhoun instructed her to wet a rag and bring it over. There'd be no salvaging his clothing without a truly thorough washing, but Sebastian hoped the purpose of the cloth was to help him clean some of the blood off his hands and face. He no doubt looked a sight.

Cook and Mrs. Calhoun fussed a bit over him. They assured him his nose wasn't yet showing signs of bruising, which seemed a good indication it might not actually be broken. The bleeding had slowed to a trickle, which they insisted was encouraging.

Through it all, Sebastian felt like a fool. He'd been eying the grounds to the east of the main house and hadn't been paying overly close attention to his immediate environs. He'd stepped around a hedgerow and directly into the path of the racquet. His assaulter had not been overly aware of her surroundings either, apparently.

"Shall I fetch the laird?" Glenna asked. "He's in the drawing room with Mr. and Mrs. Wakefield."

Sebastian shook his head, slowly on account of the throbbing pain. "A laird doesn't interrupt a visit with a fine family on account of an injury sustained by his home farmer."

General nods of agreement rippled through the group. The locals were generally quite good at separating the role he played with the intricate interconnections of his actual life. But now and then, even they forgot.

"It is quite a coincidence that the both of you should call at Burnwick House at the same time." Cook spoke as she worked at her mortar and pestle, no doubt creating a poultice for Sebastian's nose.

"He knows the grounds of this estate were neglected for many years, and he thought I might have suggestions for improvements and grounds staff."

Glenna stood a bit taller at that explanation. "My brother Archie knows all about plants and such. If Mr. Wakefield were to hire him on as gardener, Archie'd prove a fine choice."

Though she was, no doubt, partial to her brother, she was also not wrong. The oldest of the McCrory siblings was, in fact, the very reason Connall McCrory had come to work on the home farm with Sebastian. He'd learned a great deal from his oldest brother, and that made him a godsend in the work that needed doing.

The next moment, two silhouettes appeared in the doorway to the kitchen and all activity paused. Sebastian knew the ladies the moment a spill of light illuminated them: the Misses Wakefield. The one who'd laid him low with her racquet looked markedly uncomfortable. She moved with stiffness and purpose. Her expression was prim and pinched, and her brown eyes swept the room with an evaluating gaze. He suspected she was the older of the two sisters, though likely not by much. Her younger sister moved more fluidly and with more eagerness. A soft smile touched the younger lady's face. There was not a hint of such on Miss Wakefield's.

"We have come to inquire after your injury," she said to Sebastian, standing at more than a proper distance, and speaking with a directness not softened by any clear show of empathy.

"The general consensus is that it is likely not broken." Again, his voice sounded so absurd owing to his continued pinching of his nose.

"I'm pleased to hear that," Miss Wakefield said. "And I am quite sorry for my role in rendering it injured, broken or not."

It was something of an apology, he would give her that. But it was offered in a tone of obligation that wasn't precisely comforting. People of her station in life were not raised to be overly thoughtful toward those occupying the rungs beneath them. He could not entirely fault her for those predispositions which she had been raised to embrace.

Cook motioned him over toward the fire, her mortar and pestle nearby. He was not displeased to have an excuse for ending this incredibly stilted conversation. He joined Cook where she stood, lowered his handkerchief, and awaited her ministrations.

With careful movements, she dipped very narrow, short strips of linen into the poultice she had created and laid them with great care across his tender nose. He kept his winces to a minimum, somehow finding himself extremely reluctant to appear less than stalwart in front of the two visitors to the belowstairs.

Miss Seraphina moved to where he stood. There was a genuineness to the empathy in her eyes that he appreciated. "I do hope your nose isn't broken."

"I foster that same hope myself." He had a tendency to speak roughly at times, especially when he was frustrated or in pain. It was something he was working on, but often failed.

Still, she didn't seem overly bothered by the slightly

acerbic quality to his voice. She simply smiled. "I feel terribly guilty, as I pressured Cordelia to play battledore and shuttlecock when she did not wish to. Had we not been playing, you wouldn't have been injured."

"Does your sister object to games?" Society misses, in his limited experience, reached an age very early on when anything deemed childish or unsophisticated was dismissed as undesirable.

"Oh, not at all," Miss Seraphina said. "She is simply prone to silly accidents and tripping over herself. She's a very graceful dancer, which makes it all the more odd that the moment we undertake anything remotely sporting, she inevitably makes a fool of herself."

"Do her bouts of ungainliness usually end in someone being injured?" He bit back a wince as Cook pressed the poultice-soaked strips more firmly against his face, holding them in place so they would dry stuck to the skin.

"Hardly ever," Miss Seraphina said. "Mostly her mishaps embarrass only *her*. She will be pleased to know your nose is not actually broken, though I don't suspect she will feel any less humiliated."

That was an interesting evaluation. Miss Wakefield did not give the impression of being humiliated by their unfortunate collision. If anything, she seemed rather dismissive of the entire thing, more annoyed than concerned.

Sebastian generally considered himself a good judge of character. Was it possible he had misjudged the lady?

Given enough time in her company, he might manage to sort out the mystery of her. As Cook finished her ministrations and the two sisters made their departure, he resigned himself to forever being baffled by Miss Cordelia Wakefield. Sorting her required he spend time in her company, but London misses did not socialize with home farmers.

Chapter 5

HOME HAD BECOME AN uncomfortable place. Cordelia's parents were arguing more often and more bitterly. And the two of them seemed entirely determined to spend money the family didn't have on improvements the home didn't truly need.

Cordelia wanted to return to London. She had maintained some hopes that eventually she might. Those hopes were fading more each day. The family coffers would never fill enough for returning if her parents continued emptying them.

With the daily bickering already begun, Cordelia gathered up her parchment, lead pencils, and a small blanket, and escaped the house. She'd taken quite a number of walks around the estate, coming to know the fields and the overgrown gardens there. On this day, however, she wandered farther afield.

She left the Burnwick House grounds, even walked past the turn in the road that led to Teviot Castle. She walked farther from the house than she ever had before. Her steps took her to a low stone wall dividing the road from an extensive field. A large and stately tree growing near the fence caught her eye and piqued her curiosity.

Cordelia utilized a passthrough in the wall and slipped to the other side. She spread a blanket on the ground at enough of a distance to see the tree in its entirety, but near enough that she could also see it in detail. Pencil in hand, she began a rough sketch.

Painting was her preferred medium, but she also liked to sketch. Losing herself in art had always been calming, something she'd desperately needed lately.

Cordelia had not expected her removal to Scotland to be smooth or immediately enjoyable. Adjusting to a new life and place took time. But everything seemed to be going wrong.

She hadn't realized until coming to this corner of the world how disagreeable her parents could be with each other. London had offered ample diversions and the two had seldom interacted, at least in front of their children. In this place, with nowhere for them to go, no one for them to call on, they were left with only each other for company, and that was proving disastrous.

Seraphina had endeared herself almost instantly to the staff at the house and those who worked at Teviot Castle. Their one brief excursion to the village had found her sister a quick favorite amongst the merchants and their families. Seraphina had an ease with people and an ability to adjust to new situations quickly.

Cordelia had never before been in a place she didn't know well, amongst people she hadn't known all her life. And though no one had mentioned it to her directly, she was absolutely certain tales of her mishap with her racquet had already been whispered far and wide. Her embarrassment further weighed down her mind and heart.

But in this moment, she was surrounded by the beauty of

nature, indulging in a favorite pastime. A whisper of peace rested in the air. There were no parental voices raised in anger. There was no naturally friendly sister unintentionally reminding her of how naturally awkward she herself was. There was no sound but the light breeze rustling the leaves and the scratch of her pencil against the paper.

And the bleating of a lamb.

She looked up, surprised by the sudden sound. This area of Scotland was home to a great many sheep. To hear one making noise ought to have been the rule rather than the exception.

Sure enough, a little lamb was nearby. It was not, however, alone, but following close on the heels of the one everyone referred to as Sebastian of the Home Farm. He was walking through the field with a clear sense of purpose. He appeared entirely oblivious to his four-legged companion, though she suspected he was not.

There wasn't time to pack up her things and make a hasty retreat. He was too nearby and had already seen her. Determined not to make a fool of herself yet again, she squared her shoulders, summoned her dignity, and prepared herself to greet him.

He approached but didn't come all the way to where she sat. He took off his hat and held it at his side. "Miss Wakefield," he greeted.

He spoke with more of an English accent than a Scottish one, and his mannerisms would not have been out of place at a Society gathering in London. Was it possible the local people referred to him as "of the home farm," but he was not actually the Teviot Castle home farmer?

"I'm not familiar with how the land is divided up in Teviotbrae," she said. "If I am trespassing where I ought not be, please tell me, and I will move."

"These are open fields, used mostly for grazing and not claimed by any one person. You're welcome to sit here if you'd like. The flock that frequents this area is on the other side of the hill. It'll leave you be."

"And are you taking this lamb to rejoin the flock?"

Sebastian shook his head. "This little one's mother didn't survive the lambing. None of the ewes would accept the little orphan."

Cordelia needed but a moment to understand what Sebastian hadn't said, what he seemed embarrassed at the mere prospect of saying. "You have been taking care of the lamb."

"Couldn't leave her to die." Sebastian shrugged, clearly intending to look as though it were nothing at all and he had no real attachment to the tiny animal. But Cordelia was certain she saw quite the opposite lingering in his expression. "Follows me around everywhere now."

"Have you taken her as a pet?" She'd never heard of anyone having a sheep as a pet, but she wasn't overly familiar with this part of the kingdom. Perhaps it was rather ordinary here.

"I suppose she's become something like that," Sebastian said. "Though she's proving more work than I would have expected."

"Do you not have sheep on the home farm?" Here was an opportunity to see if her suspicion about his name being somewhat leading was correct without having to directly ask him.

"The purpose of the home farm is to grow food for the castle and tend to chickens and pigs and such. I've no interaction with sheep. Other than this one, that is."

He did live and work on the home farm, then.

The little lamb wandered a little bit closer to her, but kept a distance, apparently wary of her.

"Have you given your accidental pet a name?"

"Aye." That one syllable was offered with some degree of the sound of Scotland. "I call her Shadow, because she's nearly always hovering beside me."

Cordelia could not hold back a smile. He made the observation with a grumpiness that was belied by the fondness in his eyes as he glanced at little Shadow. There was a tenderness to this man that he kept well hidden. The question was why.

Shadow came near enough for her to tentatively reach out to pat its head. Though she was given a confused look by the little creature, it didn't scamper away or seem to object. Having Mrs. Seaver's little dogs as her only frame of reference, Cordelia scratched Shadow behind the ear. The lamb seemed to enjoy the attention.

Grumpy Sebastian of the Home Farm even allowed the tiniest, most fleeting of smiles. And even with the bruising of his nose, he proved remarkably handsome and not nearly as intimidating as he had proven even mere moments earlier.

Having noticed the bruising, she could not in good conscience ignore the topic. "I hope that your nose is feeling better."

He grew immediately uncomfortable. "It's a little sore, but better."

She did not mean to belabor the topic, but she felt she had done a poor job of apologizing for the injury she had inflicted, however unintentionally. Now was the perfect opportunity for rectifying that. "I am sorry for that. I ought to have been watching where I was going and what was around me."

"No permanent damage," he said gruffly and quickly.

He didn't seem overly fond of the idea of remaining. Why, then, didn't he simply make excuses and go? There was nothing about her presence here that required him to remain. She was not forcing conversation on him.

"You did a fine job sketching the tree."

She hadn't realized he'd spied her drawing. "Thank you. The tree was so lovely, I couldn't resist trying to draw it."

"Everyone hereabouts is very fond of this stately tree."

It was the first insight she'd had into the people she now lived among. Were she to finish the sketch and find a means of displaying it somewhere in the house, perhaps that would endear her a little to those who lived and worked at Burnwick House.

"You have a talent for drawing," Sebastian said.

"I do enjoy it," she said. "Though I suspect my parents wish I enjoyed something more to their liking. They are pleased with my sister's musical ability and a bit embarrassed by my artistic leanings."

He remained standing there, discomfort growing in his posture. "Family can pose difficulties sometimes." He spoke as one who knew.

"Do you have family nearby?"

His gaze dropped momentarily to little Shadow, who'd decided to sit on the grass and watch them both. "Both my parents have died," he said quietly.

She hadn't meant to cause him sorrow. "I am sorry for your loss."

He simply nodded.

Perhaps a change of subject was in order. "Did you grow up in this area?"

"I didn't, though my father did. My mother was English and preferred spending time in *her* country. That's where I lived before coming to Teviotbrae."

That explained his very English accent. "Were you also educated in England?" She didn't doubt he had an education; he spoke too formally for anything else.

"I was." That seemed all he meant to say on the matter.

"What is it that led you to come here and become a farmer?"

Stiffness returned to his posture and dryness permeated his voice. "An overfondness for lambs." On that declaration, he dipped his head to her once more, offered a quick word of departure, and trudged off, following the road back in the direction of Teviot Castle.

How had one simple question offended him so entirely? She had been glad that someone wanted to have a conversation with her; that had seldom happened since her arrival in Teviotbrae. She'd managed to make a mull of the whole thing.

A cold breeze picked up as she sat there, nipping at her and urging her to leave behind this place where she'd known a momentary peace. The serenity and calm of beautiful surroundings she could likely find again. What she never seemed to escape was the growing ache of loneliness.

Chapter 6

Sebastian thought on his unexpected encounter with Miss Wakefield over the next few days. She'd not been haughty nor dismissive as he'd expected her to be. That had, he fully realized, been unfair of him. Many of the ladies he'd known in London had been unkind and arrogant, but not all. To assume which group she belonged to before he even knew her was unlike him. He wanted to believe he was more honorable than that.

He arrived at the home farm, having been to the castle kitchen to deliver a couple baskets of vegetables. Miss Wakefield of all people stood outside his house, deep in animated conversation with Connall. Any hope Sebastian had of slipping past unnoticed disappeared the moment Shadow saw him and began bleating as if her very life depended on Sebastian noticing her there. What in the world had possessed him to take the creature in? Lambs belonged with their flock. But the flock had rejected this one.

Perhaps that was why he'd taken pity on the poor animal. Sebastian knew what a lonely thing it was to not really belong.

Connall and Miss Wakefield turned and spotted him. The lad motioned for her to follow him. "Miss Wakefield's looking for something nice to paint," he told Sebastian as he drew near. "I told her she might like the stream running behind the castle or the grand ol' tree out along the road. Can you think of anyplace else she might go?"

Sebastian might have been surprised by the request, but Miss Wakefield had expressed a deep interest in sketching and art when last he'd seen her. "You'd likely enjoy painting Loch Tev."

Connall offered a humorous slap of his hand against his forehead. "Loch Tev. Of course. Nae better sight than that."

Miss Wakefield looked intrigued. "Is it terribly far away?" she asked. "Could I walk there, do you suppose?"

"Given enough time, and very precise directions," Connall said.

"I could take you there in the pony cart." Where the offer came from, Sebastian didn't know. But he didn't regret making it.

"Oh, would you?" Miss Wakefield smiled sweetly. London ladies, he'd discovered, were often practiced at such things, but there seemed to be real sincerity behind *her* expression.

He could take her to the loch, go for a brisk walk to clear his head. Actually, he'd be grateful for it.

"Give me a few minutes to hitch up the pony," he said. "I'll take you to the loch."

Connall helped, which made the undertaking faster than it would have been otherwise.

"Best take Shadow," Connall said once all was ready. "The poor soul's been crying out for you ever since you left."

"Put her in the cart."

The lad first helped Miss Wakefield onto the bench of the

farm cart, then handed her a small box, no doubt one filled with whatever supplies artists needed. Then the lad helped Shadow take her place in the back.

Not long ago, Sebastian had been relatively content on his own at the home farm. Now he had a lamb following him about and a fine lady sitting in the cart beside him, and he was utterly confused about it all.

Sebastian set the cart in motion, the pony not objecting at all.

They'd not been on their way for long when Miss Wakefield spoke. "Connall said you were at the castle."

"I was," Sebastian said. "I was delivering vegetables to the kitchens."

"Oh." She sounded disappointed.

"Home farmers don't call on lairds," he said. "My visits to the castle are never terribly impressive."

"I hadn't asked because I wished to be impressed. I had hoped you might have heard if the laird had plans for traveling to Edinburgh in the near future."

An odd thing to be wondering about. "Are you particularly interested in Edinburgh?"

"Unfortunately, my parents are. They have made very vague plans to travel there with the laird to purchase a great many other things we haven't the money for. I'm hoping the trip will be put off indefinitely."

Things they hadn't the money for. The Wakefields, then, were in some degree of monetary distress. That helped explain a few things.

"Are you hoping there will be money enough for you to return to London if they avoid Edinburgh?"

"I do miss London, but that is not my most immediate concern. I worry a little that this retrenchment will not prove sufficient to save us from utter ruin if they spend recklessly. I almost long for the days when I was utterly ignorant of how irresponsible they can be."

It was an unexpectedly personal confession.

She seemed to realize as much. "Forgive me. That was far more than I'm certain you wished to hear. I am not usually one to confide in others. I find myself shocked at how easy you are to talk with."

"I wasn't offended." Indeed, what he felt more than anything was confused. Their previous interactions had ranged from tense to merely uncomfortable. Yet, he'd offered to do her the favor of driving her to Loch Tev, and she was telling him some of her most personal concerns. "Seems we are a mutual confusion to each other just now."

Her laugh was light and musical. The sound lessened some of the weight on his heart.

Conversation between them remained light and general as they continued on. He pointed out a few things as they passed, interesting aspects of the landscape or homes belonging to people he wasn't certain she had met. She seemed truly curious about the area and appreciative of his help.

He brought the cart to a stop at the point where the road turned and afforded the very best view of the loch and surrounding hills.

She took in a quick breath. Her eyes darted about, taking in the scenery. "This is stunning."

"Those of us from the area think so."

"How is it you resist coming here every single day? I don't think I could."

When he'd first come to Teviotbrae, he had come to the spot more than once, touched by the beauty of it. "The home farm claims a great deal of my time. And I try to be helpful to the Teviotbrae families. That leaves little time for admiring the beauty of the area. And I assure you, there are other places at least as breathtaking as this."

"I hope I have a chance to see them all."

Miss Wakefield was soon situated in the area she thought best, with her easel set up and paints at the ready. Shadow wandered about, grazing in the vast meadow, seeming to enjoy herself. Sebastian sat himself on an obliging rock and studied the area as he hadn't done in years.

It really was beautiful. He'd not taken the time to appreciate it in far too long. What little time he did have to himself he generally spent at Dalwyck, the humble but lovely piece of land his father had left him. It wasn't terribly far from Loch Tev. If not for his grandfather's firm insistence that Sebastian dedicate himself to working at the home farm, he might have made his home there.

"Did you have many opportunities for painting in London?" he asked Miss Wakefield as she worked.

"Yes, but nothing quite like this."

"Do you enjoy painting as much as you do sketching?"

"Oh, yes. There's something very soothing about it. For a time, all I need to focus on is what I'm recreating. All my other worries and concerns fade away."

That sounded wonderful. "Is that why you wished to paint something today? To escape your worries?"

"In part. My primary reason, though, is somewhat related. I've never known any home but London, and I don't imagine I will return there. I've decided that my best chance for Teviotbrae to feel like home is for me to know it well, to learn its hills and valleys, lakes and rivers. If I wander about these next few months or even years sketching or painting what I see, this may eventually feel as dear to me as the streets of London."

He let his gaze wander to the loch and the hills and the lone lamb grazing nearby, then to Miss Wakefield. The clumsiness with which she'd wielded her battledore was utterly absent in the graceful expertise of her brush. The stiffness he'd seen in her posture and expression in the Burnwick House kitchen had been entirely replaced with a calm and focused serenity. Her art transformed her.

Sebastian found himself very much enjoying this side of her. And he was more intrigued than he was yet ready to admit.

CHAPTER 7

CARING FOR AN ORPHANED lamb was no easy task. Sebastian sat on a three-legged stool in the small pen he'd built for Shadow, feeding the little lamb milk from the Breckin family's milk goat by means of a very narrow-spouted bottle. Shadow was beginning to outgrow her need for milk, having already begun eating grass. Soon enough, these time-consuming feedings would no longer be needed. To Sebastian's surprise, he suspected he would miss them. He wouldn't miss the time they took, nor how much he had to scramble to make up for that time, but there was something very peaceful about offering something so simple but so necessary to the little creature.

It sometimes felt like he had nothing of significance to offer anyone else. He'd given some thought to what Miss Wakefield had said while painting Loch Tev. Taking time to know an area made it feel more like home. Could not the same be said for the people who called that place home? If he dedicated more time and effort to knowing the people of Teviotbrae better, he could be more useful and feel more like he belonged among them.

Archie McCrory approached from the direction his younger brother had gone only a few minutes earlier. The two had likely passed each other. Sebastian rose and met him just on the other side of the pen.

"What brings you 'round, Archie?"

"I heard Burnwick House is needing a groundskeeper. Wondered what you knew of it."

"I gave the place a look over," Sebastian said. "They need a groundskeeper, for sure and certain." Archie's sister had suggested he'd make a good groundskeeper. Sebastian ought to have acted on that suggestion sooner. He meant to rectify that now. "I'll walk with you over there, and you can inquire after the position."

"I'd appreciate that," Archie said.

Shadow bleated, quite as if she knew Sebastian had just committed himself to leaving the farm for a time.

"The odd little creature seems to think I'm its mother." Sebastian shook his head.

"Connall thinks it the grandest thing that you've taken in the poor thing."

Sebastian offered a rueful smile. "I assume that by 'grandest,' he means 'strangest.'"

But Archie shook his head. "Not many who aren't shepherds have the patience to nurse a lamb through infancy. Says a lot for you that you've cared for the poor creature."

Perhaps he wasn't doing so terrible a job of winning the approval of the local people as he feared.

The two of them made their way to Burnwick House.

"I can't say if Mr. Wakefield does, in fact, mean to hire on a groundskeeper," Sebastian warned. Miss Wakefield, after all, had indicated her family was not so flush in the pocket as they'd like to be. "One is needed, but..."

Archie didn't need him to finish the warning. "What's needed most on the grounds?"

The man had a knack for looking after gardens and such things. It was no surprise that he had enough foresight to ask for information.

"The most needed things are pruning overgrown shrubbery and hedgerows and replanting the flowerbeds. The kitchen garden is in need of rethinking, as it's not producing like it ought. After that's all seen to, the Wakefields will likely eventually want to make improvements in drainage and beautification."

"The field maple on the south edge is growing well," Archie said. "Could do with a wee bit of pruning, though."

"You'll find that's true of most of the estate. Little of it is dying. Overgrowth is far more the matter of the day."

"I can certainly see to that," Archie said.

He prayed he wasn't getting the man's hopes up only to have them dashed. The McCrorys' finances were better since the father of the family had begun work as the butler at Burnwick House. But being butler meant living at the house where he worked and not at home with his family. Connall had mentioned more than once that the family mourned their father being away. If Archie found work there, Mr. McCrory might be able to return home.

They approached the servants' entrance at Burnwick House and gave a quick rap on the door. It was answered by a kitchen maid, a cousin of Archie's.

"Would you ask Mrs. Calhoun if she would inquire of Mr. Wakefield if he's available to speak with Archie, here, about the possibility of working as groundskeeper?"

"Oh, Archie'd be grand," the maid declared. "But why not have your father make the suggestion? He's the butler, after all."

Archie shook his head. "I'll not trade on that connection. I'll earn a place by m'own merits."

The young maid hurried off to relay the request, leaving Sebastian and Archie to wait in the small vestibule just inside the doorway. He heard no indication of chaos or unhappiness. It would not, of course, be his place to interfere with Burnwick House, even if he were the laird, but he listened in the hope that if there were difficulties here, he might prove in some way helpful.

They were not made to wait long. The housekeeper arrived where they stood. "Mr. Wakefield has asked you to meet him on the east lawn." She gave Archie an encouraging smile. The area was small, and the people were closely connected. Mrs. Calhoun likely knew the lad was in search of employment.

Archie looked nervous as he approached his potential employer at the designated meeting spot. Mr. Wakefield looked him over but gave no indication of what impression the younger man made on him.

Sebastian undertook the introduction. "Mr. Wakefield, this is Archie McCrory. I know you have expressed a need for a groundskeeper, and that is his area of expertise." With that, he vowed to leave the remainder of the interview to be undertaken between the other two. He didn't leave, however. He wanted first to make certain things began on a good footing.

"What experience do you have in groundskeeping?" Mr. Wakefield asked.

Archie spoke with confidence, but without arrogance. "I was an undergardener at Teviot Castle from the time I was a young lad until very recently. In the time since, I've traveled around a wee bit, doing work in other places. I've helped people hereabout with drainage on their farms and seeing to troublesome trees and plants."

"What is it you believe needs attention on the grounds here?"

Sebastian thanked the heavens they'd discussed this on the way over.

Archie reiterated much of what Sebastian said, while adding what he knew of the various insects and soil fungi that caused difficulties in the area.

Mr. Wakefield nodded throughout. "And are you able to design and build an ornamental garden? My wife and I are interested in having one here."

Archie nodded. The two began to discuss various aspects of such an undertaking; which plants the Wakefields preferred, how large they wanted the fine garden to be. Archie made suggestions about where on the estate made the most sense to build such a thing.

Sebastian was glad Archie was making a good impression, but he worried a bit. Miss Wakefield had expressed concern about her parents spending money they didn't have. He hoped, for Archie's sake, this job proved the opportunity he wanted and not a disappointment.

It was in the very next moment that Miss Wakefield herself passed nearby. She spotted them there and adjusted her path to come where they were. She had her small box with her, the one he knew contained her art supplies. Had she been drawing again? He didn't see an easel amongst her things, so she likely hadn't been painting.

"Cordelia," Mr. Wakefield said, "you will be pleased to know that we may very well be able to install an ornamental garden on the grounds."

"An ornamental garden?" She kept all sounds of concern out of her voice, but Sebastian saw precisely that in her eyes. "The kitchen garden is also in need of attention. And as it is providing our food, that seems important."

Mr. Wakefield stiffened. "We are discussing that as well, of course."

Miss Wakefield offered a quick, somewhat awkward smile. It was not unlike the one she'd given Sebastian in the kitchen a fortnight earlier after nearly breaking his nose.

"The grounds are very beautiful," Miss Wakefield said. "I am certain they will be even more so after the attentions of a skilled groundskeeper."

Archie launched enthusiastically into agreement with her. "There's a large tree south of the house, a field maple, that I'm particularly fond of. The previous residents of Burnwick House planted it, having brought it from England."

Sincere excitement filled Miss Wakefield's face. She opened up her box and pulled out a slip of parchment. "This tree?"

Archie looked at the paper in her hand and nodded, his eyes pulling wide. "Its very likeness."

"I sketched it yesterday," she said. "There's another tree on the road past the castle that I sketched a number of days ago. Sebastian of the Home Farm tells me it is also a favorite hereabout."

"I know the very tree you mean, Miss Wakefield," Archie said. "It's a grand tree."

"Cordelia," Mr. Wakefield said, a scold in his tone, "we're discussing very important matters. Please do not interrupt with your... art." He said the last word in a tone of something approaching mockery.

Though Sebastian was not in a position to speak in defense of Miss Wakefield, he felt his hackles go up on her behalf. Whether or not a parent thought art a worthwhile pursuit, to dismiss her skill in the way her father had rankled.

"Forgive me." She spoke quickly and with obvious embarrassment. "I'll cease interrupting."

She retreated without a great deal of grace. It reminded Sebastian forcefully of how she'd moved about the day she'd hit him with her racquet. What a contradiction she was. Sometimes she moved with fluidity and precision. At times, she reminded him of Shadow when she'd first been born, stumbling and awkward.

"Archie is the expert in matters of grounds and gardens," Sebastian said to Mr. Wakefield. "I'll leave the two of you to your discussion."

Sebastian slipped away from the other two. If he were smart, he would go directly back to the Teviot Castle home farm. But he clearly was something of a dolt. His steps took him instead in the direction Miss Wakefield had gone. It was easy to catch up with her; she wasn't moving very quickly.

"Miss Wakefield."

She stopped and looked back at him. She seemed pleased to see him there. That did his heart more good than he cared to admit.

"You did a fine job drawing the field maple," he said. "I can see you are taking to heart your determination to know your new home better."

"I am trying. Although, it occurs to me I might do best to not draw more of the Burnwick grounds, as those seem likely to change."

They walked along a path that ran beside some overgrown hedgerows.

"You're welcome to tell me if my question proves too personal, but know that I ask out of concern for Archie McCrory. Your father talked of a great deal of work to be done, but your discussion of other rather expensive plans he has—" He suddenly found he wasn't sure how to finish the phrase without crossing the line into something that sounded more like an accusation than he intended.

"You're worried my father will extract work from him but not pay him?" she guessed.

"Or make promises of employment but not follow through with them."

"I wish I could tell you for certain one way or the other. As the improvement efforts continue around the house, I find myself wondering if there's more money to be spent than I'm aware of. If, perhaps, our retrenchment from London was a bit premature."

"Which, while comforting in some ways, is also likely frustrating," Sebastian said. "London has always been your home. Leaving if it wasn't actually necessary would rankle something terrible."

"I feel like, regardless of which is reality, I would worry less if I simply knew. Nothing can change the fact that I've been pulled from my home. If I could know we weren't in danger of losing yet another home, I might feel more at ease."

"And if you found you *were* in danger of losing this one?" he pressed.

"Well, I might not set my heart so much on coming to think of it as home."

There was an unexpected revelation in that.

He hadn't put many personal touches on the house at the home farm, though he'd never given much thought to why. But he knew that her words, though speaking for herself, were true for him as well. The home he'd shared with his parents and, after his father's death, with his mother, remained home in his heart. He'd held some hope that Teviot Castle would be his next home, but he'd been sent away almost immediately by his grandfather when he'd gone there after Mother's death. The home farm had become his residence after that.

One was reluctant to make a home in a place that was likely to be taken away before one was ready. How was this woman, whom he'd first thought to be the very epitome of the dismissive and haughty London ladies he'd so disliked during his brief tenure in that city, proven such a source of unexpected wisdom?

"You don't intend to keep sketching and painting things you see in the area?" He found as he asked the question that he actually held his breath waiting for the answer. Though whether his anxiousness was owing to appreciation of her art or sorrow at her not thinking of the area as home, he couldn't say. He refused to examine it closely enough to know.

"I do intend to keep exploring Teviotbrae. But I will hold off on sketching the grounds of this home, at least until I know how much of it is likely to be different. Of course, that presents a difficulty."

"What difficulty?"

She was a remarkably easy person to talk to, just as she had said he was during their ride out to Loch Tev.

"I haven't the first idea where to go to find things to draw or paint. I suppose I could simply wander about, but it would be nice to know which places mean the most to people living here."

"On those days when I haven't too much pressing on my time, I'd be happy to take you to some of those places."

She smiled, and his heart fully flipped in his chest.

"You must promise to bring Shadow," she said. "Otherwise, I will never finish this."

She fished in her box and pulled out another piece of parchment. Sketched on it was his lamb, standing in the meadow at Loch Tev. The face of the animal wasn't filled in in any detail.

"I want it to be a good likeness of the dear creature but haven't been able to truly study her face."

"I believe Shadow would enjoy going on a few adventures," he said. *I would enjoy going on a few adventures,* he silently added. *With you.*

Archie came rushing up to them, a grin splitting his face.

"I'm to begin tomorrow," he announced as he came even with them. He shook Sebastian's hand enthusiastically. "Thank you for making the introduction. My family needs the money. If I can bring in enough, Father might come home again; I think Mother'd like that. We all would."

"I hope that can happen," Sebastian said.

From beside him, Miss Wakefield presented to Archie the drawing she'd made of the field maple. "I'd like you to have this," she said. "I was so very pleased to find you like that tree as much as I do."

"I cannae take this, Miss Wakefield," he said. "I've not a fine place to display it."

Miss Wakefield shook her head. "Art needn't be displayed in any particular way. All that matters is that it be enjoyed and appreciated."

"I do appreciate it," he said. "That's as fine a likeness of the tree as I can imagine."

"Please take it," she said. "Put it wherever you'd like, wherever you'd enjoy seeing it."

Archie thanked her again and again before rushing off with her drawing in his hand.

"That was a fine gesture," Sebastian said. "His entire family will enjoy having that sketch in their home."

"I'm glad. I like knowing it will be with a family who can enjoy it."

Unspoken in her declaration was that her own family didn't enjoy or appreciate her talent.

"I am certain they will more than merely enjoy it. I believe they will treasure it."

He sketched a bow to Miss Wakefield and bid her farewell. Lingering in his thoughts as he made his way back to the home farm was her beautiful smile, her kind gesture, and how much pleasure he derived from simply whispering the name "Cordelia."

Chapter 8

LESS THAN A MONTH after leaving behind London in order to severely economize, Mother and Father left with the laird to go spend a great deal of money in Edinburgh.

How Cordelia had wanted to vocalize her objections and concerns! She knew better. Even the tiniest tiptoe toward expressing her worries had led to a scolding from Father in front of Archie McCrory and Sebastian of the Home Farm.

Seraphina was as frustrated as Cordelia was. They both knew better than to discuss any of it with their parents. Nothing was ever talked about in their family—nothing that mattered anyway. Attempting to force such conversations always ended badly.

Her sister had taken possession of the small sitting room in which the pianoforte had been placed, making it their erstwhile music room. Seraphina had spent the hours since their parents' departure singing, something she did whenever feeling strong emotions, be those emotions joy or sorrow, elation or frustration. Cordelia felt certain this day's upheaval was of an irritated variety.

Feeling quite a lot of that herself, she claimed *her* artistic escape, fetching her lead pencils and her parchment and slipping from the house. It was likely not entirely proper to be wandering about without a chaperone, to call on a man she was not related to in order to indulge in a diversion her parents didn't entirely approve of.

If they had concerns, they ought to either have remained at Burnwick House or never forced the family to leave London in the first place. Teviotbrae was to be her home now. She would live *here* in whatever way afforded her a bit of happiness. And every moment of happiness she'd had involved either her sister or Sebastian.

And thus, she took her minimal supplies directly to the home farm at Teviot Castle. Luck was with her; Sebastian was working near the house, saving her the difficulty of searching him out.

"Good morning, Sebastian."

He tossed the slop bucket into the pig trough, then setting it aside, popped his hat off his head. "Good morning to you, Miss Wakefield."

She stepped onto a rock beside the stone wall, making her tall enough to easily see him over it. "It is a little odd that I call you Sebastian and you call me Miss Wakefield. Either I need to know what your surname is, or you need to call me Cordelia."

He stood facing her from the opposite side of the wall. "Would you not think me a terrible upstart if I called you by your Christian name?"

She smiled. "I call you by yours."

He dipped his head in acknowledgement of that. It was one of his many mannerisms that marked him as someone who'd spent time in fine society and had been versed in all the civilities. He was such a mystery. A rather lovely one, truth be told.

"What's brought you to the home farm, Cordelia?" He said her name with just enough of a hint of Scotland to make it sound almost magical. She liked that very much, indeed.

"If it would not cause you any inconvenience, might I work on my sketch of Shadow?"

"No inconvenience at all, Cordelia." Oh, the way he said her name!

He was everything that was considerate and kind as he saw her settled on a three-legged stool in the small hedgerow-lined pasture where Shadow was passing the morning. He asked if she was in need of anything that he might obtain for her. When she assured him she had all she needed, he insisted he was available should that change. The contrast of his courteousness with her parents' selfishness proved a balm.

"I hear that the laird left for Edinburgh this morning." He made the observation with a tone that indicated he understood why that would be of particular concern to her.

"Yes. A departure for Edinburgh most certainly occurred this morning."

Empathy immediately filled his expression. "Family ought not add to one's worries. I am sorry that yours does."

"Thank you, Sebastian." No matter that she'd been calling him by his name from their first meeting—there was something more personal in it now.

He dipped his head. "I will leave you to your art, Cordelia."

"You will come back to see it when I am finished?"

"Would you like me to?" he asked, a little more quietly.

Cordelia held back the admission that she'd very much like him not to leave in the first place. She kept herself to a simple, "Yes, please."

With another dip of his head, he returned to his work, leaving her to see to hers.

Shadow was perfectly content to wander about the meadow, exploring and occasionally taking a nibble at the grass. Cordelia forced herself to focus and not look back in the direction Sebastian had gone. She had enjoyed her interactions with him, even looked forward to more. This was, however, the first time she'd felt such a strong pull. It was somehow both pleasant and upending.

The lamb was content in her grazing, affording Cordelia ample opportunity to study her sweet little face and make adjustments to the sketch. The day was fine, a light breeze adding an idyllic quality to the setting without making the air overly chilled. The natural perfume of flowers and meadow grass wafted about. The lamb's vocalizations drifted to her, as did the thumps and cracks and heavy footfalls of Sebastian seeing to his work. Now and then, he even called out in answer to Shadow's plaintive cries.

Cordelia quickly filled in the details her sketch had been missing. She added a few extra things to the scenery, thickened a few lines where it made sense, and generally refined the drawing. Her fingers itched to make an attempt at drawing Sebastian, but she would want to sketch him as he'd looked at Loch Tev—sitting on a rock, gaze on the water, thoughts clearly far away. That moment, that look on his face, had returned to her again and again in the time since they'd made that short journey.

What had he been thinking? Where had he been imagining himself? What had he thought of her presence there?

Shadow perked up and trotted in her direction. Cordelia did not, for even a moment, think the little lamb was making the short journey on her account. Without even looking behind her, she knew Sebastian was drawing near.

He reached her side in the next moment. "I found myself

worrying that I ought to have offered you water when you arrived, seeing as you walked a distance to get here."

"You did assure me that, were I to find myself in need of anything, I was only to ask," she said.

That didn't seem to entirely reassure him. "I should have offered. My mother did raise me with manners, I assure you, but I find myself struggling of late with a tendency to neglect them."

The poor man looked both concerned about her and disappointed in himself.

"You comport yourself with admirable decorum, Sebastian of the Home Farm. So much so that I find you to be quite an intriguing puzzle."

"The feeling is quite mutual, Cordelia of Burnwick House."

A smile arose from her very heart. "Do you know, I like that almost more than 'Cordelia of London.'"

"Are we winning you over?"

She laughed lightly. "That is mostly Shadow's doing."

Sebastian bent down and stroked the lamb's soft head. "Do you hear that, wee lassie? You're to be our ambassador."

"And like any true ambassador, she has her own officially commissioned portrait."

"You've finished her sketch?" He seemed genuinely eager.

Cordelia held it out to him. He took it carefully, studying the drawing. She was often nervous when people examined her work. She didn't feel even a drop of that just then. Sebastian had shown himself to be very kind, especially in the matter of her art.

"That's her very likeness, Cordelia. She'll not be a lamb much longer. It's a fine thing to have captured her during this fleeting bit of her life."

"I'd like for you to keep it," she said. "Then you'll always be able to look back and remember her as a lamb."

"Thank you." With the parchment held between his thumb and two fingers, he showed the sketch to Shadow. "What do you think? Do you approve?"

The creature answered by snatching the paper between her teeth and running off with it.

Cordelia hopped to her feet, set her box of parchment and pencils on the stool, and rushed after Shadow. Sebastian followed the lamb as well.

The little lamb trotted faster, flicking her head in what appeared to be amusement.

"I fear she thinks we are playing a game," Cordelia said.

"Herd her in this direction," Sebastian said. "I'll see if I can't urge her to give back the paper without destroying it."

Herd her. Cordelia had never in all her life engaged in anything that might be described as "herding." Still, she wasn't averse to trying. Only Sebastian was nearby to witness—Connall didn't appear to be at the home farm that day—and he'd certainly been privy to her previous moments of humiliation. Cracking her racquet across his nose hadn't seemed to entirely sink her in his opinion; a bit of shepherding didn't seem likely to.

Cordelia was not wearing the most appropriate shoes for the undertaking. While she *had* chosen a simpler dress, one made of serviceable fabric, she was still ill-prepared for tromping about a high-grass meadow, shooing a lamb around. Even with her disadvantages, she rather enjoyed herself.

"Not that way, Shadow."

She placed herself between Shadow and the far corner of the enclosure, where the lamb had been heading. When the creature took up yet another wrong direction, Cordelia urged the lamb backward once more. All the while, Sebastian approached from the other direction, nodding his encouragement to Cordelia and placing himself in the way of any escape route he could.

Shadow still had the sketch in her mouth but hadn't done any significant damage to it. They might actually manage to retrieve it.

Cordelia urged the lamb toward Sebastian, feeling quite accomplished. She'd never have imagined she would have any opportunity to herd a lamb, let alone that she would actually prove adept at it.

She was near enough to Sebastian to hear him whisper, "Keep calm, little Shadow. I only want the drawing back."

The lamb's ears perked, but she kept a close eye on Cordelia.

"You can hear that I'm here," he continued on. "Don't be startled when I'm beside you."

Sebastian hunched down as Cordelia urged the lamb the last few feet to him. The burly man ran a gentle hand along the lamb's back, whispering soothingly to her. He carefully took hold of the parchment and gave the tiniest tug. Shadow let it go without a fight.

"We did it," Cordelia said.

"Yes, we did."

Just as he began to stand up, Shadow bolted, knocking hard into Cordelia and catching her utterly off guard. She tumbled forward, directly into Sebastian, hitting him with enough force to knock the both of them over. He wrapped an arm around her and cushioned her fall in the moments before they both hit the ground. She cringed at the sound of Sebastian's lungs emptying with a thud. How was it she continually made such a spectacle of herself around this man?

"Are you hurt?" he managed to ask, though with the heavy sound of one desperately trying to regain his breath.

"Am *I* hurt? You are the one who took the brunt of this fall." She pushed herself to a seated position directly beside him.

The arm he'd protected her with lay extended on the grass beside him. His other hand held the drawing of Shadow, now a bit crumpled. He lay flat on his back, the air clearly knocked from him.

Cordelia gently touched his face. "*Are* you hurt?"

He managed a small smile. "Only my pride, lass."

"You saved the drawing."

"I was far more concerned about saving you," he said.

It was her turn to smile. "You did manage that as well."

Seeming to have recovered from the tumble, he sat up, facing her. "It seems I'm a hero."

She knew he was joking, making a bit of a jest at his own expense. But she was grateful for his efforts on her behalf, for cushioning her against the full brunt of the fall.

Acting on an impulse she'd never felt before, Cordelia leaned forward and pressed a kiss to his cheek. "You *are* a hero," she whispered.

Filled with an equal measure of delight and embarrassment, she scrambled to her feet and rushed away, snatching up her art supplies as she went. She didn't stop until she was in her bedchamber at Burnwick House.

Somehow, someway, she'd lost a bit of her heart to Sebastian of the Home Farm, and she wasn't at all certain what came next.

CHAPTER 9

CONNALL'S ARRIVAL AT THE home farm the next day wouldn't have been so unusual, except it was not one of the days the lad usually worked there. Sebastian was happy to see him, but also concerned. There was a very good chance he had come because something was amiss.

But as the lad approached, Sebastian saw no signs of distress.

"Whit like?" When Connall had first started working at the home farm, Sebastian hadn't the first idea what that greeting meant or how to respond to it.

"I'm doing fine. What about yourself?" Sebastian tossed his bucket of slop to the pigs.

"I've come to beg a favor. Bold of me, isn't it?"

Sebastian shrugged. "Depends on the favor."

Connall was always quick with a smile. "My family and the Breckins and the Fairbarins want to have a wee *céilidh*. We've nae had one in a long time, and we got to talking about how nice it'd be. Having all three families together, we'd need more space than any of us have."

With the laird still away in Edinburgh, and knowing Sebastian's connection even though it wasn't openly acknowledged, the families likely hoped he could secure use of one of the large, open lawns surrounding Teviot Castle. How disappointed they would be to discover that his grandfather had, upon sending him to the home farm, insisted Sebastian not take advantage of their actual connection.

Connall continued on. "I mentioned to my mother that you've a big open space just to the south of your house here, and it's a fallow field this year, so there'd not be any crops at risk of being trampled. Any chance you'd be willing to let us have our wee party there?"

The request surprised him. It was his home they wished to use. And it was an opportunity to know them better, just as he'd been hoping for.

"I'd be happy to have you here," he said, with both sincerity and gratitude. "Tell me what I can do."

"There's nae much. Our *céilidhs* aren't elaborate. It's mostly music and telling stories and sitting about gabbing."

"I look forward to it."

He had heard the locals talk now and then about their *céilidhs*. The gatherings sounded delightful. He had never been specifically forbidden from attending, but he'd never been invited to one either. Now one was being held at his home, and it was exciting.

But tugging at his heart was the realization that, even with these three families he enjoyed so much, the gathering would feel incomplete if he did not also have someone else there, someone who'd managed to claim a little bit of his heart.

He wanted to—*needed* to—invite Cordelia.

* * *

"You wish us to attend?" Cordelia asked.

Sebastian had been fortunate to find the Wakefield sisters

on the east lawn of Burnwick House. He couldn't possibly have made the request otherwise. Though by birth, he was certainly permitted to call on them in the usual manner, being Sebastian of the Home Farm put him more on an even footing with the servants. It was such an odd situation to be in. None of his education or interactions with Society before settling here had prepared him for living in this in-between place.

"There will be music," he said, "and I remember you told me that Miss Seraphina has a musical talent." He dipped his head in the direction of the person they were talking about.

"I do love music," Miss Seraphina said. She was still as pleasant and sunny as she had been the first time he'd met her, but he could see that there was a heaviness in her eyes that hadn't been there before. Perhaps she missed her parents; they were still in Edinburgh with his grandfather.

"Will the families gathering there be upset if we attend?" Cordelia asked. "Sometimes having unexpected people arrive for a gathering puts a damper on it."

"If the laird came, that would cause a decided damper," Sebastian said dryly.

The two sisters smiled almost identically, clearly trying to hide some of their amusement, but not succeeding entirely.

"He did not seem a bad person," Cordelia said. "He was just high enough in the instep and just stiff enough in his manner that I can easily imagine how out of place he would be at a gathering of people with whom he does not usually interact."

"Precisely," Sebastian said. "But so long as I arm the other attendees with battledores, I feel they would think your presence a wonderful addition."

"I'm actually very selective in who I attack with racquets," Cordelia said with a feigned degree of arrogance. "You will find you are now a member of a very select club."

Miss Seraphina thrust her hand out and shook his hand vigorously. "Welcome to the exclusive club, Sebastian of the Home Farm."

He laughed out loud. "She's hit you with a racquet as well?"

"It is something of an initiation into Cordelia's world, I'm afraid."

The sisters were both so different from what little he knew of their parents. But then again, he had both been told and had seen for himself during his time among Society that many upper-class parents had little to nothing to do with the raising of their children.

"I do hope we'll see you this evening," he said to them both. "In the meantime, I need to get back to my work. Crops and animals tend to misbehave when left entirely to their own devices."

"And Shadow's likely crying her poor little heart out with you away," Cordelia said, comically shooing him away.

He made the journey home, whistling a jaunty tune and feeling rather pleased with life. Everything was far from perfect, but there was more than enough to be happy about.

He still felt every bit as pleased by the time the three families began trickling into the fallow field. They greeted him warmly and in friendly tones. They seemed quite happy to be there. More to the point, they seemed at ease. No matter that he was certain the laird had made this arrangement with him in order to be rid of him; the strategy was, in fact, working. Sebastian knew the people of this area better than he would have had his original vision of his return to Teviotbrae proven reality.

A few instruments were present. A few offerings of food to be nibbled on had been brought as well. The youngest members of the families were already running about, chasing each other and having a merry time. He received greetings aplenty. Shadow, too, seemed to be a particular favorite.

Mr. Breckin asked after the little creature.

"She hardly needs any milk lately," Sebastian said. "She seems pleased as can be to nibble on grass and wander about."

Breckin nodded. "Sheep are happiest in flocks, though. You may find as she gets a bit older that she'll be a wee bit lonely."

"As long as she has Sebastian of the Home Farm, she'll think herself in heaven," Archie said, joining them.

All three of them laughed, knowing it was more true than it likely ought to be.

"Oh, I don't doubt the wee thing thinks of you as part of her flock," Breckin said. "Keep an eye on the girl. If she starts to grow forlorn, you'll want to consider finding her a companion."

"Another sheep?" Sebastian couldn't entirely help a hint of horror in his voice.

The sound of it set the other two men laughing once more.

"It seems you've a love for this little one but nae for sheep in general," Archie said.

"Will she suffer for not being part of the flock?" Sebastian didn't like the idea of Shadow being unhappy, no matter that she was often terribly inconvenient.

"Hard to say, that. Some sheep are perfectly content being a pet, even not part of a flock."

Glenna McCrory passed by and dropped a word to them. "The Misses Wakefield are coming this way."

Sebastian worried for just a moment about the reception they would receive. He needn't have. The McCrory family rushed over, thanking Cordelia effusively for the little drawing she'd given them of the tree in the Burnwick House gardens.

Breckin asked her if she'd consider drawing a sketch of his family's humble home.

Miss Seraphina, with her sweet and open manner, had made herself a favorite as well. Sebastian had seen her make friends at the chapel on Sundays and whilst visiting the local village.

The sound of instruments began filling in the background. It wasn't a formal gathering. There'd be no insistence that music be enjoyed one moment and stories the next and something else after that. They'd all linger around, chatting if they wished, nibbling on shortbread biscuits, or singing along to the music. It was meant simply as an opportunity to be with each other.

To his delight, after amicably making her way around the gathering, Cordelia sat on the chair beside him. Perhaps she longed for his company as much as he had been longing for hers.

A bit apart from them, Miss Seraphina joined the musicians in singing a song she had, apparently, heard before.

"You told me your sister had musical talent. It was not an exaggeration inspired by sisterly affection. She has a lovely voice."

Cordelia nodded. "She has been praised often for the beauty of her voice. The music instructor she had when we lived in London was renowned throughout the Continent, and even he expressed his very real pleasure at hearing her sing."

While that reflected very well on her sister, something in the story gave him a little pause. "That musical instruction must have ended when you left Town."

She nodded and her expression turned a little sad. "I suspect that is why she's been heavy hearted of late. She no longer has the opportunity to indulge in and study music. She misses it more than she realized she would."

"Did London offer you similar opportunities for studying and enjoying art?"

She gave him a somewhat sad smile. "It did, but I found I have chances to indulge in my art here. I'm hopeful Seraphina will discover the same about her music."

"Having new things to paint and draw isn't the same as having all the benefits you had in London," he said.

"No, it is not. But when a situation cannot be changed, we are wise to find what happiness we can."

It was a good bit of advice for Sebastian, who had for so long been fighting against the circumstances he'd been put in.

Shadow nuzzled up against Cordelia's leg. Without hesitation, she reached down and scratched the little lamb behind the ears, just as one would do with a pet dog. He'd known a great many Society ladies in London and could not imagine a single one of them being anything but horrified at a farm animal wreaking havoc on their clothing or demanding attention.

He was struggling to discover a means of existing in between two worlds, but she was mastering very much the same thing. And she was managing it with far more grace and optimism than he often did. How remarkable she was, and how wrong he had been about her when they'd first met.

Miss Seraphina was being eagerly requested to continue singing with the musicians. She reminded the gathering that she didn't likely know most of the songs they preferred to sing. They all simply encouraged her to do her best. Some of the heaviness that had marred her expression earlier eased.

"I do hope our parents will allow us to come to future gatherings like this," Cordelia said. "It has done Seraphina so much good."

That one simple statement, offered as almost an afterthought, shined an unexpectedly bright light on their situation. She was a daughter of the gentry, while he was, as far as she and her family knew, merely an employee of the local principal landowner. She seemed to like him, though. She'd even offered him a sweet, tender kiss on the cheek. He'd worked very hard not to allow himself to assume there was more to the gesture than she might have intended. But the memory of it was strong and heart-pounding.

She liked him; he was certain of it. Sebastian of the Home Farm had nothing temporal or impressive to offer, and she liked him anyway. But at the same time, it was a barrier to anything beyond that growing between them.

Her parents would disapprove if they knew of his tenderness for her. She might very well be upset once she learned that he was not entirely what he said he was. Ought he try to explain his actual situation? Even if he never did, she would eventually learn the truth, living in the area as she did.

With a muttered excuse even he didn't truly listen to, he rose from the stool and wandered off past the edge of the gathering. His thoughts spun in dozens of directions. Shadow followed him, of course. But other than his little constant companion, he was alone beneath the branches of an obliging tree.

He liked being Sebastian of the Home Farm when Cordelia was about. He liked discovering things about her and talking with her without having to worry if she was being sincere. But he knew he was not being as honest with her as she was being with him.

"Is something amiss, Sebastian?" She had, it seemed, followed him after all.

He turned toward her, warmed through at her nearness. "Shadow is wandering again." He nodded to the lamb, sniffing out the best patches of grass in the open field.

"She didn't start wandering until *after* you did," Cordelia pointed out. "I haven't been able to sort out what in our conversation sent you rushing off."

"It wasn't anything you said."

Her doubtful look couldn't possibly have been misunderstood.

"I swear to you," he said. "I just have some thoughts to sort through."

"They don't appear to be pleasant thoughts." The doubt had shifted to something very near to guilt.

"You truly didn't upset me in any way."

Cordelia shook her head. "My father walks away in just that manner when I've introduced a topic he would rather not discuss."

Sebastian took her hand in his. "Let me say, then, with every ounce of sincerity, that you did not introduce any untoward topics, I am not at all upset with you, and sometimes your father drives me a little mad."

Her smile set his mind at ease, but also pushed his pulse to a quick clip. "My parents aggravate me at times as well. You will think me a terrible daughter, no doubt, but I confess I have not been overly sad to have them gone the past little while."

"Not terrible at all." He raised her hand to his lips and lightly kissed her fingers.

"Miss Wakefield!" Connall's voice broke the tenderness of the moment. "Your sister says she will only sing the song if you sing with her."

"Oh, mercy." She met Sebastian's gaze as he released her hand. "It will quickly become clear that only one of the Wakefield sisters has any musical ability."

"Best of luck to you, then."

She smiled once more, then made her way back to the gathering.

He was growing ever more fond of Cordelia, and he suspected the feeling was at least a little bit mutual. She didn't know the entirety of who he was, and that would remain a barrier between them. But Sebastian of the Home Farm didn't feel like a lie, like a deception. It was who he was, every bit as much as Sebastian, Grandson of the Laird. Perhaps *more*.

He didn't know what he was going to do, but he had the unshakable suspicion that, if he didn't sort out the matter himself, Fate, in all her unfeeling expediency, would do so for him.

CHAPTER 10

SOMETHING WAS WEIGHING ON Sebastian's mind, but Cordelia hadn't the first idea what. He was in generally good spirits and had welcomed her to the home farm in the days since the *céilidh*. She'd sat in various places, drawing sketches of the animals, the house, the distant mountains. He'd talked to her when his work took him past where she sat. He'd smiled at her often. But there was a certain pull to his mouth, a tension around his eyes that told her he was not entirely at ease. She'd half expected each time she visited that he would tell her he'd rather she not come any longer.

Cordelia arrived at the home farm on the fifth morning after the *céilidh*. Sebastian sat on the back of his pony cart, already hitched and apparently waiting for departure.

She stopped just shy of where he sat. "Are you about to leave?"

"That depends on you, Cordelia."

There was something almost flirtatious in his tone. She tried not to read too much into that.

"Did you know that you blush whenever I say your name?"

She had suspected as much. "I like the way you say it."

"And how do I say it?" Warmth filled his gaze.

"Like you've lived in Scotland part of your life. Like you think it is a nice name."

"Both true," he said with a nod, but watched her as if expecting more.

"And I think that is enough answers from me when I've a few questions to ask you."

"Fair enough." He patted the cart beside him. "Have a seat and begin your interrogation."

She set her art supplies just behind him, then sat in the spot he'd indicated. Wouldn't her London friends be shocked to see her situating herself so casually and so . . . countrified?

"Why is it," she asked, "that your imminent departure depends so much upon me?"

"Because my destination is Dalwyck, and I'm aiming for that spot specifically because I think you would enjoy painting it."

She set her hand on his arm. "You've thought of another spot for me to paint?"

He nodded. "I thought of it the day we went to Loch Tev. It's a bit farther afield, though, so I needed a day when I could take you there and back and still afford you time enough to paint."

She slipped her arm through his, even leaned a little against him. The gruff man she'd encountered in the Burnwick House kitchen was proving incredibly comforting. "I do not want you neglecting your farm, Sebastian. What little I know of the laird tells me he's likely to be very exacting in his expectations."

Sebastian pulled his arm from hers. Disappointment dropped her heart to her feet. But then he wrapped that arm around her shoulders and tucked her nearer, and all was right again.

"The laird is in Edinburgh still. I did extra work all this week to get a bit ahead on my duties. And Connall's brought his younger brother to the home farm today to help him do what remains to be done."

He'd been doing extra work that week. It did explain why he'd seemed more strained. That eased some of her worries.

"I would very much like to go with you to Dalwyck," she said. "Though Shadow will insist on coming along."

"She'll enjoy Dalwyck. Most of it is a large, open meadow. She can graze to her heart's content."

They talked of lighthearted things as he drove the cart away from the heart of Teviotbrae. She learned a little of his parents, mostly through his memories of journeys his family had made and places they'd visited. She told him of friends she'd had in London and fine works of art she'd seen there.

The miles passed so pleasantly that she was surprised when the landscape around her had transformed without warning into a glorious open glen, with mountains in the distance and wildflowers all around.

"Is this Dalwyck?"

"It is," he said.

A small house sat at one edge of the enormous meadow. "Will the people who live here be upset that we've come?"

He shook his head. "The house is unoccupied."

"It doesn't seem neglected, though."

"It isn't."

There was a history there, a story. But Sebastian gave the impression of not wishing to talk about it. She would leave that for another day and instead spend this one enjoying the beauty of her surroundings and the kindness of the man who'd thought to bring her here.

He helped her set up her easel and placed a stool for her beside it. Then he spread out a wool blanket on the ground near her. Shadow wandered the meadow as Cordelia painted. Sebastian lay on the blanket, his hands crossed beneath his head, alternately watching the sky, his pet lamb, and Cordelia.

It was a moment of utterly peaceful contentment that could not have existed in London. How had she ever believed that happiness existed only within the streets and parks and buildings of the metropolis?

"Why are you using yellow for the clouds instead of white?" he asked, his tone curious and not the least bit critical.

"The actual clouds are not, themselves, white," she said. "They contain a great many colors."

His gaze shifted to the sky overhead. "I'd not ever noticed that before."

"Have you noticed that Shadow's fleece is also not truly white? It contains various shades of gray and very pale pinks and yellows alongside the white."

He smiled, his eyes still studying the clouds. "Next you're going to tell me my hair is not actually black."

"It's not."

Sebastian laughed. He had been so cross when they'd first met but had shown himself to be a very tranquil person. Being with him calmed her usual worries. She felt less lost, less unsure of herself.

"How long have you lived in Teviotbrae?" she asked as she added shadows to her clouds.

"Five years," he said, "though my family visited a few times when I was younger."

"You said your mother was English. It was your father, then, who hailed from this area?"

"Aye. And he loved Teviotbrae. I thought, in coming back after he died, I'd feel more at home, a little less lost." His chest rose and fell with a heavy breath. "But mostly, I found myself missing him even more."

"Where do you go to feel closer to your mother?" It was a remarkably personal topic of conversation, one she wouldn't have dared broach with any of the gentlemen she'd known in London. But Sebastian was different. He was open and candid, and she never worried that he would be unkind.

"I don't truly have a place to go that reminds me of her," he said. "I've never thought to find one."

"What were some of the things that brought her joy? Other than you, of course."

He offered a grateful smile. "I do hope I was a joy to her. I'd like to believe I was. But I *know* that she loved flowers. She could not resist smelling any and every flower she passed."

"There are a great many flowers in Teviotbrae, Sebastian. Every meadow, almost every field, growing wild along the roads, poking out of every hedgerow. And this meadow is lush with them. You feel your father here, but I think you ought to feel your mother here as well."

He sat up on the blanket, his eyes scanning the area all around them. "I hadn't really thought of seeing her in the flowers and the aroma of blossoms. I do like the idea of both my parents being here with me in some way. This hasn't always been an easy place to live."

"I can imagine," she said.

"It has been easier of late." His mouth twitched.

"Has it?" She assumed a prim and proper bearing.

"The company has improved vastly." He winked at her.

All pretense of being quite calm about his flirting disappeared. Undeniable heat snuck up her neck and blotched her cheeks.

Sebastian grinned, clearly quite pleased. "I didn't even have to say your name to see you blush this time."

"Go back to watching the clouds, Sebastian of the Home Farm. I've a meadow to paint."

Hours passed. Sebastian drifted off to sleep. He was strikingly handsome, she had to admit. That dark hair of his, and the way his mouth tipped up at the corners even while he was sleeping. Her fingers itched to sketch him, to create for herself a likeness of this man who had surprised her so much and had claimed a place in her heart.

The time came to return home. She was reluctant to go, and not on account of her canvas still being a bit wet or the view still being stunning. Sebastian wasn't at Burnwick House. She missed him when they weren't together.

She recognized that for what it was: She'd fallen quite top over tail for the home farmer, with his easy smile and contradictory manners and adorably mischievous lamb. She felt certain he was fond of her, though how far that fondness went, she wasn't entirely sure.

Teviotbrae, though, wasn't London. While days seemed to fly past in a ceaseless whirlwind in Town, this peaceful corner of the kingdom felt abundant with time for pondering and sorting mysteries and discovering joy.

They stopped at the home farm only long enough to put Shadow in her pen and stable the pony. They then walked to Burnwick House, Cordelia carrying her art supplies and Sebastian carefully carrying her painting. Their conversation was not nearly so personal or revealing as the one they'd had in the meadow. But it was every bit as welcome. How easily she could imagine herself spending day after day in just this way.

As they turned down the lane leading to the back of the house, Cordelia caught sight of her parents walking along the same path toward her and Sebastian. They were not alone; the laird was with them.

"They've returned early," Cordelia said. "I wonder if that portends good or ill."

They would know soon enough. The three new arrivals spotted Cordelia and Sebastian. Even from a distance, their disapproval was apparent. Why should they be upset? They had returned early and couldn't possibly have been expected to be greeted upon their arrival. If anything unpleasant had happened in Edinburgh, that could not be laid at the feet of two people who hadn't even been present.

Mother spoke the moment she was near enough to do so without raising her voice, something she had always insisted was uncouth. "Wandering about? Without your maid with you?"

"I do not have a maid, Mother." Cordelia never argued with her parents. She certainly never defended herself to them. But the criticism had been launched without warning.

"*Any* maid would have been more appropriate than"—Mother's eyes darted to Sebastian—"a man to whom you are not related."

"He is carrying my painting for me," Cordelia said. "It was a kindness, and—"

Father spoke over her. "How many times have we told you of the need to balance this . . . interest of yours with what is right and proper?"

"There is nothing improper in painting," Cordelia insisted.

Clearly taken aback, Mother whispered harshly, "This boldness is unbecoming, Cordelia."

"Sebastian, give the offending item to Mr. Wakefield." The laird sounded as displeased as Mother and Father. "And as you return to the home farm, give some thought to whether neglecting your duties there will serve your best interest going forward. Farmers, after all, can be replaced."

It took every bit of self-control Cordelia had not to speak up in his defense. He was not simply replaceable. And he never neglected his land, his animals, or his neighbors. For the laird to lob that accusation at him was utterly unfair. But she could sense her defense would only make matters worse.

Her painting was given to Father. Mother took possession of Cordelia's box of art supplies.

"Inside the house," Father told her, his voice snapping.

She'd not thought her time spent drawing and painting was as inappropriate as her parents clearly thought. Spending time alone with Sebastian did, she admitted, push the bounds of propriety. But her parents were always so careful to present a calm and unruffled front to anyone of significance. Scolding her so harshly in front of the laird was not something they would have done for a minor infraction.

Cordelia silently followed her parents, completely at a loss. They moved directly to the sitting room where the family passed their days. Seraphina was inside, watching with concern.

"I didn't tell them," she whispered to Cordelia.

Without a word, Father tossed the watercolor painting directly into the low-burning fire.

Seraphina gasped. Cordelia was too shocked to do anything but stare in horrified silence.

Mother tugged the bell pull, then turned to face her daughters. "We have spent these past days salvaging this family's standing, reclaiming opportunities for the two of you. Imagine our shock upon returning to discover that our eldest daughter is gadding about the countryside with . . . a farmer."

Cordelia despised the way her mother spat that word out, as if there was something shameful in what Sebastian did. She was fully aware that Sebastian's station in life was considered significantly beneath hers. But her family, as far as she knew, was on painfully thin ice, financially. They had fled the very Society that would have rejected Sebastian because they could no longer afford to mingle with them. Who were they to look down on him?

The fire continued to consume Cordelia's painting. She watched the flames curl around it, and her heart sank further and further.

"The laird knows all the important families in the surrounding counties," Father said. "He means to invite them, a few at a time, to Teviot Castle and introduce us. Seeing how you conduct yourself while we are away might very well lead him to change his mind."

"For your sake and your sister's," Mother said, "we can only hope he does not."

"I merely painted a local meadow." Cordelia tried to keep her voice steady, knowing her parents did not care for displays of emotion. "And the home farmer carried it for me because it was wet, and I was struggling with it." She had no intention of telling them she'd been with him all day, indeed had spent portions of every day with him since they had left for Edinburgh.

"Young ladies are permitted an interest in art. But that interest ought never be allowed precedence in the life of a lady of standing. Fill quiet hours, yes. Allow for reflection and an appreciation for nature, certainly. But to go out of one's way to spend all one's time in . . . art"—Father never could say that word in connection with her in any tone other than indignation— "is vulgar. And now it has led you to behave with little care for your reputation. Even if this farmer were the laird himself, spending time alone in his company would still be inappropriate."

Cordelia couldn't entirely argue with that, though she took exception to the assertion that the time she spent on her art was excessive. What else was she to do in Teviotbrae? Her parents disapproved of socializing with the local people beyond polite words of greeting at church or the market square. She had no friends here that they would approve of. There were none of the diversions of London.

Glenna McCrory arrived in the room, no doubt having been sent to answer the bell Mother had pulled earlier. She dipped a quick curtsey and awaited her instructions.

Mother held out the box of artistic implements she still held. "Destroy this."

Seraphina grasped Cordelia's arm, holding it tightly but not saying a word. Cordelia couldn't breathe, could hardly think. These supplies had been obtained in London, and at some cost. They could not be replaced.

"Don't dally," Mother said firmly. "See that they are destroyed entirely."

Glenna took the box, brow pulled. "Yes, ma'am," she said quietly. She slipped from the room, having received instruction from one who had the ability to take away her employment. There was no question of not obeying the command.

"Oh, Cordelia," Seraphina whispered, emotion cracking her words.

For her part, Cordelia couldn't have spoken even if she'd thought her parents would have permitted it.

"There will be no more untoward behavior," Father said. "From either of you. I suggest you sort yourselves out quickly. The laird anticipates guests at the castle within the week."

Cordelia hadn't the least bit of enthusiasm. Her heart ached. Her parents had taken her from London, the only home she had ever known. And they had just robbed her of her art, the means by which she had begun to feel at home in Teviotbrae. The contretemps on the back pathway likely meant there was no real hope of having Sebastian's company again, not in the same way.

Love of My Heart

What had been such a wonderfully joyous day was ending in heartbreaking sorrow.

Chapter 11

Sebastian hadn't told Cordelia of his connection to the local laird. His grandfather had insisted that not be acknowledged, wanting him to make his way on his own merits. That was beginning to prove particularly problematic. The time he had spent with her had pushed the bounds of propriety, yes, but his low status had clearly been her parents' most pressing objection. That and her dedication to her art.

He'd been at the home farm only a few minutes when Archie arrived, enough out of breath to indicate he had rushed over. He held under his arm what looked like Cordelia's box of art supplies.

"M'sister was given this by Mrs. Wakefield," Archie said, "and told to destroy it. Glenna said poor Miss Wakefield looked crushed, ready to sob. We're hoping you'll keep this here until there's a way to get it back to the poor lass without landing her in trouble."

The Wakefields had ordered Cordelia's paints and brushes and other supplies destroyed? They were taking away her art. Punishing her for painting. What further punishment were they inflicting because she'd spent time with a farmer?

"I'll keep the box safe," he told Archie. "And I'll not tell the Wakefields your sister didn't follow their orders."

"Thank you." He handed the box off. "I'd best rush back. Would nae do to be caught out neglecting my work with Mr. Wakefield in such a taking today."

"By all means. Don't cause trouble for yourself."

Sebastian stored the box on a high shelf inside the house, tucked a bit behind other things. He didn't for a moment think the Wakefields would ever step foot inside the home farm of a neighboring estate, but he wouldn't risk it.

He could do little to convince them to value their daughter's talent as they ought. But he could, perhaps, save her further remonstrances by making them aware that he and Cordelia were, in fact, on equal social footing. That, however, required his grandfather's cooperation.

Shadow expressed great disdain as Sebastian walked past her pen and didn't stop for a long visit. He knew he had become the entirety of the little creature's flock, and he felt bad abandoning her, even for a brief time, but Cordelia was in such an unhappy situation that he couldn't in good conscience not try to do something.

The staff at the castle were clearly uncertain when Sebastian insisted on seeing the laird. They, no doubt, were aware that their employer had insisted his grandson be treated exclusively as the home farmer would be. Sebastian, though, knew where the old man was likely to be found and made his way directly to the library.

The laird was, indeed, there. His expression turned instantly stormy upon seeing Sebastian enter. "What are you doing here?"

"I've come on a personal matter."

Grandfather had begun shaking his head before Sebastian finished. "It is improper for you to disrupt my day with personal matters."

"But that is precisely what I've come to talk to you about. As *your grandson*, I do have that right. I have decided that—"

"For the time being, laird and home farmer is our connection. You are perfectly aware of that."

Sebastian refused to give in so quickly. Too much depended upon this. "We are family. We are each other's *only* family."

Grandfather rose from the chair he'd been occupying and crossed to the tall, diamond-paned window that overlooked the extensive grounds. "We are the stewards of Teviotbrae. For generations, we have borne responsibility for this land. Its well-being and the well-being and future of those who call it home must always be our first consideration. We would hardly be worthy of the faith placed in us if we set that aside."

It was a lecture he had heard before. "Does it automatically follow that acknowledging me as your grandson would lead to misery in this area?"

"When you become laird, they must have full faith in you. They do not know you as they did your father. There's nothing for it but to give them a chance to decide that you can be trusted."

Sebastian might have kept pushing, might have pointed out that he had earned a great deal of their trust already. But his grandfather had turned his back to him, something he had done before when discussions of a more personal nature had been raised between them. It was his way of saying he was the laird before he was a grandfather.

"I intend to make the truth of my identity and my standing known to the Wakefields."

Before the laird could speak, something he clearly intended to do, Sebastian pressed on.

"Miss Wakefield is being unfairly reprimanded for spending time with someone who is not her equal. To allow her to continue being wrongly castigated would be ungentlemanly."

Ruffled and angry, the laird spun about. "It is not for a farmer to declare what is ungentlemanly."

"It *is* when the nearest gentleman is allowing a lady to suffer unjustly."

"Your father would never have spoken to me so insolently," the laird growled through tight teeth.

"My father would never have allowed you to treat me so unfairly."

An expression of distaste twisted the man's features. "Tell the Wakefields if you wish. I will deny it. Of the two of us, you know perfectly well who they will believe."

He would literally lie to prevent being connected with Sebastian? This was clearly not a matter of looking after the well-being of the people or teaching his grandson to appreciate the land. He truly did not want any connection between them acknowledged. "What could I possibly have done to earn such disdain? I have only ever tried to be what you wished. But nothing has ever proven sufficient."

"You are ungrateful, unworthy of the inheritance that should have been your father's, that should have continued in a strong Scottish line. It ought never to have been yours." The vitriol in the laird's voice could not be mistaken. "I will not see an Englishman claim this castle, not while I am alive."

An Englishman. Because Sebastian's mother had been English, the laird considered Sebastian English as well. *Only* English.

"The Wakefields are English," Sebastian said. "You seem to approve of them."

"I approve of them for Burnwick House. This is Teviot Castle. I am its laird. And you are—" Grandfather stopped himself but did nothing to hide his angry disapproval.

"I am Sebastian of the Home Farm. In your eyes, that is truly all I am."

"Even that is more than you ought to be."

To Sebastian's surprise, the hurtful words didn't pierce or stab. They were less a matter of discovery as confirmation. His grandfather resented his very existence. Deep down, Sebastian had suspected as much.

"You truly mean to lie to the Wakefields should they ask you the truth of my family connections?" Again, he was looking for confirmation, not asking because he didn't know the answer.

"It will not be a lie. I consider myself to have no family."

No family. For so long, Sebastian had exhausted himself attempting to make the bitter old man accept him. He'd clung to the thread of family, a thread the laird had long ago severed.

You feel your father here. You ought to feel your mother here as well. Cordelia had, in her quiet way, taught him something valuable and remarkably timely that day. The laird was not the only family connection he had. He could feel his parents with him. And he felt them especially at Dalwyck.

He didn't need the laird to love him. "Very well. I know how to proceed."

"And how is that?" For the first time, the laird looked a little uncertain.

"It is not for the home farmer to take up the valuable time of the laird." He dipped a bow and turned and left without another word.

Sebastian felt more than a little foolish standing at the far edge of the Burnwick House grounds. But Connall had learned from his sister that Cordelia and Miss Seraphina took morning walks in this area of the estate. He needed to talk with Cordelia but didn't dare attempt to do so at the house.

He'd spent the night before sorting things out in his own mind. He wasn't entirely certain how to make the Wakefields aware of his true identity, but he would not leave Cordelia in the dark on that matter any longer.

Connall and his younger brother were tending to things on the home farm again so Sebastian could make yet another unexpected journey away from home, this one far shorter than the last.

He'd been standing where he was for nearly half an hour when Fate finally decided to smile upon him. The two sisters came around a turn in the path and spotted him there. Wanting to give them the opportunity to avoid him if they chose, he stayed where he was and waited. Neither hesitated, neither seemed upset. They both came quickly to where he stood.

"Our parents will be upset if they see you here," Cordelia warned.

"I'll be quick, I promise. I have been worried about you since yesterday. Your parents were very cross. I've feared they might be mistreating you."

"Nothing so—" Her stalwartness dissolved, and tears filled her eyes. "Oh, Sebastian."

He wrapped his arms around her. She leaned immediately into his embrace.

"They took my paints and my pencils and everything." Her voice broke with emotion. "And they have absolutely forbidden me from seeing you."

"Clearly that declaration is proving efficacious," Sebastian said dryly.

He felt her laugh a little. A very little. Sebastian glanced to Miss Seraphina, hoping for a little more information without pressing Cordelia to speak while so upended.

"They are being utterly terrible about all of this," Miss

Seraphina said. "They destroyed all of her art supplies. I think they would actually lock her up if they saw her talking with you."

"And if they saw me holding her like this?"

"They'd probably shoot you."

"Lovely." He pushed out a breath. "Cordelia, dear, allow me to set your mind at ease on the first matter." He set her just enough away from him to look into her tear-splotched face. "Glenna gave your art box to her brother, who brought it to me. It wasn't destroyed. It is safe and whole at the home farm, hidden from view and waiting for the day when you can safely reclaim it."

Hesitant hope entered her eyes. "Truly?"

He nodded. "If we can find a way around your parents' edict where I am concerned, you can use them whenever you are at the home farm."

Her brow pulled low with concern. "They'd likely dismiss Glenna on the spot if they knew she'd disobeyed their instructions."

"We will make certain they never know."

Cordelia leaned against him once more, fitting rather perfectly in his arms. "I hate hiding things from them, but I am discovering their view of the world is terribly different from mine. They despise the idea of you and I even being friends yet have already decided that the laird's visitors are worthy of association even though they haven't met them yet."

This was news to Sebastian. "The laird is having visitors?"

Cordelia sighed, the sound filled with exhaustion. "Other people of rank and position who live somewhat nearby. They will stay at Teviot Castle, and we're meant to meet and visit with them."

People of standing who lived nearby. Sebastian didn't have much difficulty guessing who those visitors were likely to be. He knew a few families from this area of Scotland from his brief time in London. He even knew of one gentleman his same age who lived only a bit more than a day's journey from Teviotbrae and had also been educated at Eton.

An idea began to form in the back of Sebastian's mind. "Do you know what is planned for the gathering?"

"A dinner is to be held at the castle and another will be held here." Cordelia's hands, which had been pressed to his chest, slipped around him so she embraced him in return. It was at once comforting and thrilling. "I don't believe there will be enough people for a ball. Perhaps an afternoon might be spent in the castle gardens."

The castle gardens were accessible to him in a way the interior of the castle was not. That presented some intriguing possibilities.

"I'm certain if extra things are needed from the home farm, you will be informed." Cordelia had shown herself time and again to be very thoughtful of his situation. It was time she understood what that actually was.

"Before these visitors arrive, I need to tell you something," he said. "And I will confess, I'm not certain how you will react to it."

Cordelia looked at him, both curious and concerned. Seraphina had already slipped back a little, offering them a bit of privacy.

"Will you walk with me while I explain?"

She nodded, pulling out of his embrace but, before he could even miss having her in his arms, setting her hand in his.

"Everyone hereabout calls me Sebastian of the Home Farm," he said as they walked slowly along the path. "It's what I am known as, because it is what I do here. *Now.*"

She nodded again. "You said you lived here when you were very little, that your father grew up here."

"I do have a surname," he continued. "The local people don't use it because they have been instructed not to. I don't use it because I felt obligated to the one who has forbidden me to."

"I don't understand."

He was doing a poor job of explaining.

"I likely ought to have told you this sooner. You will, no doubt, think me selfish for doing so now, only after your parents have expressed such disapproval of me. But please know that revealing this is a matter of wishing to save you further disapproval from your parents."

She squeezed his hand. "I have never thought you selfish; I am unlikely to start now."

He hoped that proved true. "My full name is Sebastian Coburn."

Her brow furrowed on the instant, clearly recognizing the name, as he had suspected she would. "That is the same surname as the laird."

"My father was his only son. He grew up here in Teviotbrae. More to the point, he grew up at Teviot Castle. I was born there. We left when I was very young. My mother wished to spend more time in England."

He could see thoughts spinning in Cordelia's mind as she was piecing together a puzzle she hadn't even realized she was facing. "Your father has passed away."

"He has."

"That means, barring the laird marrying again and having another son, you will inherent Teviot Castle."

"I will. And I'll be the Laird of Teviotbrae."

She blinked a few times as she slowly shook her head. "Why do you live at the home farm? Why does the laird not refer to you as his grandson?"

"The reason he originally gave for my situation was that

he wanted me to come to know the local people and the area, that I would be a better steward of it for having worked the land. But he's become more and more insistent that the connection between us never be acknowledged. I finally pressed the matter with him and discovered what I think I knew all along: He resents me. He resents my English mother. He resents that my father's little family took him away from home. The laird doesn't acknowledge me as his grandson because he wishes I weren't."

Cordelia rested her head against his shoulder as they walked on.

"If your parents knew my actual station," Sebastian said, "they might be kinder to you about our . . . friendship."

"For what it's worth," she said, "your circumstances don't change how *I* feel about our friendship. It does not change how I feel about you."

He lifted her hand to his lips and pressed a gentle kiss to her fingers. "That you cared for me as Sebastian of the Home Farm is a gift, Cordelia. My only remaining family member does not wish to have me around. I didn't find a place in London Society when I was there. I've felt lost for years. The fact that you saw me and liked who I was, *as I was*, means the world to me."

"My parents will likely feel conflicted. They will recognize we're on even social footing, contrary to what they thought. But if the laird disapproves of you, they will likely feel they ought to as well."

He paused and turned to face her. "The laird has warned me that, should I attempt to tell your parents my connection to him, he will deny it. He will denounce me as a liar, an opportunist, and I very much fear your parents will believe him."

She sighed. "I suspect even if they don't believe him, they

will support him in his lie simply to remain in his good graces."

"I will think of something," he said. "I'm not willing to simply give up."

Cordelia brushed her fingertips along his jaw. "Neither am I."

He wrapped his fingers around hers, then turned his head enough to kiss her hand. "I hope you can sort a way to visit the home farm and continue pursuing your art," he whispered. "That ought not be taken from you."

"Is that the only reason you wish for me to visit you?" She kept her voice low.

"It most certainly is not."

He brushed his lips over hers and cradled her face in his hands, his fingers threading gently into her hair.

"Oh, Sebastian," she sighed as she hooked her arms about his neck.

He deepened the kiss, moving his hands down her back and wrapping his arms around her waist. She returned with fervor the longing and love he felt.

Somehow, they would find a means of sorting the maze that lay between them and their happiness.

Somehow.

Chapter 12

The laird's guests arrived three days later. Cordelia hadn't seen Sebastian since he'd kissed her on the Burnwick House grounds, but she wasn't worried. Their connection had not begun on the surest footing, but he'd shown himself dependable and kind. They had obstacles to overcome, but she didn't mean to give up, and she knew Sebastian wouldn't either.

"Please pay attention, Cordelia." Mother's frustrated voice cut through Cordelia's distraction. They were riding in the family carriage to Teviot Castle for a gathering in the gardens. "Three different families will be there, all of whom I've heard mentioned around London. Among them, though, are the Lithgows."

Cordelia had heard of that family. They held some significance in London Society. She hadn't realized they lived in this area of the kingdom.

"You are not to babble on about your art." As always, Father spoke of her passion in tones generally reserved for something truly distasteful. "As we are not likely to return to London for years yet, this is your best opportunity for making beneficial connections."

It was not difficult to understand the meaning behind his declaration. Those "beneficial connections" were not of the casual variety. They meant to see her married advantageously, no doubt having been struck with fear of the contrary upon hearing she had been spending time with a local farmer.

Before coming to Teviotbrae, she'd likely have simply shrunk under the weight of her parents' demands. She knew now what she wanted and the future she meant to claim. Her parents could scheme up all the matches they wanted; she would not bow to those schemes.

As the family stepped into the formal garden at Teviot Castle, Seraphina slipped her arm through Cordelia's. They were, as always, each other's unfailing support.

They were greeted by the laird, whom Mother and Father treated with deference. For her part, Cordelia knew she would never be able to entirely respect him, knowing how he had treated his own grandson.

"Allow me to make introductions." The laird motioned to a group of finely dressed people and began doing precisely that.

The MacGregors were a family of long standing in the area, with claim to a large estate closer to the coast. They spent time every Season in London, though they were not there for more than a few weeks.

They were next introduced to the Rutherford family, who lived closer to Teviotbrae than the MacGregors and had a daughter of an age with Seraphina, but who hadn't quite the same standing in Society as the MacGregors.

The last introduction was to the family Mother and Father had anticipated most: the Lithgows. They were well known in London. Cordelia had seen their very fine carriage from a distance in Hyde Park and had, from almost as far a distance, observed them in their box at the theater. She hadn't ever met them, though.

The son of the family, Mr. Douglas Lithgow, looked to be about Sebastian's age. The silks and laces he wore spoke of prosperity without ostentation. Literally nothing about him was off-putting. Cordelia might have enjoyed meeting him if not for the gleam that immediately entered her parents' eyes.

He offered a bow to Cordelia and Seraphina in turn. Cordelia was careful to execute her answering curtsey with precision but not encouragement. Seraphina seemed a little upended but managed the interaction with aplomb.

"We will allow the young people to interact." Mother went so far as to nudge Cordelia closer to Mr. Lithgow.

Seraphina, good sister that she was, slipped her arm once more through Cordelia's, keeping the two of them quite close together. "Miss MacGregor, do join us." Adding a fourth to their numbers was a stroke of genius. Nothing in the interaction could be viewed as intimate.

"How fortunate that your family has come to live in Teviotbrae," Miss MacGregor said. "None of us travels to London as often as we would like. We simply must visit one another at our homes here."

"An excellent suggestion," Mr. Lithgow said, his manners everything that was warm and welcoming, but not the least bit overly familiar.

"How far do you live from Teviotbrae?" Seraphina was doing a fine job of leading the conversation. They had decided ahead of time that, should Cordelia be pushed toward someone by their parents, she would simply make herself an observer and Seraphina would take the lead.

"Not far," Mr. Lithgow said with an admittedly handsome smile. "A bit more than a day's journey is all."

Seraphina colored up a little.

From just beyond the gathering, someone approached. At first, Cordelia didn't recognize the new arrival, clad in a coat of striped, gray silk and a deep red waistcoat, wavy black hair pulled back with a red ribbon. After a mere moment, she knew him: Sebastian. She'd only ever seen him in the clothes of a home farmer. Dressed as he was then, he very much looked the part of heir to a laird.

Cordelia did her utmost not to draw attention to his arrival, though he stole her breath a little. The laird would be livid. The guests would be confused. Her parents would likely blame her for anything that went wrong.

Sebastian walked directly to where she stood, moving with confidence and assurity. She held her breath. Miss MacGregor caught sight of him, her brows lifting in appreciation.

As Sebastian joined them, Mr. Lithgow turned to see who had stepped up beside him. His face split into a broad grin. "Sebastian, old boy. I hadn't heard you were back in Teviotbrae."

"It is good to see you again, Douglas. I have not been to Town since we last saw each other there. How have you been?"

"Fine." Mr. Lithgow looked quickly at the ladies gathered around. "I am assuming you know the Misses Wakefield, as they are your neighbors. Have you made the acquaintance of Miss MacGregor?"

Sebastian dipped a perfectly executed bow. "I believe we met once a number of years ago, when I was visiting Teviot Castle."

"I seem to remember that as well," she said. "The laird is your grandfather, if I am recalling correctly."

"You are absolutely correct."

"Mr. Coburn." Mrs. Lithgow approached with a pleased smile. "We did not realize you were visiting your grandfather. How delightful that we should be here at the same time."

Sebastian once more offered a bow and a word of

pleasure. Cordelia began to understand. He was known to these people not as Sebastian of the Home Farm, but as Sebastian Coburn, heir to the Laird of Teviotbrae. His true identity would be made known to her parents under circumstances that prevented the laird from calling him a liar. He, after all, was not the one declaring himself the man's grandson. The laird would not accuse his distinguished guests of spreading falsehoods.

Mother and Father could not possibly have looked more perplexed. Father found his voice first.

"You know this man?" he asked Mr. Lithgow, standing near him.

"Certainly, I do. This gentleman"—Mr. Lithgow didn't overly emphasize the correction of Father's chosen term, but it was a significant change— "is Mr. Sebastian Coburn, grandson of our host."

That brought Cordelia's parents' confused gazes to the laird. With tight lips and tense jaw, the laird gave a single, quick nod of his head.

"Miss Wakefield," Sebastian said, "have you had the opportunity to meet the other guests?"

"I have been introduced, yes."

He offered her his arm, and she happily threaded hers through it.

"I had hoped you would join us today," she said.

"I am very pleased that I did."

He walked with her a bit away from the group and toward a small table holding little pastries for the guests to enjoy as they mingled.

"Has this made you terribly uncomfortable?" Cordelia whispered. "I know you did not care for Society when you were in London."

"The MacGregors and Lithgows are not terribly high in

the instep. They aren't the sort to make one feel inferior or out of place. And they know who I am, which serves my purposes quite well."

She allowed her amusement to blossom on her face. "That was very cleverly done. I daresay my parents are utterly befuddled. The laird, however, gives every indication of being boiling angry."

Sebastian went through the motions of placing a finger sandwich on a plate for her. "I fully expect the laird to exact some sort of punishment."

With worry, she met his eye once more. But he smiled softly.

"Do not fear, sweet Cordelia. I have planned for the edicts he is likely to make."

"He will take away your home, won't he?" How she knew that so suddenly, so entirely, she couldn't say. But she hadn't a doubt her hunch was correct.

"He will likely require that I vacate the home farm." Sebastian walked at her side away from the table, giving the impression to all who might be watching that they were simply having a pleasant conversation while enjoying a bit to eat in the lovely garden.

"Where will you go?" Her heart dropped to her toes at the prospect of Sebastian leaving.

"I have lived at the home farm not because I hadn't any other options, but because I did not wish to antagonize my grandfather. As he has made quite clear that he does not think of me as family, I no longer give that priority."

"You have another home?"

He nodded.

"Is it terribly far away?"

With another of his tender, reassuring smiles, he said, "Not far away at all."

"I would miss you if you left," she confessed.

"I do not intend that either of us will be required to miss the other."

They had not wandered far, her untouched finger sandwich still on the plate she carried, when the laird stepped in their path.

"This is unacceptable," he whispered through clenched teeth. His posture gave nothing away. The other guests would not be able to see his face and would not realize how angry he truly was.

"You are welcome to tell the Wakefields that what they have learned today of my connection to Teviot Castle is a lie, but I suspect the MacGregors and Lithgows would be both confused and insulted if you did so."

The laird's nostrils flared. "I will not endure this insolence."

"I had not expected you to."

Clearly the man had believed the grandson he refused to acknowledge would crumble under his disapproval. "You live at the home farm by my generosity. You will—"

Sebastian held up his hand even as he spoke over the declaration. "I have lived at the home farm as a matter of patience. But no longer. All of my belongings were removed yesterday and this morning. As of this moment, you no longer have a home farmer. I would suggest you secure one."

He offered a quick bow and offered his arm to Cordelia once more. She accepted. As they walked past the laird, she stuck her plate into the sputtering man's hand, taking advantage of his confusion. They continued on, making a slow circuit back in the direction of the guests.

"You have already moved out?"

"My father left me a bit of land, free of the entail connected to the castle. It is time I lived there, as my own man, out from under the thumb of the laird."

"And it is nearby?" she pressed.

His smile turned to a grin. "So much so that you are familiar with it."

On that mystery, they reached the others, and she lost all opportunity to quiz him. Her curiosity was piqued. But more than that, her heart was at ease. He was nearby. Her parents could not object. The laird could not keep them apart.

There was every reason to live with hope for a bright future.

Chapter 13

A GREAT MANY LOCAL families had gathered at Dalwyck for a *céilidh*. As had been the case at the gathering held at the home farm, Sebastian was playing host. Dalwyck, after all, belonged to him, an inheritance from his father. And the empty house Cordelia had asked about when he'd brought her here was his as well.

So many had helped him quickly leave the home farm and settle here. They'd shown him such acceptance, such kindness.

He'd spent his sojourn in London waiting to be accepted rather than finding where he belonged.

He'd done everything demanded of him by the laird without giving any true thought to himself. He'd very nearly let his conformity to those demands tear Cordelia from him.

No more.

Connall, standing near Sebastian, motioned with his head out into the glen. "Shadow seems to like her new home."

"We both do, though I suspect Mr. Breckin is correct in saying she needs a friend of some kind to give her the feel of a flock."

"Another sheep?"

Sebastian laughed. "Not likely, though I won't rule out the possibility should another lamb be orphaned next lambing season. At the moment, Breckin is suggesting a donkey."

"A donkey'd be helpful," Connall said, "seeing as you had to leave the pony at the home farm."

That had been Sebastian's thought as well. "I simply need to get myself a cart to go along with the animal, since that was left at the home farm as well. Truth be told, I'm more disappointed that I've had to leave *you* at the home farm, though I know it's a good position for you."

Connall grinned. "I'm not old enough to run it on my own, but my father's happier there than he was as a butler. We McCrorys belong to the land. Always have."

Sebastian looked out over the meadow at the distant mountains. "The land has begun calling to me these past years as well. I love it more the longer I am in Teviotbrae."

"A good laird always cares more about the land than about his claim to it."

It was praise of Sebastian, something he'd heard from more than one person that day. He needed reassurance. No matter that he knew the current laird thought poorly of him; he wanted to know that the sentiment was not general.

Connall looked in the direction of the house Sebastian now called his own. "You've new arrivals for the *céilidh*."

He did, indeed: Douglas Lithgow, whose family had been visiting for nearly a week, as well as Cordelia and her sister. He'd hoped they would come. Douglas had been kind to him while in London. Miss Seraphina's spirits had seemed a bit higher of late, and Sebastian wanted to see that continue. But Cordelia was his focus. Lovely, wonderful Cordelia.

Sebastian rushed over to greet them, not particularly caring that his haste would lay bare to the people in attendance his feelings for Cordelia. They likely already knew.

"Welcome." He made a show of offering the greeting to them all.

"I am certain you've been awaiting my arrival with bated breath," Douglas said dryly. He offered his arm to Miss Seraphina. "Shall we join the lively gathering, seeing as we both know we are, at the moment, wished to Hades?"

Miss Seraphina laughed lightly. "I think we had better."

And they did precisely that. Sebastian wasn't about to complain.

"I worried your parents wouldn't allow you to come," he said.

"The younger Mr. Lithgow convinced them, though it was not difficult. I suspect they aren't certain what their best position is where you are concerned. The current laird's approval might earn them the disapproval of the future laird. I do not envy them the fine line they are attempting to walk."

Sebastian took Cordelia's hand and raised it to his lips. "If that confusion means we needn't be separated by their edicts, I welcome it."

Cordelia slipped her arm around his, leaning a bit against him. "Why did you not tell me when we came to this glen that it belonged to you?"

"Let us simply say I, too, was attempting to walk a very fine line."

She sighed, the sound full of pleasure and relief. "I think you will be happy here."

"At the moment, my dear, I am utterly ecstatic."

They passed the remainder of the *céilidh* talking with the others gathered there, enjoying lively music and diverting stories. Though no one spoke their congratulations out loud, Sebastian had no doubt everyone present knew it was merely a matter of time before the current connection between their host and Miss Wakefield became a more permanent one. Even Douglas took the opportunity to goad him about it.

Sebastian didn't mind. He fully meant to make good on all their assumptions.

By the end of the gathering, only Douglas and the two sisters remained. Miss Seraphina was quite smitten with Shadow and was giving the quickly growing lamb a great deal of attention. Douglas was teasing her a bit about it.

"I wish I didn't have to go." Cordelia smiled, a bit of embarrassment and a lot of regret in her expression. "I miss you when we're apart."

"An experience that is entirely mutual, my dear." He slipped his arms around her. "Someday, I very much hope you will not be required to go at the end of the day."

"I would like that," she said quietly.

"If I offered you a humble home in a beautiful glen, a future that was not entirely devoid of possibilities but a present that is filled with rejection from the one person who might make it more temporally comfortable, would that be enough?"

She pressed a kiss to his cheek. "More than enough."

Her declaration encouraged him to be bold. "You would consider marrying a man who was, days ago, a home farmer?"

"I would more than merely *consider* marrying Sebastian of Dalwyck Glen. There is nothing I could ever want more."

"Not even a return to London?" He knew how much she loved Town, how much she missed it.

"Not even that."

"And if the laird never bestows any approval or favors on us?"

She touched his cheek lightly. "I am not in love with the laird. Not the *current* one, at least."

He could not have hoped for a better answer. There, standing near the house he ought to have claimed from the moment he returned to Teviotbrae, surrounded by the land he'd learned to love, and holding in his arms the lady who'd claimed his heart, he felt at home in a way he hadn't in years.

She offered a sweet and affectionate kiss, one he accepted and deepened. Life, in all its uncertainty, had brought them together. And Fate, in all her glory, was offering them the hope of a very bright future.

Shadow had grown in the months since Cordelia had first encountered her as a small lamb. As Cordelia painted the idyllic scene, making certain to include the sweet creature and the newly obtained donkey, she was struck by how much Shadow was beginning to resemble the grown sheep she would one day be.

But it was not Shadow nor the donkey that held her attention. Her Sebastian, her husband of only a few days, stood across the glen, looking out at the mountains, the breeze rustling his waves of dark hair.

Leaving London had felt like the greatest of tragedies. How she'd mourned and railed at Fate. But that departure had led her here to this time and place and a love she could not have even dreamed of. It had happened so quickly, so unexpectedly. She couldn't have been happier.

With careful strokes, she painted Sebastian into the landscape she'd been recreating on the canvas with the paints he had safeguarded for her. She filled the painting with the rainbow of colors and variety of textures found in this magical meadow. She painted their small, welcoming home, the garden plot they carefully tended, the no-longer-tiny lamb and newly arrived donkey. She created a picture of the most beautiful moment she could imagine.

As she put the finishing touches on her work, Sebastian slowly crossed the meadow toward her. A skip of delight disrupted the calm beating of her heart. She never tired of having him near.

He smiled as he approached. "You always look so happy while you're painting."

"And you always look happy here on your own land."

"*Our* own land." He sat on the empty stool beside hers. "I see Shadow managed to make an appearance in this latest painting."

"So did you. She would not wish to be in any painting or meadow or place where you weren't." Cordelia leaned a little against him. "I cannot say that I blame her."

"She will have to learn to be apart from me for a time." Sebastian set his arms around her. "A sheep, however loyal, cannot be brought to London."

Cordelia turned to look at him. "To London?"

"I wish to see the city through the eyes of one who loves it. And I wish for you to return to the museums you have missed and obtain more supplies and canvases."

"Truly?"

He nodded. "And I believe we should bring Seraphina so she can enjoy the music she has longed for."

"Have we the means of doing so?" She dared not get her hopes up until she was certain.

"We do. Our visit will not be extravagant, but we can go for a time. And Douglas will insist on making certain we are introduced to anyone in Town we do not know yet."

"I know you did not care for London when last you were there." She would give him a means of escape if he wished for it.

"I am convinced, my darling Cordelia, that I disliked it only because I was not afforded a chance to meet you when I was there. Had Fate been kind in that, London would have instantly become my favorite city in all the world."

Love of My Heart

"I think you like me, Sebastian of Dalwyck Glen."

"I *love* you, Cordelia, Love of My Heart. Utterly and entirely."

Sarah M. Eden is the *USA Today* bestselling author of multiple historical romances, including Foreword Review's 2013 "IndieFab Book of the Year" gold medal winner for Best Romance, Longing for Home, and two-time Whitney Award Winner Longing for Home: Hope Springs. Combining her obsession with history and affinity for tender love stories, Sarah loves crafting witty characters and heartfelt romances. She has thrice served as the Master of Ceremonies for the Storymakers Writers Conference and acted as the Writer in Residence at the Northwest Writers Retreat. Sarah is represented by Pam Pho at D4EO Literary Agency.

Visit Sarah at www.sarahmeden.com

Miss Smith
Goes to Wiltshire

Rebecca Connolly

Chapter 1

NO ONE OF SENSE married for love.

Apparently.

Martha Smith was unconvinced of the assertion her mother had attempted to engrain into her mind for the last six months, if not more, but she could certainly concede that it was not the standard nature of Society's marriages. The majority of her acquaintances who had made matches since they'd all been presented at court had done so for connection, for fortune, for status, and even for appearances, but no one, as far as she knew, had married for love. Or even affection.

It was a commoners' match, her mother insisted, and hardly a mark of good breeding. She had not married for love, and her marriage had been all the more successful for it, she claimed. Martha's father could not refute or support the statement, as he had been deceased for ten years now, but as he had been at least twenty years more senior than Martha's mother, it was not difficult to presume that he felt the same.

Why, then, did Martha feel so convinced she ought to marry for love?

It was a question that had been shouted throughout her home in London, usually in her mother's voice, and asked within Martha's own mind at a much more reasonable volume. Her life might have been infinitely more simple had she given up such an idea and made a match for a less fanciful reason, but every attempt to do so had left her cantankerous and sullen. She did not want to have a marriage for appearances or to tolerate her spouse on the occasions required of her.

She wanted to feel as though she were flying when she was with him.

According to her mother, this was likely due to entirely too much reading of novels.

That might have been true, but it did not follow that Martha should have to ignore the impulse.

The fight that had ensued with her mother on the very subject had led to her present position, sitting in a coach heading for the country, riding post, and being jostled into the shoulder of the dozing lady beside her. She had been sent with no chaperone, shockingly enough, though the aforementioned slumbering woman had insisted on acting the part when they'd been introduced at the coaching station. It hadn't proved all that necessary as yet, as all other occupants of the coach were presently sleeping or attempting to, but it was a pleasant comfort all the same.

Martha could not sleep, which she might regret upon arrival at her final destination, but it was not even a consideration for her. She had never been very far outside of London in her known life, and now she was going into Wiltshire. Every glimpse of rolling hills and streams, every acre of ground not containing a building, was of intense interest to her. Her adoptive companion, Mrs. Rhoades, had grown weary of her questions about the country, and the driver was now accustomed to her inquiries as to their present county at every change of horses.

Thus far, she had seen London, Sussex, Surrey, Hampshire, and Berkshire. They'd stayed the night at a coaching inn in Reading, wherein she had shared the room with Mrs. Rhoades to save them both the cost, and the entire company had again got the morning post to continue on. The last change of horses at Swindon had seen them in Wiltshire at last, and this was what captured Martha's attention most.

Wiltshire, the county she had been exiled to for six weeks at minimum. The punishment her mother had devised for Martha's romantic sensibilities, if not for her outright refusal of Mr. Standish and Sir Charles Stark last Season. From what Martha was now seeing through the windows of the stagecoach, it did not seem a particularly poor exchange.

The countryside was beautiful, and she wished there were a better word to describe it. She had never seen so much green, and in so many natural shades. It was better than any landscape she had seen captured in art, and more fascinating than anything she had conjured up in her mind. She had heard so many complaints about the country from her companions in Society, but felt unable to contribute to any conversation on the topic, as she had no knowledge or experience in any such thing.

A ten-year-old girl did not comprehend such a thing, so the entailment on her father's family estate had been no wrench for her. Even her father had not favored the country, so Martha had never been. Worley Park was a sty, by her mother's record, and they were better off without it.

Martha had needed to look up the definition of a sty upon hearing it, and now she wished to see one in truth for proper comprehension.

Someday, she had vowed, she would make the journey to

Oxfordshire to see the place. She was not entirely certain her mother's account of things could be trusted.

Then again, she had yet to see Lanfare, her cousin Eliza's house.

That was her mother's true punishment for her.

Eliza was fifteen years older than Martha, and the daughter of her father's younger sister. She had married for love when Martha was a young child, and now lived in a small village in Wiltshire with her many children. Her husband had not come from a wealthy family, but Eliza had been determined to marry him, so her family had consented. She had not been cut off, which Martha's mother, for one, could not condone, and her dowry had helped to purchase the house in which they had been raising their family.

Their particularly large family.

Which was her mother's point. She wanted Martha to see what a marriage of love would bring her to and, presumably, what it had brought Eliza to.

Thus far, Martha had no complaints about her journey. The coaching inn was exciting, if a trifle simple and quaint, and the food was excellent. Her bed could have used some fluffing, but even her bed in London was occasionally uncomfortable, so she could not lay blame on the innkeeper for that. The stagecoach was comfortable, as far as coaches went, and there was nothing to be done about the state of the country roads when traveling at these speeds. Yes, they were a trifle cramped with five of them sitting inside all squished together, but how much comfort did one expect to have when traveling post?

Though she was a veritable heiress, and though her station was enviable, she was not so fine a lady that she could not endure a little discomfort where it was reasonable. And she did not expect grandeur wherever she went, only decency. No frills, only kindness. No flattery, only respect.

Thus far, nothing in the country had prevented her from any of that.

But if it so happened that Eliza lived in squalor surrounded by babies, Martha might look very differently upon the state of affairs in her mind. It was vulgar to speak of money, but she was quite certain her dowry was considerably more than her cousin's had been.

Surely, that would keep her and her prospective husband out of the poorhouse.

Martha knew very little about such matters, and it was infuriating. Ignorance was acceptable for young ladies, even encouraged, for there was nothing more dangerous than an informed woman.

Ignorance was not bliss, in Martha's mind. Ignorance was madness.

Not that she wished to be a bluestocking or a busybody, but she did wish to have some modicum of intelligence about topics relating to her life and existence. And Society. And the world in general.

There was nothing about being blank inside that was enjoyable for Martha.

Which was leaving her more and more frustrated with Society and its collection of vapid ladies of fortune and breeding, despite being one of them herself.

One of the more promising ones, in fact.

But in Wiltshire, she could be no one, if her cousin truly lived in as remote a portion of the country as her mother had led her to believe. What in the world could that be like?

"I don't know what you're so fascinated about, Miss Smith," Mrs. Rhoades grumped from beside her. "You've seen one country hill, you've seen them all. There's been nothing but hills for miles and miles."

Their three companions across the way grunted in acknowledgement of her statement.

Martha turned and gave her adopted chaperone an exasperated look. "For a young woman who has only ever seen London, and at the furthest, Richmond, every hill stream is extraordinary, Mrs. Rhoades."

Mrs. Rhoades's expression turned pitying. "My dear child, that will not last long. How much time are you spending in Wiltshire? A week? Two?"

"Six, I believe," Martha replied, smiling blandly.

That prompted a deep bark of laughter from Mrs. Rhoades. "You will find nothing remarkable to look at on the return journey. It will be boredom from start to finish, and you will crave the sight of cobblestone."

The idea of so much misery building up from her time in the country that she would hate the view from the window, which was so exhilarating to her now . . .

It didn't sit well with Martha.

"Heavens," Martha murmured as she turned to gaze upon the rolling countryside, wondering how anyone could become bored with the sight of them. "I hope not."

"Hope does not water flowers, child. I doubt your mother is sending you to Wiltshire to appreciate the countryside." Mrs. Rhoades paused, then patted Martha on the knee. "Your optimism does you credit, Miss Smith."

Did it? Martha was less convinced of her optimism as she was about her obstinacy, perhaps her determination to ruin her mother's plans.

She would see as much of the countryside as her cousin and Wiltshire could show her while she was in this part of England. She would embrace what she discovered, admire what goodness she found, and continue on as she had done, albeit with a less naive image of England in her mind. There would be no coming to whatever sense her mother feared she lacked, and there would be no accepting of proposals simply because the man could further her popularity in Society.

Surely, there was some sense in seeking more from life than that, even for a woman.

But the rolling hills of Wiltshire had no answers for Martha on that score. Time would tell if they ever would.

"I hesitate to ask, for fear of becoming a nuisance," Martha announced, avoiding the temptation to bite her lip as she looked back at her fellow occupants in the coach. "But . . . when do you think we will arrive at our destination?"

The portly man directly across from her chuckled with what appeared to be good nature. "I expect we will be reaching Chippenham within the next quarter hour, miss, if I am any judge. From there, it would be a less expeditious drive to wherever you are bound. Stagecoach only goes through the market towns and more."

The term caught Martha's ear for no other reason than because it was foreign to her. "Market town?" she repeated, sitting forward just a touch. "Is that what Chippenham is?"

His smile spread, his stained teeth not particularly off-putting, given the warmth in his eyes. "Aye, miss. Wiltshire has more sheep than people, and Chippenham more than most, so the wool market is popular. Have you ever seen a sheep, miss?"

"Only in storybooks," Martha quipped without shame, her own ignorance over something that was so simple to her companions becoming amusing to her. "I take it I will see several?"

Most of her companions were chuckling now. "Look out of the window, miss. The white bunches on the hills are sheep."

"What?" Martha whirled to the window once more, her eyes scanning for any specks of white among so much green. They were scattered everywhere in the distance, and she realized she had been seeing them all along, but somehow, she had never considered them to be animals. They had seemed so remote, so natural, so part of the landscape that she had presumed them to be part of the regional flora.

But they were sheep!

A childlike wonder began to seep into her as she tried to make out the details of the sheep from her place, wishing one or two would come closer to the road without encountering any danger. She wanted to see what was so common and ordinary for the country, wanted to find it common and ordinary herself, although not too quickly. She wanted the novelty to linger a while, giving her something to be curious over and admire while she began her exile.

If she despised the sight of sheep by the time she returned to London, so be it. At least she would have seen sheep.

Perhaps that was the more important notion. If she gained nothing else on this excursion but the satisfaction of her mother and the separation from Society's emptiness, at least she could also claim to have lessened her ignorance.

The carriage turned from the rough country road onto smoother, more even streets. Not quite cobblestone as in London, but certainly an indication of a change in scenery. Buildings began to dot the view from the window, homes and businesses alike. Some villagers walked nearby, while others rode on the backs of fine horses. All were simply dressed, but not necessarily cheaply. Even from her position here, Martha could tell the difference.

None of the people paid the stagecoach any attention, no doubt accustomed to the sight and event, which certainly occurred on a near daily basis, if not more. Why should it disrupt their day and their routines? But surely, someone cared that a spoiled Society miss from London had arrived in Chippenham as punishment for being too whimsical about marriage.

It seemed like something that ought to have garnered some attention from somebody.

Alas, she was a nobody after all.

Martha Smith from London.

It wasn't the first time that the simplicity and utter banality of her name had struck her as ironic, but it was the first time it had truly made her want to laugh.

Perhaps her mother ought to have thought of that as a detriment to her prospects.

The carriage rolled to a stop and Martha released a breath. She wasn't entirely certain what Eliza's husband looked like, or how he would know her, but she supposed she was the only young woman on the stagecoach in Chippenham today, which would make his chances of finding her all the greater.

"End of the road for you, miss." One of the drivers stood at the door of the coach, offering a hand to her.

Martha nodded quickly and took his hand, allowing him to help her down. "Thank you," she told him with a smile when she was firmly settled.

He returned her smile, seeming far younger when he did so, and tipped his cap. "Nothing of it, miss. I'll see to your trunks."

Martha smiled into the coach as he moved to do so. "Safe travels to the rest of you. Thank you, Mrs. Rhoades. I am indebted to you."

Mrs. Rhoades simpered a little. "Oh, child, it was a pleasure. I'm just down the way in Melksham if ever you need. Write to me, won't you? I must know how you get on."

"Of course." Martha curtseyed with all politeness, then turned to remove herself from the road, now giving in to the temptation to bite her lip as her nerves flew into a frenzy in her stomach. She was here, wherever here was, and now she must wait.

But for how long?

"Miss Smith?"

She exhaled sharply, turning to her left. A tall man in plain clothing and a worn hat approached, smiling as though she were familiar, but more than that, as though she were a welcome sight. "Yes?"

He chuckled, sweeping his hat from his head, revealing dark hair speckled with bits of silver. "I don't expect you to remember me, as you were just a child at the wedding, but there would be no forgetting those eyes of yours. Palest green I've ever seen, then or since. George Cummings, Miss Smith." He bowed quickly, then raised a brow. "May I call you Martha?"

She liked him instantly. "I insist you do, Mr. Cummings. And now that I see you, I do find you familiar. Did you chase me around a table in my aunt's library?"

Mr. Cummings chortled heartily, replacing his hat upon his head. "Indeed I did, and you chased me back. Quite a ruckus we made, and your aunt did not find it nearly as amusing as we did."

"That is not at all surprising." Martha sighed happily, clasping her hands. "I confess, I am relieved to see you, Mr. Cummings. And to be here. Is it far to Lanfare?"

"I'm afraid we've two miles to go yet before we find ourselves there. We're settled just outside Allington, but it's an easy ride, and I've brought the best wagon." He looked almost sheepish as he said so. "It's not so fine a transport as you'll be used to, I know, but it is still comfortable for the shorter journeys."

Martha smiled with all the warmth and fondness one could possibly find on so short a reacquaintance. "Mr. Cummings, I shall be delighted to ride to Lanfare with you, no matter which wagon you have brought. I'll bump along in the back of it, if there's no room at the front."

Mr. Cummings beamed and nodded with apparent approval, if not outright cheer. "There's room at the front, Martha, make no mistake. Though I've a steady hand, and you'd not feel a single dip in the road as I drove, were you to sit in the back."

She laughed at the boast and took his arm without shame. "Excellent. I want to sit where I can see and hear everything, and plague you with questions until you tire of my company."

"I have ten children, Martha. I no longer tire of company, and questions no longer plague me."

Chapter 2

Pontcaster was a worthless estate.

Officially. It was practically written in such terms in the documents Benjamin Steele had received upon his ascension to Earl of Hillier, though the wording had been a trifle more refined. Once he had set his eyes on the place, however, he had understood the irony in the choice of words.

Rustic had meant ruins. Natural had meant wild. Vacant had meant abandoned. Solitary had meant . . .

Well, there wasn't much more to say than solitary, but what it truly meant was there were no tenants, no neighbors, and no servants.

It was simply Benj and what was left of Pontcaster Park.

Stupid name for a place, but when the Normans had made a camp near a bridge, there really wasn't a better name for it.

The house had probably looked lovely for the Normans.

Benj shook his head now as he glanced over at his ridiculous new home, or whatever one called the place where one slept.

What was the point of gaining a title and property if nothing lucrative came with it? Some distant cousin of his late father had died without descendants, or funds to retain a caretaker, and it had taken so long for the solicitors to identify Benj as the next in line for the title that the estate had fallen into complete shambles. Every tenant had abandoned their farms after tiring of their complaints going unanswered and no repairs being made. Even the estate agent had departed for greener pastures, though he had been good enough to leave fairly detailed notes for whomever would fill his position in the future.

It made for some rather exhausting reading when Benj struggled to sleep at night, make no mistake.

But he had been raised in a farming community himself, and trained up to work the land no matter the station, so his first task had been to use the funds he did possess to procure a flock of sheep and updated farming equipment, as well as a trio of pigs. He'd managed to persuade a pair of local young men to act as shepherds without pay for the promise of a salary plus pay owed when the estate began to bring in funds.

It had cost him his father's signet ring for that arrangement, but it was a price worth paying. Benj went out to the fields with them twice a week, feeling the need to act as estate manager until he had an estate worth the requirement of such a position. It was an education at every turn, but at least he was feeling more confident that he could work with the animals without supervision.

Prepare for the worst and hope for the best, his father had always said.

Benj wasn't sure how his circumstances could get much worse, unless all of the sheep caught bloat and none of the farm equipment worked. Even if both of those things transpired, he could try for a loan from a banker in Chippenham or Swindon. He had no outstanding debts at the present, so his luck there should be decent.

But it was entirely possible he would default on those loans, requiring a mortgage on Pontcaster, which was not worth the effort, and when all of that failed, he would be in debtor's prison.

He might at least be fed there, so the prospect was not quite so terrifying as it ought to have been.

He was miserable at fending for himself when it came to food, and meals at the Chippenham Inn were becoming part of the routine. It was three miles to the village, but he did have a horse, so it was not so terrible. And besides, everyone in Allington and Chippenham knew full well that the new Earl of Hillier was poor and had no tenants, so baskets of food were brought his way regularly. Clearly, he had earned their pity with his inheritance.

What exactly one did with an excess of baskets, particularly when one had nothing to fill them with, was less evident.

If they could carry water that he might presently empty over his head, he would use them thus.

He was drenched in sweat and splattered with mud, somehow also accumulating dust despite the softened earth beneath his feet, and he was fairly certain he had been bitten by at least three different insects on the back of his left thigh just above his boots. The horses were fine, and seemed to give him pitying looks at every turn they made in the field, which grew in significance the more filthy he became.

It could not be helped, he supposed. After all, he had no tenants, just the two work horses, and this plow, which was hardly the newest innovation, but was widely accepted as the cheapest and best plow to be found anywhere.

There were several farms associated with the estate, though all of them had been left fallow for at least a year, some longer than that, and while Benj was intelligent enough and realistic enough to understand that he could not turn each back into properly treated and planted fields, he was also desperate enough to do more than he should. He had sent word out to the neighboring villages that he had positions for any laborers looking to earn a little to pad their coffers, but the responses thus far had been minimal. Which was why he was out here dragging himself through the least poor of the remaining fields and driving furrows into the ground that would then be followed by seeds of wheat.

Then he would go on to the next field that was among the least poor, and do the same. And the next, and the next, and the next.

Five fields remaining. Surely, that wasn't so unrealistic.

Unnecessary, perhaps, but he was attempting ambition.

So long as he did not kill himself in his attempts, there was no reason he should be unsuccessful. He could not predict a harvest, of course, but any profit would be an improvement. After the fields were completed, he might turn his attention to the tenant farmhouses and see them cleaned, updated, and renovated into something that might actually persuade people to come to Pontcaster, let alone to live there.

Then he could begin to think about rents as well as farm prosperity.

Then he could consider what he might do with Pontcaster Park for himself.

Then he could think of his inheritance as something worth having.

Then, and only then, could he consider the prospect of eventually passing it on.

His mother would have had him married and bringing forth children tomorrow, but his sisters kept her plenty occupied with grandchildren to distract her from the topic adequately.

It did not keep the subject from resurfacing whenever he visited home, but he supposed that would be the case until he actually brought children home to meet her, regardless of his marital status.

Heaven help the poor woman he would manage to convince to marry him.

"Afternoon, my lord!"

Benj looked up from his mindless plowing, continuing his path straight ahead as he looked around for the source of the voice. He knew some of the locals from the last few weeks, and those that, like himself, dined at the inn, but as far as who might call out to him while he was in the fields . . .

His eyes widened as they settled on the now approaching figure, and he pulled the horses to a stop. "Mr. Jepps?"

Jepps chuckled his usual booming sound. "Surprised, sir? My oldest boy practically begged me to leave the anvil for a few minutes, so I thought I'd drive up and deliver your mended harness myself." His eyes cast across the field, and a faint crease appeared between his graying brows. "How many of these have you done, my lord?"

Benj thought about the question for less than a heartbeat. "A few," he replied with a bland smile.

The blacksmith returned his attention to Benj directly. "And how many more do you have to do?"

"After this?" Benj asked, hedging the question. "Four more."

"Alone."

"Well, I do have the horses."

"But no workers."

"Not many men will do this amount of work with the small amount I can pay, particularly when I am an unknown figure to them." Benj shrugged, shifting his position against the handles of his plow. "I make do."

Jepps nodded once. "Yes, so I see. Well," he said as he began shucking off his jacket, "I've a few minutes. Allow me to drive a few furrows for you, sir. Finish this field, at least."

Benj blinked at the idea. "Thank you, Mr. Jepps, but I can manage. Truly. You've your anvil and bellows, and surely you have work to be done before you close up this evening."

"Not a bother, my lord," the man replied as he tossed his jacket on the grass and started to roll his sleeves. "My son has everything in hand. He'll take over the business, you know, and could do so now. The shop is in good hands."

Excuse after excuse lit into Benj's mind, any protestations he could conjure, and the only thing that managed to make its way out of his mouth was, "You're a blacksmith."

Luckily, Mr. Jepps had an excellent sense of humor, and gave Benj a laughing look, gesturing for him to step away. "I wasn't always a blacksmith, my lord. I can plow a field."

There wasn't anything else to do but step away and let the man take a turn, but it tasted bitter to do so. What was he supposed to do while someone else plowed his field? He wasn't planting yet, and there was no need to lead the horses while Jepps drove them. He could, he supposed, but it might look odd to anyone who knew what they were about.

Jepps was giving him a respite, but he hadn't had a respite since he'd begun this whole project.

What did a country earl working his own land do for a brief respite?

"I feel awkward and useless," Benj informed Mr. Jepps as the man expertly snapped the horses back into their rhythm.

"Take a breath, my lord," Jepps called back. "Take a walk. Take a . . ."

"If you are about to say wife, you can get off of my property now," Benj interrupted with a lightness he thought himself too exhausted to drum up.

Jepps barked another loud laugh. "I was going to say ride, my lord. I would never suggest a man get a wife until he was ready to do so. I've been married long enough to know one must be fully prepared for such a thing."

Benj gave him a firm nod of approval, then, seeing that the man was quite set on his course, opted to walk back to the house just to look around. He'd done so prior to this, of course, but it had been a few days since he had let himself really see the situation for what it was and start to plot a strategy towards its restoration.

Even on approach, his eyes were drawn to the left of the house, the wing pointing west. Or mostly west, at any rate. The balustrades of the roof were crumbling on that side, as well as the short wall extending out towards the remnants of the garden, and the half-dead ivy encasing the walls made the place look more darkened than it truly was. He did not quite understand why the eastern wing was completely ivy free, but as it was the least damaged of the wings on the interior, he would not ask too many questions.

He needed to keep Pontcaster intact for the time being, unless there were true issues with the structural integrity. He could adjust whatever he liked when he had the funds to do so, but for the present, it was best to make do with what he had. Which meant clearing, cleaning, and . . . whatever word could be used for attempting to refine that which could not be refined. For covering up that which ought to be hidden. For being too poorly off to renovate and too proud to expose the truth.

If there was a word for such a thing.

Benj grunted softly to himself as he looked over this undoubtedly once-fine façade of a house. The style was fairly modern, all things considered, though it had been so neglected, it looked to be much older. There had been some renovations in the last century, but a few aspects were original, which likely accounted for the crumbling in parts. He'd have to examine the rest of the house in depth once he'd removed the distraction of mess and decay.

He didn't mind the work. He would rather strive for something than be idle for nothing. And if looking at Pontcaster told him anything, he would be striving for a very, very long time.

The sound of hooves hitting the ground pulled Benj's attention from his house to the surrounding hills, his eyes narrowing as he tried to spot the source of the sound. It wasn't exactly common to have riders out here on his lands, and his present position was too far from the road to hear hooves so clearly.

Then he caught it: a fine chestnut bay horse galloping majestically along the hills just behind his estate. His eyes moved to the rider, and his eyes widened.

A woman in a plum-colored riding habit managed the horse beautifully, even at such speeds and terrain. No hint of nerves, no hesitation, no maidenly reserve in her riding or handling of the creature. She was almost reckless in her manner, forgoing the ladylike posture Benj was used to seeing and leaning close to the horse, and it was impossible to tell if she was managing sidesaddle or riding astride. This far removed from Society, it would not matter either way.

But he wondered how she chose to ride as her form faded over the rise of the hill. He was positive he hadn't seen her in the area before, but he would also admit that he hadn't exactly been paying attention.

He hadn't seen her face, and her figure had been difficult to observe from this distance, but if she could ride like that in hills like these, he would be looking out for her from now on.

It added significantly to the interest of the area.

More than Pontcaster could ever hope to.

CHAPTER 3

"Martha, I do wish you would be more careful. How would I explain an injury like that to your mother if it were serious?"

Martha laughed as she removed her hat, sinking down onto a chair in the kitchens, where she usually removed her mud-caked boots and outerwear. It saved the housekeeper the trouble, and the cook didn't mind so long as she was not in the middle of something. A daily walk or two and a ride had become a routine since arriving, and this afternoon's walk had been glorious, indeed.

Eliza, however, did not seem to think the same.

"It was only a slight turning of my ankle," Martha assured her, still laughing. "I was too impetuous and attempted to walk across a fallen log. I fell off straightaway, but only my ankle suffered. It was a silly thing, and I feel minimal pain."

Her cousin frowned, her expression perfectly capturing an exasperated and worried mother.

Not Martha's, but the ideal mother everyone wished for.

"Still, I would feel much better if you were able to walk your usual distance before this evening without pain," Eliza told her, folding her arms. "Perhaps I might send you into Allington for bread. That is not far, and you would be able to send word hastily if your pain is too great."

Martha sighed as gently as she could manage while feeling patronized. "My pain will not be too great. The boots you and Mr. Cummings purchased for me are remarkably sturdy, just as you said they should be. I have tested them now, and find them more than satisfactory."

"You've tested them," Eliza repeated, her tone less than enthusiastic.

Resisting the urge to bite her lip, Martha nodded, smiling.

There was a beat of silence, then Eliza released a heavy sigh, smiling herself and shaking her head. "Well, I suppose that is one way of putting it. Really, cousin, what am I to do with you?"

Martha laughed and bent to remove her boots. "Continue with your hospitality and let me breathe in the countryside, as you have done. The greatest weapon at my disposal presently is finding great enjoyment in my exile, and I aim to use it."

Eliza waited for her to finish the removal of her dirty boots, then took them over to dry by the fire. "There, they'll be dry in no time, and then you can see if your ankle truly is as unaffected as you think."

Her tone still held notes of skepticism, which made Martha's smile spread. "If I am mistaken, cousin, I give you full leave to lord over me and treat me like one of your children for the rest of my visit here."

That made Eliza laugh as she came back to Martha's side. "If I did that, I would not have you for conversation."

Martha pushed to her stockinged feet and put her arm around her cousin's waist as they moved out of the kitchen. "Do you not have a husband to talk to?"

"When one has been married as long as we have, dear, variety in conversation is much appreciated." Eliza's small smile spoke of restrained laughter, and Martha could understand why.

Her few days spent at Lanfare thus far had already given Martha proof enough that Eliza and Mr. Cummings were as devoted to each other now as they had been when they wed. Perhaps not as demonstrative or so obvious as in courtship, but there were enough shared smiles and stolen glances to convince Martha of their mutual adoration. More than that, they seemed to genuinely like one another.

They were friends, not just lovers.

The word made Martha blush, even as she walked beside her cousin. It was silly to be embarrassed by the fact, considering there were so many children dashing about the place, but she would give credit where credit was due. Her ignorance saved her from feeling anything besides embarrassment, for good or for ill.

A victory for ignorance, in this case.

Martha saw nothing wrong with the way her cousin's family lived. Yes, it was perhaps lacking in finery, but there was such joy within the walls of Lanfare! Laughter in abundance, and even in her short time here, Martha had laughed more than she had in her entire life, she was convinced of it.

And when the youngest of her cousin's children was eagerly crawling across the floor, there was nothing to do but love on that little cherub and tickle her mercilessly just to hear the musical gurgle of her laughter.

Eliza was a sort of mother that Martha had never seen. One who managed the home and seemed to know what every child was doing at any given time. One who could somehow show individualized love and affection to every single child despite the intimidating number of them. Who enjoyed every moment with her children, even when she was exasperated. Who still managed some kind of energy to share smiles and winks with her husband.

And Mr. Cummings...

Martha had never imagined seeing a man crawling on the floor on all fours with his children, but Mr. Cummings did so every evening. He read stories to the children before bed, helped the younger children cut their food, and answered every question with either a calm answer or a humorous one. Never once had he raised his voice, never once had he appeared stern, and never once had he insisted they go elsewhere.

The phrase "seen and not heard" was not uttered in this home.

She rather enjoyed the change from the formality she was raised with.

Everything about her life had been formal until she had come to Wiltshire. She hadn't known there was another way to live before she had arrived here, and the revelation was something she was still reeling from. Eliza had seemed to sense Martha's confusion in the first few days, having come from the same sort of home and upbringing, and she had taken the time to answer her questions and expand her understanding.

It had given Martha a sense of freedom she had not expected from her exile here. Permission to breathe and relax the perfect composure she had spent years maintaining at the behest of her mother. An opportunity to explore the parts of her personality and manner that she had never been able to before.

She was becoming a newer version of herself, for good or for ill, and she had a feeling her mother would not like that at all.

Martha's mother wanted her to be a reflection of her own image, rather than herself. The truth of herself.

Martha had never given much thought to the truth of herself.

Until now.

Various crashing sounds from above them paused their quiet stroll through the house, prompting both of them to look upwards as though they could see through the ceiling.

"Oh dear," Eliza said mildly, despite the heavy sigh. "That will be the twins. I predict tears or shouts shortly."

Martha winced. "Perhaps I should go into the village now, then."

Her cousin gave her an almost aghast look. "No! I wanted you to rest so that your ankle might heal."

"I promise, my ankle is well," Martha assured her, smiling for effect. "I will even put a poultice on it before I retire to ensure it is even better tomorrow. Will that satisfy you?"

"I suppose," Eliza grumbled. "You will need to wear different boots. The ones from your walk are far too muddy. The village paths are dry, so your London boots should suffice."

Martha nodded as though instructed, wondering if it was difficult for her cousin to recollect when she was a mother and when she was not. "I will fetch them and go now. Will you be so good as to create a list for me of what exactly you would like me to purchase?"

"Of course," Eliza said, dropping her arm from Martha's waist. "It is only some bread, but there may be additional items available. I'll have it for you momentarily."

It was odd, Martha thought as she hurried out of the corridor and up the rickety stairs to the family rooms, that she was now about to go on an errand for her cousin. Her mother would never have dreamed of doing anything that could even remotely resemble something a servant could or, in her mind, should do. And she would have been particularly aghast if she knew that her daughter was doing so.

Yet Martha felt no shame in what she was about to do. No irritation or embarrassment, no resentment that she had been thus relegated. Eliza had walked to Allington several times since Martha's arrival for various errands, and there had been no chagrin in her manner about it. The fact of the matter was that they did not have the staff in their home for others to do such things, and in all honesty, it was likely a great relief for Eliza to take such an expedition herself when Lanfare was so full of jubilant noise and chaos.

Martha had even gone with her the second day, and there was something intimate and quaint about such a venture.

One would never do such a thing in London. Not anyone of her station, at any rate. It was simply unfathomable.

But here in Wiltshire, it was not only fathomable, but expected and unremarkable.

It was blessedly freeing to have so much opened to Martha since her arrival. Fewer restrictions and more opportunities. Fewer airs and more humility. Less reliance and more resilience.

Resilience. That was the word. There was something resilient about life in Wiltshire, and that was fascinating, indeed.

Martha's London boots, as they called them, sat on the floor of her bureau, and she pulled them out after a bit of shuffling other items aside. It had become supremely evident very early into her time at Lanfare that she had overpacked, and had brought wholly unnecessary items with her as well, which had led to the bureau housing her clothing becoming overstuffed.

The London boots were perfectly suitable for outings in

Hyde Park and walking along Bond Street, but would never do for walks in the country lanes in Wiltshire. They were a softer leather, a perfect partner for the subtle fabric used in ladies' slippers and heeled shoes, and while Martha had opted for a simple pair without adornment, other young ladies chose shoes that took as much design and elaboration as any ballgown in the world.

Considering the voluminous nature of skirts in current fashion, one did wonder why footwear required so much attention when they were rarely seen.

A scant few minutes later, Martha was out of doors once again, list in hand, London boots on her feet, walking towards Allington. She inhaled deeply, then sighed in delight at the freshness that filled her lungs. Allington was so close to Lanfare, it could be seen once one stepped outside the door. A small, well-worn walking path extended down to the road, and then it was simply over the stone bridge before one was at the edge of Allington proper. Apparently, it was the stream over which the Allington bridge sat that dictated the boundaries of the village, which kept Lanfare as private property, in the most technical sense. As Lanfare had little land beyond the house itself, it was hardly worth contention.

It was astonishing how comfortable she felt taking this path without someone accompanying her. Or any of her walks and rides, for that matter. In London, she was never alone. Had never been alone. Was not permitted to go anywhere alone, unless within the walls of her home, and under those circumstances, there were servants everywhere, so she was never alone even when she was. But here, she was completely without escort or companion, and it would not garner a second look from those who saw her.

Where was the insecurity she ought to feel because of such independence? Where was the feeling that her safety was in jeopardy? Where was her sense of prim propriety?

Nowhere in sight, she realized. Nowhere in sight.

What did that say about her true nature?

"Good afternoon, Miss Smith," a cheery voice called from Martha's right.

She glanced over, and found herself beaming at the smiling countenance of Miss Holmes, the eldest daughter of a local lawyer. They had met twice before when Martha had come into Allington, and Martha was impressed with the completely unspoiled nature of the girl. They were of an age, Martha thought, and seemed as though they would suit well, should they wish to become friends.

Martha would only be so fortunate.

"Miss Holmes!" she greeted, waving at her and turning her course to move in that direction instead. "What a pleasant surprise!"

Miss Holmes bobbed a quick curtsey of greeting, the light dusting of freckles on her nose creasing a little as she smiled in return. "I am fetching meat from the butcher for my mother. What brings you into Allington?"

"Bread," Martha told her simply, shrugging her shoulders slightly. "My cousin sent me with a list."

"Well, Mr. Nelson is packaging my order and said it might take some time. Why don't I go with you?" Her cheeks colored slightly. "That is, if you do not object to my joining you."

Martha smiled and shook her head. "Not at all. Please, come with me. I know where the bakery is, but I've never entered it. I would welcome familiar company."

Miss Holmes nodded and came to her side, starting to walk with her. "Have you settled into Lanfare, Miss Smith? Mr. and Mrs. Cummings are wonderful people; I imagine they have been warm and welcoming."

"Very much so," Martha informed her. "I feel quite at

home there. A trifle trampled with all of the children, but they are so darling. This morning, Sophie came into my room and asked if she could climb into my bed and if I would tell her a story." Martha paused, smiling more broadly at the memory. "She is just six."

"What a dear girl!" Miss Holmes laughed to herself, something just as natural in that sound as there seemed to be in the woman herself. "I have a sister who is that age, and she is rather prone to do the same. She and Sophie would likely be great friends." She gave Martha a questioning look. "Are you missing London, Miss Smith? I have never been, but one hears such grand tales."

Martha's smile turned rather rueful at the question. "I cannot say that I am, no. There is much of grandeur to be found in London, but hardly substance. At least not in my circles. One does get so tired of ceremony and bored with pretense. Everybody is playing a part, and one is always on display."

Miss Holmes made a soft tsking sound of sympathy. "That sounds fatiguing."

"To say the least," Martha agreed. "Even with my own mother, I am never certain what is genuine. Although I am quite sure her obsession with my marriage is true and honest."

"Are you to be married, Miss Smith?" Miss Holmes cried out in surprise, grabbing Martha's arm with an eagerness that reminded her of the girls in London, yet could not have been more different. This was a young woman whose eyes were wide open as to the realities of life and marriage, who had less ignorance than the girls in London, and still found the prospect of marriage something worth celebrating.

This was a person with whom Martha could easily form a true friendship.

"No," Martha told her with a laugh. "And that is why my

mother is so angry. I've refused good marriage proposals, which is unforgivable. She does not share my view that a marriage ought to be made for love and affection."

"What other motivation should there be?" Miss Holmes asked in outright bewilderment. "Surely, she would not have you marry for money."

"She wouldn't mind money," Martha said, "though I've a dowry one might call fashionable. I think she would like me to marry a title, or some pristine pedigree. More preferable if he needs money, as he will then value a connection with me more."

Miss Holmes frowned now, her brow creasing. "But that has nothing to do with you. The money is not even yours. Surely, it would be better to wed someone who values you rather than your money."

Martha gave her new friend a speculative look. "I like you, Miss Holmes. I insist that you call me Martha."

"I think our difference in position might make that impolite," Miss Holmes murmured, ducking her chin. "You are a woman of status, Miss Smith. I am the daughter of a country lawyer."

"And I am staying with my cousin, who has one maid, a housekeeper, and a cook," Martha replied at once. "There is no ceremony to stand on, and I would be most pleased to call you a friend. I have very few, and I would like to look past what other people have decided are barriers preventing me from honest friendship. Please, will you indulge me in this? Unless you are feeling differently, of course. I will not force this."

Miss Holmes made a quick sound of disbelief. "I would be delighted to form a friendship with you, Miss Smith. I cannot pretend those barriers do not exist, nor that a friendship with me will be considered fashionable, but I do admire you, from what I know, and would be pleased to be your friend."

"Then let me be Martha to you," she insisted, beaming at Miss Holmes. "And may I call you by your given name?"

Miss Holmes nodded, sharing a smile now. "I would be honored. My name is Cassandra. My family calls me Cassie."

"Delightful!" Martha looped her arm through Cassie's, the elation of having a friend making her feel oddly childlike. "Now, Cassie, will you tell me about the local society? I know absolutely no one but my cousin's family and a few of the shopkeepers. Are there great secrets in Allington one must know about?"

Cassie laughed and continued to walk along with her. "I don't know about many great secrets, Martha, not in Allington. We save those for Chippenham. Here, we're really rather quiet. Comfortable, simple, and rather familiar. The most exciting venture is when there are assemblies in Chippenham. There is one in a few weeks, if you will still be here."

"I certainly hope so!" Martha exclaimed brightly. "I should love a country assembly ball. I've never been to a dance where my mother has not arranged every dance and conversation for me. I shall not know what to do on my own!" She giggled at the ridiculous idea, and was relieved when Cassie did the same.

"Well, you won't have to worry over our country lads making love to you, that is almost certain," Cassie told her with a smile. "There aren't many in the area that are eligible, and those who are take some prodding to make an introduction."

Martha shook her head with a playful sniff that reminded her of her mother's disapproving sounds. "I have absolutely no interest in making a match while I am here, I thank you."

A mischievous smile captured her lips as she gave her new friend a sidelong look. "Though it would utterly gall my mother to do so."

"Might be worth a look, then?" Cassie quipped with a laugh.

"It just might." They continued to laugh together, making polite conversation that kept Martha occupied enough to avoid paying much attention to any of her surroundings.

Which was likely why she stepped directly into a pile of horse droppings.

"Oh dear," Cassie whimpered when the pair of them paused at the horrible squelching sound. "Martha . . ."

Martha looked down at her foot, now trapped in rather unpleasantly textured excrement, and hummed in disgruntlement. "Now that is unfortunate. Serves me right for forgetting this is the country, and not minding my surroundings." She raised her eyes to Cassie's horrified ones and gave her a crooked smile. "Any advice?"

Cassie bit down on her lips hard, as though she feared Martha would shriek. "Take your foot out gently. Don't move it much. And then we could clean your boot. My home is not far; we could go there directly."

"Don't be silly, we are both on errands." Martha waved the idea off, and removed her foot from the mess, twisting her lips at the stain that remained, though gratified there did not seem to be all that much substance on the surface. "I don't know that I should enter the bakery with this muck on my boot. What do you think?"

Cassie giggled softly, releasing the pressure on her lip. "I think others have walked in with much the same. You will want to clean your boots soon, so the stain does not set in. And such fine boots, too. Oh, Martha, what will you do?"

"Walk," Martha said simply, grinning at her. "And mind my step. I'll not make the same mistake twice. Come on, the bread will not wait."

Chapter 4

"Hey-ohhh. Hey-ohhh, hup, hup, hup!"

Benj watched in fascination as Harris and Thorne managed the sheep with such ease, calling out wordlessly to them in such a way that the sheep did as they were told. Of course, there was also the dog darting around and keeping the sheep together, but as Barney wasn't actually barking orders, Benj wasn't sure how much credit he ought to receive.

His own dogs would never have been bright enough to herd sheep, he was quite certain of that.

"It's really quite simple, my lord, once you learn the way of it," Harris assured him, mistaking Benj's fascination for confusion. "The sheep don't know what we're asking them to do, they just know when we correct 'em. Barney is the one to give 'em direction."

"I wondered about that," Benj admitted sheepishly, shoving his hands into the pockets of his well-worn trousers. "They're well trained."

Harris barked a laugh. "If you want to call it that. We'll be starting on the shearing once we're down at the barn, if you care to see that. It's not all that difficult, but it does take some maneuvering."

"Love to," Benj replied with a firm nod. "Anything I can do to help. Does it hurt them? Shearing the wool?"

"Does it hurt you, my lord, to get your hair cut?"

Benj blinked at the question. "No, of course not."

Harris gestured his response to the answer. "There you have it, sir. Much the same. Keeps them clean and tidy to have it done. Wool grows continuously, so it must be sheared for their health and safety. Best to do it before lambing as well, as it's easier to nurse when the ewe has been sheared."

"I had no idea." Benj looked at the sheep as they walked behind them, Thorne ahead of them, towards the front. "What do you think about lambing this season?"

"Hard to say, sir." Harris scanned the sheep in front of them, his eyes plainly taking note of things Benj wasn't seeing. "I reckon you've a dozen at least that are carrying, thanks to whoever brought in the rams for 'em before they came to you. Maybe more. About a third of the ewes seem fairly young, so they might not be mature enough to carry. Next season, though, you should be able to do a fair bit come lambing season. Afraid this year might be a surprise."

Benj frowned and sighed. "I hate surprises. I've had too many of them lately."

Harris chuckled good-naturedly. "I daresay you have, my lord. Pontcaster was no treat when you got her."

"She's not much of a treat now," Benj assured him, managing a smile. "I've got ages of work to do on the house, now that the fields are done. Heaven knows if we'll bring in much for harvest, but I've got to start somewhere if we want the farms to be worth anything. Can't really prosper without tenants, you know?"

"They'll come, sir. Mark my words, give it a few weeks, maybe months, and word will spread."

Benj glanced over at his shepherd, strangely encouraged by his words. "I'll take any help spreading that word you can give me, Harris."

"Already doing so, my lord. I've got brothers, and they've got friends and neighbors in their own places." Harris shrugged, then frowned as his eyes moved to something in the distance. "Who's that, my lord? Friend of yours?"

Benj followed his look towards the east, only to see a young woman on a familiar-looking chestnut horse watching them walk with the sheep as though she had never seen anything like it. At once, he knew it was the woman he had seen riding in the hills the other day, and when her eyes landed on him, he also recognized her as the young woman he'd seen yesterday in Allington who had stepped in horse droppings. He'd been struck by the minimal reaction she had given to such a thing, given her obvious finery and station, though she had hardly paraded such about. It had been the quality of her clothing, the perfection in her posture, and the precise manner in which she'd held her chin.

And she'd laughed off stepping in horse droppings as though she'd been raised on a farm herself.

Benj had never seen anything like it, and had decided he may need to venture to Allington more often, if that was what the village had to offer.

She was closer now than he expected, given he hadn't recalled hearing the horse gallop, but the sheep did create their own symphony of sound, so he supposed that was reason enough. He noted her position, seeing she rode sidesaddle, which made her reckless and skillful riding all the more impressive.

"Can I help you, ma'am?" he called, starting in her direction and realizing how much like a farmhand or shepherd he would look, rather than the landowner.

She shook herself at his question and almost seemed surprised to see him there. "Pardon?"

Benj offered a polite smile. "Can I help you? Only you seem a trifle lost."

She blinked her impossibly pale green eyes, made even more brilliant by the dark, luxurious hair coiled and pinned beneath her hat, curls draping along one slender shoulder. "I'm not lost."

There was no crispness to the words, no haughtiness or airs, and he was fascinated further still. But this was not the time for that, nor the situation. "Forgive my presumption, ma'am."

"I've never seen sheep before," she admitted, as though he hadn't said anything. "Not so close, at any rate. I've seen them in the distance and in the fields when I ride, but . . . I've never seen sheep."

Those eyes of hers moved back to the animals, and a childlike wonder entered them. Benj had never been as interested in anything as she was by these sheep, and there was something almost sweet about such an intensity over such a simple thing.

Venturing further than he probably ought, he asked, "Would you like to see them closer, ma'am? You can ride alongside, or walk with us, if you wish."

"I don't want to be in the way," she said quickly, though her eyes hadn't left the animals.

He hid a smile. "You won't be, ma'am. We're only walking them down to the barn for shearing. The cutting of their wool, that is. Harris and Thorne have them in hand, so there's no harm in joining us."

Her eyes returned to him. "You're certain?"

"Quite, ma'am," he replied, praying he was right.

She nodded before looking down at her horse for a

moment, frowning slightly. "Hmm. How to manage this without a mounting block. I am quite adept by now with it, but this . . ."

It was all Benj could do not to laugh in wry amusement. "I can help you down, ma'am, if that is your wish. And if you've hobbles, your horse will be safe here. Or we can walk him down to the barn. It is not far."

"I wouldn't know hobbles from a horseshoe," the woman admitted without shame. "I'll accept your help down, if you please, and walk the horse with us for safety."

"His or yours?" Benj quipped before he could stop himself.

She tilted her head slightly, a faint smile crossing a rather perfect pair of lips. "Both, I imagine."

Fair enough.

Benj moved towards the horse, patting its neck fondly as he reached them. "Right, then. If you'll just put your hands on my shoulders, good and secure, then I'll have to set my hands at your waist. It's the safest way to help you down."

She nodded without hesitation and set her gloved hands firmly on his shoulders, gripping a little. "Ah. You seem stable enough."

He bit back a laugh and ducked his chin in an almost nod. "I suppose that's a compliment of sorts."

"As good as," she replied, a quick smile flashing. "Next?"

"Next," he went on, still trying not to laugh, "my hands will go to your waist, and I'll lift. You press down on my shoulders, and you'll be flat on the ground in no time."

She nodded, and he took her waist in hand, determined not to think about its slenderness, and lifted her gently from the horse as she pressed her hands into his shoulders obediently.

She was lighter than he'd figured, and smaller in stature,

once he'd set her to the ground, but there was something rather perfect in her proportions. With her natural grace and command of comportment, he'd expected more in height. A woman to tower over all and intimidate with a glance.

Yet she was perfectly average in that regard.

And somehow not average at all.

"Rather expeditious, all things considered," she said lightly as she adjusted her gloves before smiling up at him. "Thank you, sir. And you are?"

"Benjamin Steele," he said simply, not bothering with his title. "At your service."

"Martha Smith," she replied, with a quick curtsey he almost missed. "The most common name life could bestow, I believe."

The unexpected jab at herself made him chuckle. "I've heard worse."

"Have you, indeed?" Her already wide eyes somehow went rounder before she grinned fully. "I suppose you must have met a Bess or an Anne Smith somewhere in the past. Or a Jane Smith?"

"I believe I did," he said with a nod. "Perhaps all three."

Her nose wrinkled up in a hint of a laugh that did not have sound. "I don't doubt it. One could never credit my mother with originality." She adjusted her gloves again before tugging them off entirely with a small huff of frustration. Turning towards the horse, she took the reins and looked at Benj expectantly. "Shall we follow the sheep, then?"

He gestured the way, and fell into step beside her as they walked. "And where are you from, Miss Smith?"

"London. I was born there, I was raised there, and I've never left there." She smiled again, though this time it was a bland version of the majestic thing. "Which is why I've never seen sheep."

"You can hardly be the only one so relegated to London," he said politely, trying to soothe her.

Her smile turned wry as she glanced over at him. "Most of the other girls like me in London have country houses to retreat to after the Season. Ours was entailed after my father died, so London is all I know."

Benj had never heard of such a thing, but he could not say that he had spent all that much time in London. He'd always preferred the country to Town, and had never been of a status to find it worth his effort anyway. No wonder the country looked so strange and interesting to her.

Interesting, and not disgusting.

That was significant.

"Do you ride in London?" Benj asked her, clasping his hands behind his back.

"Some," Martha admitted, her tone brighter than before. "But not all that much. My mother made sure I was an accomplished rider, but one can hardly become truly skilled trotting around Hyde Park for show, can they?"

He'd never thought of that; he and his siblings had practically been raised on horses, so the idea of never riding freely with the wind in one's hair seemed as foreign to him as London's finery.

"I suppose not." He tapped the back of one hand into the palm of the other, trying to follow up on something connected to the topic that would not be patronizing or ridiculous.

He was not having much luck.

"I've been riding every day since I've come to Wiltshire," she said without prodding, her hold on the horse's reins loose, but the animal docile enough to trod after her without fuss. "It's exhilarating. I don't know how I'll ever go back to the sedate pace a lady keeps in London."

"I've seen you ride," Benj admitted, wondering if that was something that should even be uttered. "You're quite good."

Martha gave him a wry look. "And you're an expert on the subject, are you?"

Benj laughed at the direct question, and its tone. "Not at all. I'll admit to being a fine enough rider myself, perhaps reckless at times. No one would give me excessive praise. But I've seen enough to know a bad rider, and you are certainly not that."

Her smile lit something within the walls of his chest. "What a relief." She stopped suddenly, her eyes widening before squeezing shut. "Oh dear. Please tell me I have not stepped in animal excrement once more."

It took a moment for her statement to register in his mind, and when it did, he glanced down, horror welling within him.

Relief fell hard on horror's heels, and he took a moment to collect himself, as laughter nearly took over.

"Not this time, Miss Smith," he informed her with all the sageness the moment called for. "What you have stepped in is good, honest Wiltshire earth. A trifle softer than our usual fare, but there has been a great deal of rain lately."

Only one of Martha's magnificent eyes opened. "Earth. You're certain?"

Benj looked down at the ground again. "Hmm," he mused, frowning despite his complete certainty. He crouched as though to inspect the situation more closely, and she obliged the study by raising her skirts just enough to reveal the entirety of her boot. It sat only a trifle submerged in slurry, and could easily be retrieved, but the exact shade of the material might never return to its full luster. She did have an almost delicate-looking foot, despite its covering in boot and slurry, but the length of it seemed standard enough, if he recalled the size of his sisters' feet accurately.

He had never made an exact study of women's feet, but there did not seem to be anything out of the ordinary here.

"Mr. Steele?"

Her voice brought him out of the strangely fascinating faux study of feet, and he peered up at her, grinning unabashedly. "Wiltshire earth after all, Miss Smith. Not to worry."

She exhaled heavily in a rush of air, laughing to herself. "What a relief. I couldn't possibly be so unfortunate as to step in animal mess twice in the space of two days."

Benj waited for any sort of reaction regarding her situation, or the previous day's situation, anything to indicate that her station in life dictated her behavior or thoughts.

Nothing spoiled or fussy in the least.

"Remarkable," he said to himself as he rose, brushing his hands off, though they had not touched anything.

"What is remarkable?" Martha asked, her brow creasing ever so slightly, which did nothing to lessen the brilliance of her eyes.

He allowed his mouth to curve into the natural smile that was gently pulling at its corners. "I'll confess, I saw you yesterday in Allington. I might not have noticed apart from when you stepped in the horse excrement. I expected disgust, at the very least. Laughter and nonchalance were not anticipated. And today, though it is earth and not something worse, more of the same. It is quite remarkable, Miss Smith."

"Is it?" Her brow cleared and she tilted her head again in that same adorable manner from before. "I have never been squeamish. Only ignorant. I am hoping that it can be cured."

Whatever other plans he'd had for the day, he would have given them up just for more time in her company. She was refreshing, amusing, fascinating, beautiful, and constantly full of surprises, and all of this in just a few minutes.

Had any person in the world had such a profound effect on him so suddenly?

"I think it could be cured, Miss Smith," Benj told her, entirely unaware of the details of his smile, only that one remained. "And I think you are well on your way."

Chapter 5

"Wait. You mean to tell me that Mr. Steele from the fields is not one of the shepherds?"

The pitying look on Cassie's face as they walked in Allington again was enough to clench Martha's stomach for the second time in the space of a minute, and it was no less unsettling.

She had spent over an hour with Mr. Steele and his companions the other day, talking about everything and nothing, walking after the herd of sheep and watching in fascination as they sheared most of them. No one had given her any indication that Mr. Steele did not belong with the others, no one had been uncomfortable with the situation or the company, and no one had addressed Mr. Steele in any specific way to indicate he was anything but what he had said.

No one had addressed him at all, as she thought about it.

They had spoken to him, of course, but they had never called him Mr. Steele or sir or any title to distinguish him from the others.

She had genuinely liked the man. He was handsome, to

be sure, but he had seemed so earnest and genuine, so comfortable in his surroundings and in her company. He had been at ease with the sheep and among the others, had not flattered her or given any offense. His speech had been careful and refined, and yet held no elegance to it.

He'd seemed an honest sort, just as she expected Mr. Cummings to be at any given time or place.

Yet what she had felt for him in no way resembled what she felt for Mr. Cummings.

At all.

Not that she could describe her feelings as something significant. But she would admit to fascination, for certain. And a tendency towards his direction when she rode. Or walked. She hadn't seen him again when she rode, and her walks had not taken her so far as yet, mostly because she had yet to find a manageable walking route that did not exhaust her. But she had been drawn in that direction, it was true.

Now, however . . .

Well, now she was determined to march in that direction quite directly and ask the man what he meant by intentionally not revealing the nature of his identity. She had no doubt it was his name in truth, but he had clearly let her assume that . . .

That what? That he was a man, just as the other men were? That he had no airs or high opinions? That he did not see himself as above others in rank or situation? That he could walk among the animals and the land without offending his sensibilities?

Which, she had to admit, she was also doing.

She didn't know much about animals or land, and the only sensibilities she had were the ones she didn't care for and sought to replace, but she was certainly acting outside of the realms to which she had been accustomed. She was doing so proudly and with great determination. She was throwing off the bindings Society had placed on their young ladies and deciding her own identity.

But for how long? How deep was this adjustment of hers going to sink? How permanent would these changes become?

And how could she judge Mr. Steele for doing exactly as she was in his own way?

Martha shook her head now, frowning more at herself than anything regarding him. "I must speak with him. I must know why he did not tell me." She turned and started away, still shaking her head.

"Why does it matter?" Cassie asked as she hurried to walk along beside her, the skirts of her blue cotton gown rippling with her quick steps. "If Lord Hillier did not offer his title when he met you, why should you care?"

"Lord Hillier?" Martha repeated without altering a single step. "More to be questioned, then. And truth be told, Cassie, it might not matter. I spent a lovely afternoon learning more about sheep than I could possibly imagine, and I enjoyed it immensely. But what purpose did it serve to keep me in ignorance as to his identity? I don't know why, but I do care about that very much."

"Perhaps it was to spare you mortification?" her friend suggested, one hand clutching at the top of her straw hat to keep it from dislodging in the breeze. "By your own account, you happened upon them unexpectedly."

Martha considered that, her strides continuing to be long and purposeful as her arms swung in time with them, insofar as her trim redingote would allow. "That would be a rather pretty, gentlemanly way of managing the error. I cannot say if my conversation with Mr. Steele would have changed overly much had I known he was Lord Hillier, but we will never know for certain. I have interacted with earls and lords and viscounts in London, and it is rare to find good conversation among them. Perhaps I might have borne some prejudice had I heard his title."

"Exactly," Cassie said with some relief in her voice. "Lord Hillier is somewhat new to the area, Martha, and I think new to the title. Perhaps he is not comfortable with it yet? I have heard only good of him when he comes into Allington. Even Papa says so, and he is a stern judge of character."

"Does he know Lord Hillier himself?" Martha asked her, something eager leaping within her chest at the idea.

Cassie pursed her lips a little. "Not directly, no . . ."

Martha nearly groaned at so swift a disappointment. "Then how can he say so? I must meet his lordship as he is and ascertain for myself if he is the man I met or a pretender."

"You intend to walk to Pontcaster from here?" Cassie's distressed disbelief gave Martha some pause, but her feet would not listen to reason and kept their pace.

"Evidently," she grunted. "How far is it?"

"Four miles, at least!"

Martha glanced at Cassie with a raised brow. "That is not so far, is it?"

Cassie did not adjust her expression. "Pontcaster is in the hills north of Chippenham, three miles outside of it. And it is difficult walking, despite the distance. I was born and raised here, Martha, I know of what I speak."

This made Martha's feet come to their senses, and they slowed, then came to a stop as her mind spun on the idea of walking so far, followed by walking back. She would admit to being a better walker now than she was when she had arrived in Wiltshire, but she would not go nearly so far as to claim a hardy stamina.

It would be mortifying to present herself at Pontcaster to question its master and then be forced to ask if he might drive her to Lanfare to save her aching feet.

"Perhaps I was overhasty," Martha allowed slowly, the image of rattling along beside Lord Hillier in a cart while they sat in stony silence a harrowing one she would not soon forget. She turned to stare at her friend in consternation. "What other options have we?"

Less than half an hour later, the pair of them were driving away from Allington in the Holmes family's wagon, Cassie expertly managing the horse, who was well used to the terrain over which they would travel.

It was undoubtedly the wiser course, under the circumstances. And they were a rather lively pair on the drive, regaling each other with stories from their youth. Cassie's usually involved her several siblings or locals in the village, while Martha's were almost always about someone or something she witnessed in Society. The subject matter could not have been more different, but the humor and entertainment to be found in each was the same.

"Have you ever been in love before, Martha?" Cassie suddenly asked when their laughter over the last story had faded.

Martha stared at her, almost startled by the question. "No. Not even remotely."

Cassie shrugged a shoulder. "You have had one London Season, have you not?"

"I did not interact with a single gentleman whom I wished to see a second time," Martha assured her firmly. "Never mind finding one I wished to give my heart to. My mother was very selective in her choices of whose company I should keep, and while I heard of agreeable men, I certainly never met one."

"If she did not allow you your choice in company, why did she allow you your own decision on any proposals?" Cassie gave her an almost bewildered look. "Surely, she knew you would not give her the satisfaction once you had a say."

Martha shuddered at the thought. "Pray, do not speak to my mother on that score. She will see your point and have me arranged off to the next portly viscount in need of a second wife."

Cassie laughed at that and sighed almost whimsically. "I always envied girls who would go to London and dress in finery. Who could meet such dashing gentlemen and find themselves vied for. I never thought it would be so restricting and callous."

"You have a beautiful freedom here, Cassie," Martha said, patting her arm gently. "I would not wish that away for the world."

The two shared a smile, and Cassie's eyes drifted just ahead of them. "I believe we are here, Martha. And I think that is Lord Hillier tilling the ground."

"What?" Martha whirled on the wagon bench, turning to look at the land where Cassie indicated.

There, in a very similar linen shirt of uncommon plainness and trousers any farmhand might don, was the man she had spent such an enjoyable time with only a few days before. Benjamin Steele, who was apparently Lord Hillier.

Working his own land.

"Why is he tilling his own field?" Martha whispered. "And what in the world is tilling?"

"He's preparing the field for planting," Cassie explained, a hint of laughter in her voice. "Turning the soil over so that he . . . Never mind, I very much doubt it matters. Would you like me to stop here, or . . . ?"

Martha nodded and adjusted the shawl about her shoulders, swallowing with some difficulty as the wagon pulled to a stop and she prepared to climb down.

Lord Hillier saw them now and raised up slowly. He laid his farming implement down, whatever it was, and started in their direction, hands going into his trouser pockets.

He might have been any farmer in the world. Yet she was quite certain no farmer in the world would look half so attractive or make her heart skip the occasional beat in a pattern she hadn't a hope of recollecting.

"Martha?"

She barely heard Cassie's voice as she climbed down from the wagon, praying she could do so without embarrassing herself in any way. Thankfully, she managed the thing without any injury, and could walk towards him while appearing remotely sedate, though she was anything but.

"Miss Smith," Lord Hillier greeted, bowing just enough to betray his rank, though his expression was as open as it had been before.

And he was confused.

Not displeased, thank heavens, but certainly confused.

That would make two of them.

Martha managed a curtsey, and took care that it should suit. "My lord."

His confusion cleared as she rose. "Ah."

"Hmm, yes," she said with a humorless laugh. "Ah, indeed. Why did you not tell me you were an earl?"

His mouth curved in the crooked smile she'd seen before, the one that had made her toes scrunch then and did so again now. "I don't hear much recrimination in your voice. Is that good manners or a genuine question?"

"Both, I should hope." Martha exhaled and folded her arms, tucking her shawl tightly. "You had an opportunity to introduce yourself properly and you did not. I do not seek to judge, only to understand. Surely, you can see how uncomfortable the revelation was to me."

"I would never wish you to feel grief or mortification, let alone from something I have done," he said quickly, taking a step forward. "Please, forgive me."

Martha nodded without much effort, a breeze dislodging a bit of her hair beneath her hat. "I know it was not your intention, my lord. But still I ask why."

Lord Hillier continued to stare at her for an uncomfortably long moment, his smile turning almost sad. "I've spent my entire life being Benjamin Steele and nothing more. I've found myself turned into Lord Hillier, and I barely know what that means. Look at my land, Miss Smith. What do you see?"

She did look, and she wasn't entirely sure what she saw. Countryside, for certain. Fields, none of which seemed to grow anything. And in the distance, there appeared to be some sort of a house, large enough to be the estate's manor, but derelict in nature.

"Nothing, Miss Smith," Lord Hillier answered for her. "Nothing. And since Lord Hillier is Earl of Nothing and No One for the present, I much prefer to continue being Benj Steele until the two men are reconciled into one."

Martha looked at Lord Hillier again, something shifting within her chest and releasing a warmth that she had felt in his presence when they'd last met. Something comfortable and easy, something natural, and almost affectionate. "I think that is rather rational and sound, my lord. It must be difficult to be brought into a status with little to show for it."

"Feels rather impossible, actually," he admitted with a sheepish smile. "Who would believe that an earl would plow his own fields and till his own earth? Or go out with his shepherds twice a week to oversee the investment that is his flock? Or chop an old armoire into pieces for firewood?"

"Did you really?" Martha asked before he could go on, laughing in surprise. "Why?"

Lord Hillier gestured dejectedly in the distance. "Do you see the house, Miss Smith? Pontcaster is a relic, and not a covetable one. The exterior is the least offensive of its parts. I shall have to scrap nearly everything within it before I can do much in improving it, and I've barely been through the place enough to know where to start."

"You chose to focus on the farming first?" Martha started walking in the direction of the house, keeping her pace slow.

"I did," he confirmed, falling into step beside her as though it were the most natural thing in the world. "Given the time of the year, I thought I might try and give the estate some sort of revenue as soon as possible. No tenants, you see, and it's a poor prospect to convince new ones to come in. I must give them something to want. I did not come from money before I inherited, but what I had saved up I used to procure the sheep, some pigs, and the equipment. There is some put by for other purposes, and if I do any of this well enough, more will come." He paused, then chuckled easily. "I beg your pardon, here I am discussing money and income, of all things. You must think me dreadfully crass."

Martha smiled to herself. "Must I?"

She could almost feel the ripple of air as he jerked to look at her. "You don't?"

"How could I?" She looked up at him, allowing her smile to deepen. "We were speaking of your estate, your manner of caring for it, and that includes a financial responsibility. You are relying on abilities rather than assets, and given the state of those assets, how could that not be an admirable thing? Do you know how many people would have thrown up their hands already at such a prospect? Who else would roll up their sleeves and change the fortunes of their estate with their bare hands? No earls that I know, that I can say for certain."

"When you put it like that, I almost feel this is a noble thing and not a hopeless one." Lord Hillier grinned, instantly ridding Martha of the capacity of her left lung. "You have a luminous way of looking at things, Miss Smith."

Martha's cheeks colored slightly. "I don't believe I do. I think what I have is an ability to see things as they really are, and a hope that something can be improved upon. It does not always serve me well."

"No?"

She shook her head. "It is why I find myself in Wiltshire. My mother has sent me here to learn the error of my ways."

He laughed once. "And what was your great error?"

She could not laugh in return, but somehow she managed a weak smile. "I refused marriages of convenience. I cannot consign myself to the fate that seems so paramount in London and Society. I do not want to make a match that improves my status, but not my nature. I realize that young ladies like myself are raised to become some man's property in a game of connection and strategy and money, but I do not want to do so. If this is all I am to be, I find my life to be so vapid and pointless." She exhaled roughly, her arms unfolding as though fatigued by the whole idea. "I just seek a purpose that values the fact that I live and breathe as myself, and not for the purposes of someone else."

There was a long stretch of silence, though not a moment of it made her uncomfortable amid the softness of the natural Wiltshire music. "And you led me to believe that you were ignorant," Lord Hillier said.

Martha blinked, returning her gaze to the handsome man beside her. "Pardon?"

His smile eased something within her chest, made her want to draw closer. "The other day, you told me you were only ignorant. I find nothing of the sort in you, Miss Smith. On the contrary, I believe you may be more enlightened and astute than any person I've met in my life, and without a doubt, the most refreshing."

"You make it sound as though I am akin to taking the

cure in Bath." Martha laughed, the sound seeming somehow breathless to her ears.

"I'm not altogether sure you won't be a cure here," he said simply, as easily as one might comment on the weather. And his smile never wavered.

It was as though her heart had sprouted wings and fluttered around each of her ribs, striking them with feathers before darting across to another, and another, until every rib quivered and felt bruised from impact.

What was one supposed to do about that?

Somehow she smiled, and it was then that she felt she truly saw Benj Steele, just as she had the other day, through the new image that was Lord Hillier.

There was something perfect and profound in that.

And something almost magical about Benj.

"Will you show me Pontcaster?" Martha asked, when she could find her voice. "Perhaps I can help you see what might be done. Unless you must get back to tilling this field."

"The field can wait," Benj said without hesitation. "I'm rather interested in seeing the place through your eyes. I have no doubt you will change my mind on that score too." He glanced behind them quickly. "What of your friend there? She's more than welcome to join us."

Heavens. She'd forgotten all about Cassie.

Martha looked back, and saw Cassie smiling widely in return. She waved them on, climbed out of the wagon, and moved to the head of the horse, rubbing his nose gently, then waved insistently again.

There would never be another friend like Cassandra Holmes in all the world.

"She'll be along," Martha told him, returning her attention to the fascinating darkness of his eyes. "Miss Holmes is a sensible girl with excellent manners and a healthy appreciation of the time. And she is very clear-sighted, I find, which must always be admired."

Benj raised a brow, his smile crinkling his eyes. "Miss Holmes must be very useful as a friend."

"You have no idea."

They walked towards the house without much haste, Benj pointing out the fascinating details of the exterior as well as the failing ones. Martha asked what he thought to do about the repairs and the landscaping, and he confessed to not having given much thought to the thing, his mind being more full of the land itself than the house.

"Perhaps if you look at the house as what it could become rather than what it is, it will not seem so very dreadful," Martha suggested with a smile as they moved to the dark entrance. "I think it could be charming. It's already a lovely, stately home. Imagine its luster when you've done away with the decay!"

Benj laughed, glancing over his shoulder as they entered the cavernous entry. "Lovely and stately, eh? Martha Smith, I think you will need to see this entire house so I know exactly where you find luster."

There was something rather ticklish in what he said, a compliment without so many words, and there was no help returning his smile as she did her best to find beauty around her.

It really was not so very hard, once the signs of neglect were passed over. The western wing had rooms that still bore something resembling furniture, but all were beneath sheets that Benj said he dared not remove. He was certain that at least two animals had died in the western wing, especially in the old ballroom, and that a new species of moss had taken over the gallery. Combined with the general fragrance of moth, dust, and various animal products, a venture into that part of the house was an experience in nasal distress unlike any other.

Even Martha could agree with that, though she laughed about the experience more than anything else. She was positive, she told him, that there were places in London that smelled far worse.

She could not name any, of course, but there had to be some.

The eastern wing had less furniture, and less cobwebs, and was generally in better condition. The family rooms had no beds apart from one, and it was there that Benj had made his bed. It was a tragic sort of establishment, the one moderately lived-in room in the entire house, but Martha was impressed by it all the same. There were not many men who could live and breathe in such a space, without furnishings, finery, or true comfort. Yet he was sleeping in a bed that had no frame, a room with no curtains, and using half of a bureau, as the other half was missing.

This room, at least, had no cobwebs at all, and bore an almost charming simplicity.

Rather like Benj, actually.

The main of the house was somewhere between the condition of the two wings. Relatively inhabitable, though sparse in setting and furniture, it did not have any known animal inhabitants, and did not smell of any particularly foul stench. There was no obvious damage in this area, and a hardy bit of cleaning and refurbishing would surely set it to rights.

Something about that made Benj laugh, when Martha gave him that opinion. When she demanded to know the humor in it, he only shook his head and smiled at her in a way that twisted her stomach and curled her toes.

She would need to spend more time with Benjamin Steele, Lord Hillier, Martha decided as Cassie joined them at last.

A great deal more.

If only to feel her toes curl in such a way again.

Chapter 6

There could be no doubt about it now. Benj was in trouble.

Only it didn't feel like trouble. It felt exciting and bright and stirring, occasionally terrifying, and wildly entertaining.

And also it had a peculiar effect on time. One minute never matched another in length, and hours that had dragged on in the morning were gone in a blink during the afternoon.

Two weeks of this madness, and it was only getting worse.

Martha Smith was upending his world.

Even thinking her name made his pulse skip and drew a smile from his lips. He had seen her several times since she had surprised him on the estate and demanded an explanation for his lack of forthcoming upon their first meeting, but he always came back to the sweetness of that day. Their tour of Pontcaster had been perfection, going from room to room while he had given her his thoughts, and she had followed that with a few of her own. Where his vision had been realistic, hers had been very much optimistic. No room was hopeless or beyond saving, in her eyes, and though she might not have the understanding of what her version of improvements would entail, it did not seem mountainous or impossible.

Pontcaster was less of a disaster when Martha looked at it.

If there was nothing else miraculous about the woman, that would have been enough. But she also made him smile without any effort at all. He was not a surly individual, but he was not overly jovial when under his own influence. Martha made him smile from the blessed moment she arrived to the unfortunate moment she departed, and for hours on end in her absence.

He felt less burdened in her company, less unfortunate than his circumstances, less prone to gloom. He was less of an imposter to his title when she was with him. Less of a misfit. Less uncomfortable.

He did not need to be anything but what he was with Martha, and she saw him just as he was.

It was unlike any other experience Benj had known in his life with any other person.

To be enough as he was and yet feel called to be more, not for his own interests, but to be of more benefit to someone else.

The cacophony of his internal thoughts and sensations was enough to give him some trepidation, though what exactly was unsettling could not be easily identified. It was the change in him, it was the feelings that Martha alone conjured, it was the shift in his view of his home and land, it was . . .

Well, it was everything.

Which was why he was in trouble.

All that he had planned to accomplish in the next few months required his undivided attention, and, for the present, his attention only wanted to be on Martha.

She was the most beautiful woman he had ever known,

let alone seen. Her raw honesty, her openness, her perspective on life and purpose and manner of being were all just as captivating as the incomparable shade of her eyes. And he had a particular interest in the degrees of her smile, all of which made something dip in the small of his back.

He was greatly concerned about this near-obsession, the complete consumption of his thoughts, and the ridiculous smile the image of her brought to his face. He feared that none of this would ever fade, and that the rest of his life would be uprooted because of it.

Yet it was exhilarating rather than terrifying.

Which meant it was either perfectly right or perfectly foolish, and he was not sure how one made the distinction.

Or when.

All he knew at the moment was that Martha was due to visit him at Pontcaster again, and he needed to accomplish a few more tasks before she did so. Primarily, he needed to look in on his sow, who he had not known to be pregnant when he'd purchased her, but who had recently birthed a dozen healthy piglets.

And unless his eyes were presently deceiving him, all of the piglets had somehow escaped their pen and were running free on the estate.

Mr. Harris had been assisting him with the care of all of the animals, and he had been minding the piglets and their mother since the birth. Today he had other calls upon his person, and Benj had assured him he could take care of checking the piglets and changing out the straw. He'd been raised in a farming community, after all, and was more than capable.

Arriving at the sty to find only the adults within and not a single piglet had not exactly been the ideal situation to enter upon.

Mr. Thorne was out in the fields with the sheep, and likely would not be back for another hour, if not more, and there were no other farmhands for the present.

No neighbors for some miles, and no servants.

Just Benj and a dozen piglets to be rounded up.

Panic shot into the pit of his stomach, and he took off running, his eyes scouring the green and brown of his surroundings for any splash of pink. New piglets likely wouldn't get so very far, but there were many dangers that awaited them, and they would not take kindly to being chased.

He remembered that from his youth all too well.

He spotted one lurking behind a bush and dashed to pluck it up, his hold slipping twice before he finally managed it. The piglet must have been hungry, for she darted for her mother the moment he deposited her in the pen.

They would not all be so easy, and Benj knew it well.

Three piglets later, Benj found himself wondering how in the world he could manage eight more piglets on his own. There was no telling how long they had been out, or how far they had gone, or how long it would take to bring them all back in. But one thing was certain: There was no possibility of him completing this task before Martha arrived.

And that was a travesty.

"This is an interesting manner of attire."

Her voice warmed his heart yet froze his limbs at the same time. Benj sighed as she rode over, looking stunning in a rich green redingote over ivy-embroidered cotton. Her eyes had never been so luminous, he was certain, and this was broad daylight.

He wanted nothing more than to stare into those eyes for quiet conversation and a dash of carefully placed flirtation.

His lack of response brought a slow rise of her brows beneath her hat. "The dirt? Hoofprint? Benj, you look trampled."

It wasn't often that he was taken aback, but her use of his name arrested him, sent him reeling into a warm abyss that he only just resisted succumbing to by the feel of the cool, hard ground beneath his feet.

"The piglets escaped," he explained, when his ears ceased their ringing. "I've brought in four, but I must find the rest. I am so sorry, Martha."

If she used his given name without hesitation, he was not about to be reluctant in using hers.

"What for?" she asked him, sliding her crop into an elegant satchel on the saddle. "They are not my pigs, I was not about to scold you for it." She waved him over to help her down.

Benj went, frowning up at her in confusion. "No, I was apologizing because it will keep us from our plans today."

Martha brushed a dismissive hand in the air before placing both hands on his shoulders. "Plans change all the time, Benj. No matter. We'll gather the piglets and see what time is left when we are done."

His hands had gone to her waist as she spoke, and lifted before she'd finished, but he froze as he set her on the ground, gaping at her in shock. "We? You're going to help me retrieve them?"

"Of course," she replied, as though the answer was obvious, her eyes searching his. "What else would I do?"

What else would she do, indeed. Her hands were at his shoulders, his still at her waist, and what he hoped she would do was kiss him soundly when he would inevitably kiss her first, but he was too stunned for that.

The reflex to kiss her had yet to be built up in him, but the impulse was there.

She patted his shoulders fondly and her hands moved to her hat, unpinning it easily. "I don't suppose this will do me any good, will it?" She laughed and pulled from his hold, setting the hat on the ground and removing the redingote with deft motions, folding the garment before setting it beside her hat.

Benj watched her, still unable to move. She was truly the most remarkable woman he had ever known, and he was in desperate need of stronger adjectives.

"Will you set the hobbles?" Martha asked, nudging her head at the horse. "I don't fancy tracking down the horse after we've managed the piglets."

"Of course," Benj finally replied, the words somehow dry in his mouth. He absently moved to do so, his eyes flicking back to her at regular intervals just to be sure he wasn't imagining this fine woman preparing to gather up dirty, squirming piglets.

She gave no indication she was having any second thoughts or doubts whatsoever.

"Now, then," she said when the horse was secure, "where have you already been?"

Benj grinned at her for no particular reason, only that she was here and entirely herself, and quickly relayed where the first four piglets had been. The pair of them devised a plan for scouting out the rest and started out, deciding to stay together rather than divide up, for their own safety as well as increasing the likelihood of spotting the piglets more speedily.

Martha's eyes proved to not only be beautiful, but sharp.

"There!" she called when they'd been walking a few minutes, pointing two fingers toward some puddles lingering from the recent rainfall.

Benj saw the two piglets and nodded. "Right, now carefully make your way around the puddle . . ."

Martha gave him a hard look. "Really, Benj, I've spent my entire life chasing my mother's infernal pugs around our house in London. This cannot be so different."

He bit back a laugh and shrugged. "I mean no offense, nor do I intend to be patronizing. But pigs are . . ."

His voice trailed off as she darted out at the pigs, grasping one, but splashing hard and off-balance into the largest puddle. Filthy water and slurry kicked up on her skirts, some flecks even managing to strike her bodice, and the piglet himself, wriggling against her, bore even more muck.

"Difficult," Benj finished lamely, watching as the other piglet trotted a moment before stopping to sniff something.

Avoiding looking at Martha at all, he moved to this piglet and snatched him up without too much bother. Then and only then did he face Martha.

Her expression held no horror or disgust, but he did detect an air of laughter in her eyes and the corners of her mouth. The piglet in her arms had settled, but Martha still held him tight.

"Ah," Benj murmured as he came to her, his own laughter rising up. He switched the piglet in his hold beneath an arm, and extended his hand to her. "Might I . . . help you out of the puddle, Miss Smith?"

Martha dropped her head back on a merry laugh, the sound dancing majestically across the hills and grass, the mud and the brush almost discordant with her appearance, and yet so incomparably perfect. "You may, my lord," she eventually giggled, grasping his hand and taking a marked step out of the puddle, then releasing his hand to clutch the pig once more. "I can see I shall have to take your advice rather than my own in this."

"Oh, I don't know," Benj mused as they started towards the barn with their piglets. "You did, after all, manage to snatch him. The effect was quite resounding."

"And staining," she quipped, glancing down at her dress. "Fine idea to wear pale cotton on a day like this, but there is no help for it now."

Benj gave her a sidelong look. "You don't have to do this, Martha."

She met his gaze evenly, still grinning. "Oh, I know. But I might as well. Spending time with you was all I had in mind for this afternoon. Why not hunt your property for wandering piglets?"

Gads, he could have kissed her for that, and were his arms not occupied with a fussing piglet, he might have done.

It seemed he would have to one way or the other before the day was out.

The next four piglets were less complicated, though there was a great deal more running involved for both Benj and Martha. With that running came laughter, and with that laughter came the realization that life at Pontcaster, as derelict as the place was, could be glorious with the right woman beside him.

With Martha beside him.

It was far too soon to make any statements or ask any questions of her, and he was not at all convinced that the good-natured woman with shocking clarity of sight would have any interest in joining him in such a long and uncertain prospect, but it was the only thing that made sense to him since his turmoil had begun.

He was falling in love with Martha Smith, and he highly doubted anything would stop that.

He glanced over at her now as they walked away from the barn in search of the final two piglets. Her dark hair still maintained most of its elegant hold, though several tendrils had dislodged themselves, and short wisps danced in the air at her brow and over her ears. Her gown was smudged in countless places, likely filthy beyond saving, and her petticoats bore at least five inches of mud.

Yet even like this, she was the most beautiful creature he

had ever laid eyes on, and the sheen of perspiration on her face only made her beauty more pronounced.

What woman in the world would have done this with him? Would have done this for him? Would have taken the situation by the reins and willed it to her own ends? Did nothing disrupt her serenity of spirit?

She was extraordinary. And suddenly, he wanted nothing less than extraordinary.

Martha caught him staring, and her smile was quick even as her cheeks flushed. "What are you looking at? My hair must look a fright, and heaven only knows how much mud has landed on my face, but I must tell you, my lord, you are not one whit behind me in dishevelment and dirt."

"Nothing looks a fright," Benj murmured, shaking his head. "In fact, I was just thinking that I've never seen anything lovelier."

Her eyes widened and her smile faded. Not entirely, thank heavens. She seemed almost amused by his statement, yet there was no mistaking the astounded air about her. He had struck something with his statement, something she had not anticipated and perhaps could not see. But how would she respond?

That would tell him more than anything else could.

"I'm not often speechless, Benj," Martha said softly, her smile growing just a little, "but you have rendered me so. Were you any other person, I would think you flatter me, but you are no flatterer, are you?"

Relieved beyond measure, Benj shook his head very firmly once more. "I am not."

She hummed a quiet laugh, her eyes bright. "Thank you. And despite my previous statement, you wear the dirt and dishevelment rather well."

Benj barked a laugh. "You are very kind."

"I mean it!" Martha insisted, giggling along with him and stepping closer to his side. "You are no less attractive for your present state, and it suits you. Not all men would be so fortunate. I can name several in London who would look quite a fright."

"Then it is fortunate this is my lot and not theirs," Benj replied as he smiled at her, heat coursing through his veins as the word attractive pulsed in his mind.

"None of them could do this," Martha went on, exhaling a sigh he could not interpret. "Not a one. No one could, except you."

If she was trying to keep him from kissing her, she was doing a poor job of it. The temptation was reaching heights and depths and strengths he had never heard of, and the only reason he had not given in was . . .

Why was it that he hadn't given in?

Martha suddenly stopped, her eyes narrowing. "Is that one of them?"

One of what?

He looked over, his head swimming with thoughts of kissing her, only seeing a brief flash of pink on the other side of the rock wall.

Ah, right. The piglets.

"How in the world did that one get over the wall?" he pondered aloud.

"There must be a hole somewhere," Martha said, eying the entire portion of the wall they could see. "A weakening, perhaps, where some of the rock has given way."

Benj exhaled in irritation, his previously pleasant thoughts gone now. "I'll come out tomorrow and examine the lot of it. It should span most of the property, so no doubt there is more to be mended."

"I can help."

He smiled over at her, irritation abating. "I couldn't ask that."

"You didn't," she quipped. "I offered. More than that, I could bring my cousin's husband out as well. You'd like Mr. Cummings, and I think he'd like you as well. You're not exactly neighbors, but with distances like this, who is?"

She had a point there.

"I don't want to steal your time with your family, Martha," Benj told her softly. "Not for hard labor on a worthless estate."

"It's not worthless," she retorted almost defensively, reaching out to take his arm firmly. "And I am giving my time to you while I am here because it is worth that as well. Believe me, it is no sacrifice." She squeezed his arm gently. "Now help me over this wall so I can get your piglet."

If more romantic words had ever been spoken, he wasn't sure what they were. Before he could change his mind, Benj cupped her cheek in one hand and pressed his lips to hers. To her credit, Martha did not jerk in surprise, though she did stiffen.

For a moment.

Then she leaned into his kiss, her hold on his arm tugging him closer. He did not dare press further, kiss more deeply, give in to the roaring fire within his chest, for fear that any of it would consume him completely. His thumb stroked against her cheek as his lips took hers again, tenderly caressing their softness, their sweetness, their fullness. It was a heady delight, and her fervency humbled him to the core.

Benj broke their kiss as gently as he could while shuddering with restraint. He brushed a loose portion of her hair behind her ear before brushing his lips over her brow.

"Forgive me," he whispered, barely finding his voice. "I had to try."

"Good," she breathed as her fingers moved against his sleeve. "I'm rather pleased you did. I wouldn't have known... would never have..."

He smiled and turned her face up to his, seeing where his thumb had left an additional smear of dirt against her cheek. "Speechless again? I rather like that."

Her nose wrinkled up on an almost laugh. "At least one of us does." Sliding her hand from his arm to rest in his hand, Martha tilted her head. "Shall we fetch your stray piglet, my lord?"

Benj brought her dirty hand to his lips, making her laugh in earnest when he playfully sniffed it first. "We shall, Miss Smith, and with any luck, his sibling will be somewhere close."

Chapter 7

"Oh, Martha. You look so lovely! I only wish Chippenham had a ballroom worthy of your splendor!"

Martha snorted a soft laugh as she finished adjusting the paste gems in her wig. "I have no doubt, Eliza, that I look a fashion plate, and will be gawked at like a strange-plumed pigeon." She sighed at her appearance in the looking glass and fussed with the lace at her throat. "I trust that here, at least, my wearing a muslin will not be seen as lowering myself."

Eliza gasped in outrage, her reflection showing Martha just how much. "Is that what they say about you?"

"They say all sorts of things," Martha informed her, keeping her tone as light as possible. "But my distaste for silks is generally frowned upon."

Her cousin made a sound of disgust. "I invite any of those individuals to look upon you in this exquisite muslin gown and find anything in it that could be improved upon in silk."

It was a kind thought, and Martha was delighted by it. Looking at her reflection now, she felt only hope and panic. Hope that she looked as lovely as she wanted to for Benj, and panic that it would not be enough. That he would prefer the country-trudging girl to this more finely arrayed one. That her efforts would be in vain, and he would regret the kiss they had shared in the fields the week before.

But they had talked and laughed so much in the days following, particularly when they and Mr. Cummings, and a few others whom Mr. Cummings had brought along, had walked the boundaries of the Pontcaster estate, examining the rock wall. Benj and Martha had separated from the rest, which had enabled them to walk hand in hand. He taught her how to repair the parts of the wall they found, and she did her best to avoid ruining the process. According to Benj, she had done better than he expected, but that did not tell her much.

She wanted to be useful to him. She wanted to be beautiful to him. She wanted to be worth something to him. She wanted to be with him.

She had no idea what to expect from the evening, only that he would attend and had asked her to reserve a dance for him. Given she hadn't met any other young men whom she might have considered for a dance, she doubted it would be any difficulty to ensure he could partner her for at least one of them. Were she in London, she would have entered the ballroom with nearly every dance spoken for, as her mother would have arranged everything.

Fortunately, Martha was fond of dancing, so it mattered little to her.

Tonight, however, it mattered very much.

Everything did.

Her gown was new, something she'd procured in London before she'd left and packed on a whim, and she could not have asked for more from a gown. Sheer layers of pale green muslin in a fashionable *robe à l'anglaise* style, embroidered with leaves and flower petals in gold wire laying over a deeper, rich green pleated-satin skirt that almost shimmered in the candlelight. Her sleeves were tight down to her elbow, then draped with gauzy white lace cuffs that would have reached nearly to her wrist, had they had fastenings. The neckline was fairly modest for her, though a differently endowed woman might have told another story. White, green, and gold ribbons and bows adorned the edges of her muslin as it lay over the satin skirts beneath, accompanied by matching bows at the sleeve edges, at the neckline, and along the train of satin-lined muslin that extended from her shoulders down to the hem, trailing a foot or more behind her.

It was an exquisite garment, far too whimsical for her London events, but perhaps not out of place in Chippenham's assembly dances. Fashions allowed for less padding than she had worn the year before, and being in the country was more freeing as well, so she had chosen to only wear the minimal hip padding rather than the full false rump London would have required. That, at least, was a small comfort.

Martha already felt overly aware of her appearance. She did not wish to be uncomfortable in her attire as well.

"We must go, dear, or the dancing will be half over," Eliza said softly, her tone full of unspoken understanding.

Nodding, Martha straightened, exhaling shortly. "I suppose this is the best I can manage."

"Lord Hillier will find you exquisite, cousin," Eliza assured her, extending a hand.

Martha turned in surprise, her cheeks heating, before she chuckled sheepishly. "Is it so obvious?"

Eliza's smile was all too knowing. "Only to me, I think. Mr. Cummings told me all about how the two of you were together in the fields at Pontcaster. I'd think it a fine thing, should the two of you form an attachment."

"Does it require both parties for an attachment to form?"

Martha murmured as she came and took her cousin's hand, covering it with her own. "I will not pretend to know what his lordship thinks or feels, but for my part, I think I am very much attached. Can such a thing happen in just under a month?"

"There have been stranger things." Eliza winked at her and led her out of the room. "And I think you might rest easy on his lordship's score. But his manner and expression this evening will likely tell you for certain."

Martha barely managed a smile for that, her pulse pounding in at least five places in her body. That was what she was most afraid of at the present. One look at Benj and seeing some obvious sign of displeasure or distaste, some evidence that she was not the woman he thought, and her heart would be crushed beneath the dancing feet of the assembly guests.

Everything was easier when she had no emotion attached to an event, she decided. Perhaps that was why people of sense did not marry for love.

It was much safer for one's heart to do otherwise.

They met Mr. Cummings downstairs and donned their cloaks before loading into the carriage. The drive to the assembly rooms would not be long, but every minute would bring additional anxieties for Martha. She could not stop thinking about the feel of Benj's lips on hers, the pressure of his fingers curling against her own, the delicious tingling that extended from the top of her head to the soles of her feet when he smiled at her . . . It also did not improve the state of things that Benj was the handsomest man she had ever seen in her life, so any glimpse of him must be appreciated by a working pair of eyes.

And she would dance with him tonight.

It did not matter if he was a skilled dancer or not. The mere opportunity to turn about in his arms, however briefly, to press their hands together in a way that would not shock, to gaze into each other's eyes in front of others rather than in secret—every aspect of the dance, whatever it was, that she had taken for granted in all other dances she had participated in were suddenly more important than she could have expressed.

The carriage pulled to a stop sometime in the midst of her whimsical imaginings, shaking her from them and making her throat clog with nerves. The assembly room windows were all alight, and the strains of lively music could be heard from within, though none of it brought great joy. A burst of excitement, perhaps, but with that excitement came the desire to retreat.

She could not retreat. Not now, not tonight.

Martha exhaled a little, starting towards the rooms, then stopped as she glanced within the windows.

The dancing had begun, along with the revelry associated with country dances, but it was the dancers themselves that caught Martha's notice.

Not one of the ladies wore a wig as she was, and as every lady in London did. Not one of them wore a gown so elegant, though all were dressed in fair enough finery. No sign of silks, or much of satin, and while the décor was certainly charming, it was hardly grand.

Martha would look like the queen herself among a party of peasants, entering as she was.

"I cannot do this . . ." she whispered, shaking her head.

"What?" Eliza asked, coming to her side. "Do what?"

"Martha? What is wrong?" Cassie's voice called from somewhere behind them, then her friend suddenly took her other arm.

Martha blinked at the sight before her in the windows. "I cannot go in there like this." She frowned in thought, then shook her hands free of her cousin and friend. "Quick, take my wig down. We can put it in the carriage before it goes to the mews." She fumbled along her scalp for the pins, plucking them out the moment her fingers gripped them.

"Martha!" Cassie hissed in distress. "Don't, it is so fine..."

"It will be ridiculous in there," Martha insisted, feeling the wig totter a little on her head as she removed another pin. "I will not be gawked at, and I will not give any the impression that I may not belong with the others. I must join them, not sit above them. Come on, pull those bows off of my train, they are unnecessary."

With girlish giggles, the three of them went at various pieces of Martha's appearance, ridding the garment of anything they could that made it in any way outré. She couldn't do anything about the gold-wire embroidering, but if the rest of the fuss could be removed...

"Here, let me plait your hair," Cassie said, taking the pins that had been used for the wig and setting them aside. "I should be able to set it fairly quickly. Do you want ribbons, too?"

Martha shook her head. "No, I want to be as simple as possible without looking a peasant."

"I don't think you'll pass for a peasant, should you wear your hair down and be without half of your skirts," Eliza laughed. "I could draw up your train, make it *a la polonaise* from the start, rather than waiting for the dancing."

"Please do!" Martha urged as she yanked the lace cuffs from her sleeves. She felt Eliza fumbling around the skirts at her back even as Cassie worked at her hair, and she brushed at her cheeks quickly to rid her face of the rouge she'd foolishly added. It was all ridiculous, and she ought to have seen that from the beginning.

Still, no one had seen her yet but those she loved, so there was no harm done.

Mr. Cummings cleared his throat as he stood nearby. "Incoming," he told them all in a low tone, coming to stand in front of his wife's attempts to adjust Martha's skirts.

"What I wouldn't give for a fan to hide my face," Martha muttered to herself as she tried to hide behind his frame.

His low laugh was not the answer she'd expected. "I don't think that would be necessary, in this case. Good evening, Lord Hillier."

Martha closed her eyes slowly, her lungs seizing up. Of all the times and places to be seen by him, her frantic readjustment of her appearance outside of the assembly rooms was certainly one of the worst.

"Good evening, Cummings. Mrs. Cummings. Miss Holmes. Good evening, Miss Smith."

There was no mistaking the shift in his tone when he said Martha's name, and her eyes snapped open, darting to him at once.

He smiled at her in a manner she had never before seen, something tender, hot, amused, and proud all at once. And nothing in his expression held the slightest sign of distaste.

She could have collapsed where she stood as relief poured over her in waves.

"Good evening, my lord," she murmured, curtseying with all the elegance one could manage while one worked at her hair and her skirts.

He looked over their efforts with an assessing eye before returning his attention to Martha. "This seems interesting. Was there a need to adjust your appearance?"

She dipped her chin in a playfully regal nod. "Indeed, and my evening shall be all the better for it."

"Done," Eliza exclaimed as she brushed at the now

drawn-up train and the rest of the skirts. "No one will ever notice." She stepped to the side and curtseyed belatedly to Benj. "My lord. Apologies for my tardy greeting."

"You were rather importantly engaged," Benj told her with a warm nod. "No apology needed. Miss Holmes, you are clearly quite adept at the fashioning of hair. I never saw a more becoming arrangement. One would never know it was not set at home before Miss Smith departed."

The compliment was so easily given, so sincere, and knowing Benj was the giver, there was no alternative but to believe his words implicitly.

"Thank you, my lord," Cassie said as she placed a final pin. "Having several rather opinionated sisters, one gets a good deal of practice at the thing."

"Your modesty does you credit, Miss Holmes," Benj said, "but I have several sisters, and I have not these skills."

Cassie laughed easily and came to Martha's side, brushing away a thread that remained from a removed bow. "If you've an interest, my lord, I shall teach you the way of it at another time. If you will excuse me, I will go inside and rejoin my parents."

Eliza and Cummings followed her in, both grinning at Martha before they did so.

Martha moved to do the same, but Benj took her hand, holding her back. Heart pounding, she looked up at him, afraid and thrilled at the pressure he exerted.

His smile had faded some, sitting barely present on his lips but abounding in his eyes. "You are the most beautiful woman I have ever seen," he confessed without hesitation. "I can barely speak, Martha." He brought her hand to his lips, kissing the back of it, then turning it over and pressing his lips to the palm.

"You should have seen me when I arrived," Martha

whispered, rambling as her head swam with ecstasy. "Utterly ridiculous, not at all pleasant to see."

Benj chuckled against the skin of her hand, his eyes raising to hers. "I did see you when you arrived. I've seen the whole thing, Martha. I thought you were as beautiful then as you are now."

Something about the tone of his voice made her tilt her head, even as her stomach burst with a thousand fireworks at his words. "But?"

"But what you've done . . . what you've said, why you've done it . . ." He shook his head, his smile spreading further. "Darling, I've never admired you more, and I did not think that was possible."

Darling . . . The endearment wrapped itself around her heart like a warm blanket, brought tears to her eyes that she prayed would not fall, and had her tugging his hand to her own lips for a quick brush of affection.

They could not share a kiss in truth with the assembly room windows so near, but this . . .

"Dance with me, Benj," Martha pleaded, clinging to his hand as much as she dared. "As many times as you like, no matter what anyone says."

He nodded, offering his arm to her. "Things are not as structured in Chippenham as they are in London, Martha. There is a great deal more freedom when it comes to dancing. One might dance three or four dances with the same lady and think nothing of it, gentlemen dancers being as scarce as they are in the country."

"Such a trial for local society," Martha tsked, shaking her head playfully as they entered the building. "However does one manage with such a limited selection?"

"They seem to manage well enough."

Once their outerwear had been taken, they made their

way into the rooms themselves, and Martha felt her heart begin to dance within her just as the other guests were doing before her eyes.

"Martha."

She looked up at Benj, the catch in his voice making her breath stop. He had never looked more handsome than this, his fine evening wear no less striking than on any other figure she had seen in London, though somehow more perfect on him than ever seen before. His hair was dark and neat, a hint of shadow across his jaw where the stubble would appear in the morning, but for now he was only glorious.

"Benj," she whispered, smiling as she did so.

His look was a kiss in itself. "Candlelight makes you a goddess, darling. Nothing less."

How did one survive a night such as this?

She was spared the necessity of words by Benj leading her into the dance, sweeping her away as though they were the only two people in this room, in this dance, possibly in the entire world. There was nothing like it, and that was the best part of it.

Nothing could compare.

They barely said a word as they danced, rather gracefully, as it happened, and the music was just as lost on Martha as the other dancers. There was only the touch of Benj's hand, the smile on his lips, the adoration in his eyes.

If this was not love, she wasn't certain what was.

And this . . . this was worth refusing safe proposals.

Should Benj have any such ideas in his head, of course. It was rather soon. But they had weeks before her return to London, and in that time, a great many things could happen.

"Martha."

The sound of her name in a voice that was definitely *not* Benj's startled her out of her bliss and back into the crowded assembly rooms.

Her cousin stood there with her husband, expression apprehensive.

"What?" Martha asked, coming out of the line of dancers at once. "What is it?"

Eliza looked at her husband, clearly pleading for him to speak.

Mr. Cummings looked at Martha with sympathy. "An express came just now, Martha. From your mother. She insists that you take the next stagecoach to London. Apparently, there is some son of a viscount that has just returned, and she wishes for you to try for him. She writes in . . . rather determined terms."

"Yes, she usually does," Martha grumbled, something cold sinking into her core. "No doubt my lack of correspondence has worn away at her patience."

"She does suggest that if you had kept her more apprised of your situation here, she might have given you more notice," Mr. Cummings relayed. "She believes this sudden news will inconvenience you, but will, in the end, lessen the suffering you have endured here."

Martha snorted softly in derision. "I've had a more pleasant time here than I've had in the last five years combined, and she won't wish to hear that." She looked over at the dancing couples, seeing Benj make his way towards them with concern. "And if I refuse her? If I decide to stay in Wiltshire for the time originally allotted me? She thinks I'm miserable. What if I explain that I am not?"

"She will come out and fetch you herself," Mr. Cummings replied sadly. "If you are not in London by the week's end, she will come."

That stopped Martha cold. It was nothing for Martha to spite her mother and feel the wrath of it, but if her mother came to fetch her, showed herself at Lanfare, it would be mortifying for Eliza. There was no mistaking the disdain that Martha's mother felt for her niece, and the barbs would certainly be thrown about. Eliza was too good a creature to retaliate, and Mr. Cummings too congenial to rage in defense. The children would hear all that was being said, and would doubt their family's worth and standing within the extended relations.

She could not subject her cousins to the shame her mother would shower down upon them.

"I must go, then," Martha whispered as her limbs began to slowly tingle into a frozen numbness. "When is the next stagecoach?"

"Tomorrow," Eliza whispered, near to tears.

Martha nodded absently, wetting her suddenly parched lips. "Such a lovely stretch of time here gone, and no more to be had." She swallowed hard, taking her cousin's hand and turning to the approaching Benj. "What do I tell him?"

"The truth, I expect," Mr. Cummings advised. "Then enjoy the rest of the night to its fullest. 'Twill be a fine memory."

She could only nod again, already pained by the thought. A memory only. Not a reality.

Something within her cracked, and the sound of it seemed to echo in her ears.

Chapter 8

From the moment Benj had heard of Martha's required return to London, he had begun to plan. His mind had spun on every option, every obstacle, every minute detail that could remedy the situation. He could not force her to stay, not if the stories about her mother were true, and if he were to truly solve the dilemma, he would need more than a sleepless night to bring it about.

So she had left, and he had mourned. He had worked his land, and he had sheared his sheep. He had tended his pigs, and he had rid the rest of Pontcaster Park of its ruined interiors.

None of it seemed to matter anymore. Not for himself, not for his title, not for anything.

And that was when obstacles faded and only the answer remained.

He needed Martha Smith.

It was madness. He didn't even know if he loved her yet, only that he was miserable without her. Was that enough? Could that be enough to put a hold on whatever plans were being made for her? If she could wait for his estate to be suitable, if she could love him at all ever, then perhaps...

It would take time, and time was something he did not have. If her mother was truly determined to have her marry the son of whomever it was in London, Martha might not have much power or say in the matter. He knew her mother controlled her, and her time in Wiltshire had been due to her stubborn refusal to marry her mother's choices. But what if her mother removed that choice for her? He had heard of worse things happening, arrangements without consent of the parties, and the like.

He could not bear to think of Martha forced into a marriage of such a nature, something stale and distant, incapable of bringing joy or contentment. Something that would benefit others but not herself. Something that would never allow her to be herself, only the version of herself that had been created.

No, he needed Martha to have more. He needed her for himself, but even if her feelings did not match his in fervor, he would fight to allow her the comfort of any marriage of affection she chose, even if it was not with him.

Although if it was not with him, he would likely sell Pontcaster for whatever money he could get and hide away in some remote corner of Ireland.

He had to try his hand for her, at least. He'd never forgive himself if he did not.

And this was how he had managed to bring himself to London mere days after Martha had left, his estate in the care of Harris, Thorne, Mr. Jepps, and Mr. Cummings, all of whom were now dedicated to helping him prosper however he could.

Benj had been to London before, but not recently, and certainly not as a man of influence. He'd never thought of himself in such terms, but apparently, being a country earl with a finely situated estate made him so, and the cards that had piled up in his rented room from those wishing to meet him were laughable. Clearly, none of these people had heard of Pontcaster's present state, nor of the particular state of Benj's finances. Were he truly seeking a match to further his ends, however, he would have had plenty of options.

One could never accuse Society's finest of being particularly intelligent, but they did have a knack for opportunity.

It had taken him a full day and a half to make connections that would enable him to get to the next Society event. Knowing no person of standing and influence in London, he had been at a bit of a disadvantage, but a few key uses of his title, and the invitation presented itself. He could not remember the name of his new connection, or the host, for that matter, but he knew the address well enough, and that was all he needed.

Now he was walking into that address, trussed up like a peacock of sorts, wearing a silvery blue frock coat embellished with an embroidered leaf motif in silver and black threads along the lapels and buttons. His weskit was cream, and faintly textured, though he had no idea how or what the texture was, and his breeches were nearly black. Stockings and buckle shoes finished him out, and he greatly disliked them both. He could dance in boots in the country, but apparently that was a problem in London.

One more reason to dislike the place.

The ballroom of his host and hostess was unlike any place he had ever seen, glistening from top to bottom, candles in every part he could see, chandeliers catching every sliver of light available and reflecting them onto the guests below.

This was the world to which his Martha had been born, and to this world she should belong. Would she ever wish to leave it for him?

Thinking of her brought his eyes back down from the surrounding finery and onto the guests around him. He had no assurance that she would be here, but if her mother was as determined as he thought she was, no event of this magnitude would go unattended.

The nature of the evening required him to mingle, to be introduced endlessly, and to make his way around the room, even dance with a young lady or two as politeness required. Doing so also gave him further opportunity to examine the room, which was rather convenient. He was one of a few men in the room who had not worn a powdered wig this evening, but as he was not the only one, he did not feel so out of place. The wigs on the ladies varied from outrageous to minimal, but it seemed that all wore some sort of faux headdress. Again, some were powdered, and some were not. It would appear the fashions in London were changing, and some were eager to change with it.

He had just finished his second dance with a very nice young lady when he spotted Martha, and all of the sound in the room suddenly seemed to focus on her.

She was more beautiful and ethereal than he had ever seen her, dressed in a white gown that was detailed only in silver and the slightest hint of pink. Her wig was unpowdered, he was pleased to see, and matched the beauty of her dark tresses almost perfectly. Pink flowers and silver gems darted in and out of it, while long tendrils curled and coiled down her neck, beautifully encasing the elegance of her neck and throat, where a diamond choker sat as though to tempt the eye to its location.

He could not have pictured anything more lovely.

What was he thinking of? He was going to tell her whatever romantic, personal notions were swirling in his head in the hopes that she would . . . what? Not marry whomever her mother wished? Come back to the country and watch him work on his land? Stay there for him?

She was a fine lady of high standing and fortune, and he was an empty earl. He could not consign her to live in a cottage for months or years until the estate was fit for inhabitants. They could not live together at the inn in Chippenham.

She was a goddess of this fine, elegant world. What could she possibly want with him and the nothing he had to offer?

Her incomparable eyes landed on him then, and widened in recognition, her full lips parting.

There was no retreating now, and Benj could not resist her. He strode over to her without hesitation, and bowed deeply. "Miss Smith."

"Lord Hillier," she breathed, her voice barely audible over the music. "How . . . how are you here?"

He smiled as he straightened, his heart thudding painfully against his chest. "I found myself drawn here, Miss Smith, when I had a rather startling realization."

She blinked, not seeming entirely steady. "What was it?"

Benj took a quick glance at his surroundings, then stepped closer, the distance between them still technically polite. "I realized I am terrified that, for the rest of my life, every woman I meet is going to be lacking in my eyes because she isn't you."

He heard the faint exhale that passed her lips, watched as she wet those lips carefully. "Benj . . ."

"I want the full six weeks with you in Wiltshire that I was promised," he told her, lowering his voice. "I believe I'd make an offer by the end of it, given I've fallen nearly in love with you."

Martha's lips curved into the loveliest smile he'd ever seen, one brow lifting playfully. "Nearly?"

He shrugged with a hesitant smile. "Is it really possible to fall in love in one month? I was thinking it would take at least six weeks. I want more time with you, Martha. I want those six weeks."

Her smile was sad and shimmering. "I would love to return to Wiltshire for such a time, but I am certain my mother would not let me. You see, she has designs upon the son of a viscount for me."

Benj took a small step closer, his heart dropping to his knees at the prospect of losing her. "And what are your designs?"

She bit her full lip, almost pleading. "I have none. I want to go back to Wiltshire with you, but I am stuck unless there is a stronger offer, such as a proposal, and an engagement. And you said you needed two more weeks to be sure."

He was shaking his head before she finished, his mind and his heart suddenly perfectly in tune and clear as day. "I don't need two weeks anymore."

Her mouth dropped again before she laughed, tilting her head in his favorite manner. "But you just said . . ."

"I have nothing in this world to offer you," Benj told her, even as his voice turned rasping, "but a title and my two hands, a ramshackle passel of sheep, far too many pigs, and some fields I have plowed myself and will likely have to harvest myself. But I do love you, Martha Smith, and I don't want to make anything of myself or my estate if you aren't there by my side."

Her eyes shimmered in the candlelight, their pure green brilliance shining through. "I had to leave Wiltshire for you to say that?" she asked him, laughing again.

"I didn't realize it would be this way," he protested, taking her hand and squeezing. "I didn't want you to leave, but Pontcaster became so much worse for me when you left, so you're my only hope of redeeming any of it."

"I don't see how it could get worse, but it's a sweet thought." She sniffed a little, smiling brightly. "Shall I sweep in and save your estate with my fortune?"

Benj shook his head. "I don't care about that. Just save me. Will you marry me, Martha?"

Her throat worked on a swallow, then she nodded, her smile turning tender. "Yes. Benj . . . I didn't know anything could feel this way. I wanted it to, but . . . I love you, my darling. I would love to marry you."

He laughed breathlessly at her words, none of this seeming possible or real, and yet it was her hand in his, and her scent around him, her eyes he was seeing. "It's going to take ages for Pontcaster to be ready and worthy of you, darling, but I'll work hard, and when it's ready, we can marry, and . . ."

"Nonsense," Martha interrupted firmly, taking his other hand in hers and clenching. "I want three weeks, no more. The bare minimum for the banns. Benj, I want to go back to Wiltshire with you as soon as possible. As your wife."

"You cannot." He shook his head in disbelief. "It's in no fit state . . ."

"I am neither squeamish nor ignorant now," Martha said, overriding him again. "I can manage whatever you can manage."

There would never be another woman like this one, and remarkable was too pale a word.

"Your mother will never approve," he felt duty-bound to remind her.

Martha scoffed very softly. "You're an earl. She'll approve."

He raised a brow. "She's never heard of me. Or of Pontcaster."

"She's never been to Wiltshire, either, so she'll have no idea of the state of things."

Benj's jaw dropped before he grinned at his bride-to-be. "Are you suggesting I be less than honest?"

"Not at all," Martha quipped. "Just be vague in your honesty." She quirked her brows and leaned close to his ear. "It will work, my love. Let's make haste."

A vision of his future spanned before his mind then. Laughing in the fields with this woman, looking like country bumpkins. Picking their own vegetables and harvesting their crops, both toiling hard. Children darting across the land with the sheep, playing with the dogs who should have been working. Dancing in assemblies among their neighbors, tenants, and friends. Holding each other at the end of a day before a fire, content just to be together.

Never, in his wildest dreams, could he have ever imagined anything so perfect.

"All right," he replied, eager to make that vision a reality. He brought one hand to his lips, kissing the back for all to see. "Let's make haste. We've a wedding to arrange."

Epilogue

It was spread about Chippenham with great excitement that Lord and Lady Hillier of Pontcaster had been lately delivered of a healthy son and heir to the grand Pontcaster estate. Widely accepted as the most prosperous estate for miles, and the finest, it was presumed that a celebratory party would be hosted on the event of the christening. As it neatly aligned with the harvest, a fine and bounteous harvest supper was arranged to coincide.

As befitting the occasion, there was a great many number of well-wishers whose gifts were showered upon young master William Steele, Baron Carver, in the hopes that he would bring his parents, the greatly respected Earl of Hillier, and the beautiful, much-admired Countess of Hillier, all the blessings a faithful son can bestow.

Of course, there were a few of the local gentry who wondered at the fuss being made over a seventh child, but as there had been similar celebrations for each of the preceding daughters of the earl and countess, one could hardly claim it was due to the particular birth of this heir-apparent.

Lady Cassandra Steele, aged nine, could be heard at the occasion declaring that her brother was the finest, most handsome baby boy who was ever born, and she would teach him herself the proper way to drive a team.

And not a soul in attendance would dare to disagree with the lady.

Rebecca Connolly writes romances, both period and contemporary, because she absolutely loves a good love story. She has been creating stories since childhood, and there are home videos to prove it! She started writing them down in elementary school and has never looked back. She currently lives in Indiana, spends every spare moment away from her day job absorbed in her writing, and is a hot cocoa addict.

Visit her website: www.rebeccaconnolly.com

www.ingramcontent.com/pod-product-compliance
Lightning Source LLC
LaVergne TN
LVHW021800060526
838201LV00058B/3185